8/12

THE
CURSED

Center Point
Large Print

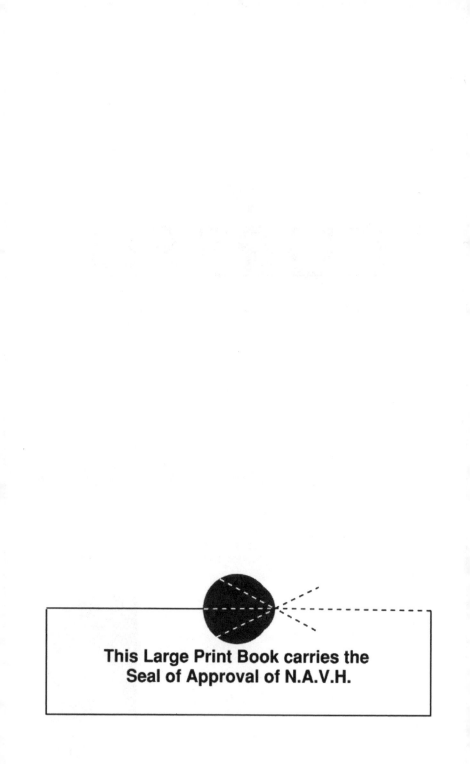

**This Large Print Book carries the
Seal of Approval of N.A.V.H.**

THE
CURSED

HEATHER
GRAHAM

CENTER POINT LARGE PRINT
THORNDIKE, MAINE

This Center Point Large Print edition
is published in the year 2014 by arrangement with
Harlequin Books S.A.

The text of this Large Print edition is unabridged.
In other aspects, this book may vary
from the original edition.
Printed in the United States of America
on permanent paper.
Set in 16-point Times New Roman type.

ISBN: 978-1-62899-167-3

Library of Congress Cataloging-in-Publication Data

Graham, Heather.
The Cursed / Heather Graham. — Center Point Large Print Edition.
pages cm
Summary: "When a man is murdered behind her haunted B&B in Key
West, Hannah O'Brien teams up with FBI agent Dallas Samson and the
FBI's Krewe of Hunters, an elite unit of paranormal investigators, to
solve the crime"—Provided by publisher.
ISBN 978-1-62899-167-3 (library binding : alk. paper)
1. Bed and breakfast accommodations—Florida—Key West—Fiction.
   2. Murder—Investigation—Fiction. 3. Key West (Fla.)—Fiction.
   4. Large type books. I. Title.
PS3557.R198C87 2014
813'.54—dc23
                                                      2014015947

To Key West—
one of the very special and unique places that
make my home state of Florida so special.

And for Stuart and Teresa Davant
and days at the Banyan; Shayne, Chynna, Bryee,
Jason and Derek for many trips to the island;
Kathleen Pickering, Mary Stella, Connie Perry,
Debbie Richardson, Aleka Nakis,
Frazier Nivens, Clint Bullard, and
so many more friends who make every trip
down to Mile Marker 1 a little more amazing.

Prologue

Ghost Stories

"The children screamed in the night as they felt the fire surround them, as they felt the ash . . . as they breathed in a smell like bad fried chicken that drifted on the air—a smell that must have been the victims' burning flesh!"

As he emerged from the bathroom, Stuart Bell waved his arms over his head in a ridiculously—he hoped—spooky way. He was trying to be funny. Not that the event had been funny. A dozen children and adults had once been killed in a fire here at their bed-and-breakfast. But that had been a long time ago.

Still, he was apparently not funny at all.

He could see that Shelly was genuinely scared—she had been since they'd embarked on the Key West ghost tour earlier that night.

The friends who'd taken the tour with them had all shaken off anything even remotely scary at their last stop, the haunted Hard Rock Cafe, where they'd imbibed a few island specialties and discussed some of the stories their guide had been telling them—despite having been told that a member of the Curry family had committed suicide in the ladies' room. Everyone was having a great time—except for Shelly. Judy and Pete Atkinson, married grad students, were living it up away from kids, school and responsibilities. Mark Riordan and Yerby Catalano had kept up, matching them drink for drink. Shelly, however, had sipped at one blue, flowery beverage all night but left most of it behind.

The others had talked about the past and even laughed at the spooky melodramas their guide had recounted.

But Shelly took such stories to heart. She was still nervous.

He and Shelly Nicholson had been a couple since their junior year at the University of Miami, and they both believed they would stay together once they graduated; she was even looking for a graphic art job in the same city, Plantation, where he already had something lined up.

Stuart loved Shelly. He didn't like to see her genuinely frightened.

She offered him a weak smile. She'd already changed into a pair of Disney pajamas—pretty obvious he wasn't getting through those cute characters tonight. He didn't care; he just wanted her to feel better. "I know you're trying to help," she said.

He caught her by the shoulders and urged her down on the luxurious bed. "They're just stories,"

8

he told her. "Sad memories of someone else's past."

"Yes, but . . . I can *feel* the stories. Does that make sense?" she asked.

In a way, yes, he thought, given where they were staying. The owner of the Siren of the Sea bed-and-breakfast—Hannah O'Brien—believed in doing it up right. The house had been built in 1839, and the care it had received over the years was extraordinary.

He had, he thought, done exceptionally well in choosing a place to stay for their trip down to the southernmost city in the United States.

But Shelly whispered, "If only we hadn't stayed *here.*"

Of course. Their tour that night had started out from their bed-and-breakfast. Hannah herself, a lovely young woman not much older than they were, had been their tour guide, and she'd started with the tale of the B and B's own ghosts.

There were several, supposedly. The most often seen was Melody Chandler, who paced the widow's walk atop the roof, eternally waiting for her lover, Hagen Dundee, to return from the sea. He had died saving lives rather than cargo when her father's ship *Wind and the Sea* had floundered just minutes after striking out from Key West, dashed to pieces on the reef by the sudden rise of a summer storm. There had been rumors of violent fighting with another salvager in the midst of the wicked storm—rumors that suggested Dundee had actually been murdered.

Melody had been convinced he wasn't dead, that she would have felt it had he perished. Two weeks later, in the midst of another storm, she saw lights on the water and believed her lover had somehow survived in the ocean and been helped by a passing boat that was returning him to shore. She had raced down to what was now Smathers Beach, only to be swept away herself in the raging gale.

Now, Melody was sometimes seen on the beach when the sun set and night came on, while at other times she paced the roof of the Siren of the Sea. Occasionally she was even observed in the backyard, where what had once been a pond was now a small swimming pool surrounded by tiled paths, lush greenery and beautiful flowers.

And Hagen . . . well, Hagen had been seen opening the doors of the bed-and-breakfast time and again, searching for Melody.

"They're real," Shelly said. "I can feel them. I just—I just can't go to sleep right now. I'm too wound up."

Stuart felt himself perk up at those words, but the feeling was quickly dashed when she saw the hope in his eyes.

"No, I do not want to fool around," she said. "Stuart, I'm sorry, but I just . . . can't."

He heard laughter from outside, soft and quiet.

There were rules here at the Siren of the Sea. Hannah didn't close the pool at night; she only asked her guests be quiet and respectful of others.

"Okay," Stuart said. "That's okay. But, if you can't sleep, why don't we join whoever is out at the pool? There's even a small hot tub. Maybe that will make you sleepy."

Shelly's nod of gratitude was worth a night of not fooling around. He felt like a hero just from the way she was looking at him.

She rose, diving for her suitcase and bathing suit. He quickly grabbed his own trunks and tried not to watch her change. Even though she was scared, he couldn't help himself and was feeling pretty hot and bothered.

Not much to see, though. She changed quickly then turned and gave him her beaming smile.

"Um, I think there are some beers in our mini-fridge," he said.

She shook her head. "No more alcohol, please."

"Soda?"

"Sure, thanks."

That was another high point of the Siren of the Sea. Every one of the six large bedrooms contained a minifridge and microwave. Stuart collected two plastic bottles of soda, grabbed a couple of towels and smiled at Shelly, who smiled back, looking a little less frightened.

They left the room quietly and headed down the stairs. Whoever had been there earlier was gone.

He set their sodas and towels on the old Victorian lawn chairs by the pool and jumped in. It was a small pool, only fifteen feet by thirty, adjoined by a small circular hot tub.

Shelly followed him in. For a few minutes they swam silently, and then, in unspoken agreement, they slipped over the divide into the hot tub. They sat together for a while, still without talking. The night was beautiful. A full moon rode high in the sky, and nearby hibiscus bushes and tree limbs thick with green leaves moved gently in the breeze.

"You okay?" he asked Shelly finally.

She nodded. "This was good. Thank you." She smiled. "I love you. Let's dry off. I think I can sleep now."

They hopped out and went to get their towels. Stuart loved the period lawn chairs. They made him think of giant mansions and croquet fields, with men in knickers and women in white gowns wearing big white hats to shade their faces from the sun.

"Wanna lie here and dry off for a few minutes?" Shelly asked him.

"Sure, great."

They stretched out their towels and lay in the moonlight, hands entwined as they looked up at the stars. Hannah kept subtly arranged lights burning in the garden that gently illuminated the lawn with their soft glow. The spring day had been warm, and the night was kissed by a pleasantly balmy breeze.

Stuart closed his eyes. "It's beautiful here," he murmured. "Too bad that massive ad agency that wants to offer me the almost-big bucks isn't down here, because I could live here."

"Easily," she whispered.

Peace and serenity surrounded him. He really did love the Keys. There was something magical that happened once you left the mainland behind.

The air was so soft and nice, the lounge so comfortable, that he began to drift off.

Then Shelly screamed. It was a scream of pure and absolute terror.

His eyes flew open as he bolted up and saw . . . a strange man standing over Shelly. The stranger was gripping his throat with his right hand and making choking noises. Stuart was too startled, too terrified to be sure, but it looked as though something was oozing through the man's fingers. Blood?

In his left hand the stranger held a knife. A huge bowie knife.

He heard another scream and realized that, just like Shelly, he, too, was screaming in pure, gut-wrenching, primeval terror.

He thought he saw the knife move, glittering silver and red in the moonlight as the stranger raised it and then sent it slashing down toward Shelly.

1

Hannah O'Brien walked into the large kitchen, ready to throw something. The past hour had been pure bedlam—guests hysterical and screaming, she herself completely baffled.

Of course she had offered to refund everyone's money and suggest a beautiful chain hotel for them to check into.

She opened her mouth, not to scream, but to call out for immediate attention. Because she couldn't think of anything else that might have happened except that one of her permanent residents had played a not-very-funny trick on her unsuspecting guests.

Melody Chandler was already there, leaning against the refrigerator in her beautiful Victorian glory, staring at her.

"What the hell was that?" Hannah demanded. "Did you bring a friend in? A dying man with his throat slit, carrying a knife and trying to kill my guests?"

"No!" Melody protested.

"That was unbelievable. I've never had guests up and leave at 4:00 a.m. before. Never. And I've never had to refund anyone's money before, either." Angrily, Hannah crossed her arms over her chest and stared at the ghost with whom she had shared this house for as long as she could remember. The original owner had been Hannah's great-great-great grandfather on her father's side, but she had actually inherited the house, already a B and B at that point, from her uncle. She had been his favorite niece, and she had loved him and the house. Sadly, he had died in his late forties from a sudden heart attack, and she had inherited the Siren all too soon. He had known how much she loved the place. She'd spent much of her time there with him, since her parents— who had lived a few blocks away on Simonton Street—had both worked.

She knew the house backward and forward— along with its ghosts.

She fought to control her temper. "Melody, a little spooking the guests is fun, but this time you and Hagen went too far. I'm fighting to keep this place, but I can't do that if I don't make a profit. You two just scared all our weekend guests away. And Shelly, the poor girl who saw you, was beyond terrified. And from what she described, I don't blame her."

"You did not listen to me, Hannah," Melody protested, staring at her with wide eyes, pleading to be believed. "We did not do it. Hagen would never do anything like that. You know how squeamish he can be. And look at me. Do I look like a bleeding man with a knife? And who do I know? The same spirits you do! I do not know of a single spirit walking around Key West with a bleeding neck and a knife in his hand."

Melody and Hagen didn't refer to themselves as ghosts and didn't like to be referred to that way. Of course, tourists and most locals called the city's haunts ghosts, but Hannah was usually careful and polite, following their wishes and calling them spirits within their hearing.

And with her temper cooling, now that the brouhaha in the house had died down, she had to admit that she really couldn't picture her resident ghosts turning themselves into the terrifying apparition described by her now-gone hysterical guests. But if her two known household entities hadn't been playing tricks . . .

"Then who . . . ?" she asked.

Someone drifted in through the closed back door and then materialized into an excellent imitation of flesh and blood.

Hannah was accustomed to such comings and goings. Hagen Dundee entered the kitchen and took up a protective stance at Melody's side, slipping a ghostly arm around her. "I heard, Hannah, and Melody is telling you the truth, I swear it. As if anyone could ever mistake her for a man! And I promise you that it was not me, either. We were not even here. We were at the Hemingway House, playing with the cats."

"Torturing the poor little six-toed creatures,

probably," Hannah said, still angry. She'd lost business tonight, business she couldn't afford to lose. And she was fighting to believe it had been someone's idea of a prank; it was too frightening to think that it might be something else. Something real.

"I love cats. I would never torture cats. You know that I love all animals," Melody said regally.

Hannah swallowed, then pursued the hope that perhaps the couple had schemed with one of their island spirit friends to scare tourists.

"Honestly," she said, "we've talked about this before. It's charming and wonderful and *helps* business when you guys fool around and moan and groan in the middle of the night. Or, Melody, when you make an appearance at dusk, pacing the roof. Or, Hagen, when someone opens a door in the middle of the night and you're standing in the hallway, looking tall and strong and desperate to find your beloved. But what happened tonight . . . it was mean. One of those people could have had a heart attack."

Hagen looked at Melody and then walked over to Hannah and set his hands on his hips. His sandy hair was worn in a queue, and his bleached cotton shirt seemed to billow around his broad shoulders. She could have sworn she even saw specks of mud on his black leather boots. "Hannah," he said earnestly, "we did not do it." Then he turned his back on her and addressed

Melody. "Dear, I believe we need fresh air—and different company. Shall we go for a bit of a walk?"

She stepped forward and took his arm. Then, heads held high, they headed toward the back door.

"Wait!" Hannah said. "Please. Help me. If you guys didn't do it . . . who could it have been?"

"This island has spirits—and spirits," Hagen told her. "Most of your ghost tourists stay on at the Hard Rock when you are done talking, and maybe they imbibed too heavily of spirits of an alcoholic nature. What I do know is that we did not do it—and you have deeply insulted us by suggesting we would do something so horrible. I really cannot stand here discussing this any further, Hannah. I am sorry. Melody, shall we take our stroll now? Perhaps down to the beach?" he asked, then bowed in a courtly manner and moved as if he were really opening the door for Melody. She sailed out, and he looked at Hannah again then strode off in Melody's wake.

Hannah watched them go, surprised—and more than a little shaken.

She'd grown up in this house with the two of them for company. Nothing like tonight's events had ever occurred before. She couldn't believe they would do anything so vile, but if not them . . . She didn't even want to think that a murderous ghost might be stalking the streets of the city she called home.

She sank down on a chair at the kitchen table, exhausted. She'd been sound asleep when she'd been startled awake, stunned and terrified herself, by the sound of screams. And Melody and Hagen were right. They didn't begin to resemble the knife-wielding apparition that had threatened her guests out by the pool.

She winced. It hurt to lose so much business. Weekdays in the Keys were slow this time of year. The Siren of the Sea wasn't a major hotel to be found on every travel site on the web, though she did have a great website of her own. During Fantasy Fest and other Conch holidays, she had it made. And she had wonderful reviews on the sites where she could be found. It was still hard to make ends meet, though. She didn't want to overprice, but she only had six guest rooms.

Her house was worth a small fortune—she knew that. She'd received enough offers for it. But she didn't want to sell—there was certainly nothing else in the area she could afford if she sold, and Key West was her home. She'd seen a fair amount of the world, many wonderful places, but she loved Key West.

"So . . ." she murmured aloud, drumming her fingers on the table.

Petrie, her humongous, long-haired, six-toed "Hemingway cat," leaped smoothly up into her lap and meowed as if in deep sympathy.

"What's going on, big guy? You're a cat—you're supposed to sense things."

He merely swished his furry tail.

Hannah stood, gently sliding Petrie to the floor, and poured herself another cup of coffee before giving the cat a few treats.

It had all happened so fast. She had heard the screams and shot downstairs to see what was going on. Everyone in the place had been out by the pool within minutes, one college boy wielding a dive knife and Mr. Hardwicke, an elderly regular along with his wife, a heavy boot. But there had been no one there other than Shelly and Stuart, both of them hysterical. Their friends had been less than kind, insisting she'd freaked out over the ghost tour, that was all. But Stuart had been adamant that there had been a ghost—a vengeful ghost—and only their screams had driven him away. Someone had suggested they call the cops; someone else had snorted and said that cops couldn't arrest ghosts.

The next thing Hannah knew, they were all leaving. And while they'd spent most of the night, she'd decided it would be bad customer service practice not to refund their money.

Now the sun had risen on another beautiful Key West morning. Bright and early, just about 7:00 a.m., a westward breeze was coming in, the foliage was moving gently in the breeze, and the dead heat of midday was not yet burning the pavement.

She went to right one of her Victorian lawn lounges, which had toppled over in the commotion.

And that was when she saw them.

Drops of red that led off through the bushes and . . .

Disappeared.

She hunkered down to study the spots and froze.

They were blood. Real blood. Not astral blood, spiritual blood, ghostly blood or imaginary blood from an apparition of some kind. Real blood meant that someone or something living had come through the yard—not a ghost. There were outside lights by the pool, but at night these drops would have been invisible.

Hannah pushed her way through the foliage where the blood trail seemed to end, though the drops might have disappeared into thin air or they might have been soaked up by the dirt. She couldn't really tell. The yard here in back of the pool grew rich and lush all the way up to the bushes that lined the brick wall and the white wooden gate that led to the small alley behind her house. Vehicles couldn't traverse the narrow way; it was a footpath, normally used only by those who already knew it was there.

The gate was unhooked. There was a bloody handprint on it.

Gingerly, afraid of what she would find, Hannah pushed it all the way open.

And there he was. A man lying just two feet from the gate, sprawled faceup, staring wide-eyed up at the sun.

A brilliant crimson ribbon ran around his neck.

And his fingers curled as if he had been holding something. . . .

Like the hilt of a knife.

"How did you know there was a body in the alley?" Dallas Samson asked, after introducing himself and flashing his FBI badge.

The young woman who had summoned the police was standing behind the crime scene tape that now stretched across the alley and up to her gate. Detective Liam Beckett was with her. Beckett was a city cop—and a friend of Dallas's. Apparently Beckett was a friend of the young woman's, too. She was extremely attractive, Dallas noted almost dispassionately. He filed away everything he noticed about possible suspects and witnesses in the back of his mind, so it was second nature to make a physical assessment. She was about five-five, maybe a hundred and twenty pounds, sleek and slim, with deep blue-green eyes and a mane of golden hair. She was, however, tense. She stood straight— almost frozen. Not panicked, but icy. Almost as if she were battling not to show any emotion, doing everything in her power to remain stoic and calm. He realized he'd barely taken his eyes off her. And the tension he was feeling himself was making him come off like a drill sergeant. He couldn't help it—not with a dead body lying in the alley and her standing there not answering his question.

He sure as hell wasn't helping her any, but it rankled that she'd been talking easily with Liam when Dallas had arrived, and now she was just staring at him without saying a word.

Her brows hiked up as she finally considered her reply to his query.

She was taking too long to answer. The tension he was feeling increased.

He pursued his question even more impatiently. "Let me rephrase. Do you usually wake up bright and early and come out to the alley looking for bodies?"

Liam cleared his throat reprovingly, and Dallas winced inwardly. He'd let his temper get the best of him, making him rude and sarcastic. He wasn't usually that way, but he was feeling a hell of a lot more tense than the blonde—than any of them, at the moment.

But, then, he'd known the dead man.

And he didn't like the way the man had been found.

"Hannah called me immediately," Liam said, frowning. "And, I assure you, it's the first time she's ever called me about a body."

"Of course," Dallas said. "Sorry. So, you knew

he was here because—" he paused, looking at Liam "—because he was in your yard—and still alive—last night?" He realized the implication that she might have saved him was in his voice. He hadn't meant it to be, but that didn't mean it wasn't true.

He looked around and noticed that there was a lot of confusion at the scene. A couple of uniformed officers had been first on the scene, followed by Liam—and he'd been right behind. Now techs were dusting and setting out numbers by everything they found, and looking for evidence, and the medical examiner was with the body. She had touched the body, trying to see what she could do for him before realizing he was dead. If she'd been a screaming basket case, he would probably be having an easier time dealing with her. But though she was calm now, she had been screaming when she'd dialed 911. The uniformed officers had probably arrived within seconds—they were just down the street from Duval, because the department always patrolled the bar and club scene there, no matter how late—or early—that was.

"I never saw him in my yard. Two of my guests—former guests—saw him. But they didn't realize he was real. They thought they were seeing a ghost."

The young woman—Liam had introduced her as Hannah O'Brien—seemed to be growing aggravated with him. He didn't really blame her. He was usually a lot better at a crime scene.

"They thought a real man—mortally injured and bleeding—was a ghost?" Dallas demanded.

"Yes."

"How the hell . . . ?" he muttered.

"I can't read their minds," she said sharply. There was something almost regal about her. Maybe that was what bugged him. It compelled him, and that irritated him. He took a breath and tried to regain a professional calm.

"All right. Can you start at the beginning for me?" he asked.

"I was sound asleep. I heard a scream and came running downstairs—they were in back of the house by the pool. I looked out and saw two of my guests. One of them was insisting she'd seen a ghost in my yard," Hannah explained. "She—her name's Shelly Nicholson—had been on my ghost tour. She and her boyfriend, Stuart Bell, were absolutely convinced they'd seen a homicidal ghost. But there was nothing there.

"I tried to calm them down. I told them . . . I told them that ghosts weren't real, and even if they were, it wasn't likely they'd be able to kill anyone. I got them to quit screaming and talk it through. Nothing budged them. They insisted they'd seen a bloody ghost holding a bowie knife. By then, everyone in the place was out there and freaking out. So I got everyone checked out and sent them down to the Westin, and then, when it was light, came back out to look around." She hesitated for a long moment, glancing at Liam. "I don't even know of any Key West ghosts that supposedly run around bleeding and carrying a bowie knife." She stopped, struck by the thought that the man on the ground was now eligible to be a Key West ghost legend.

"A bowie knife?" Dallas demanded.

She nodded. "That's what Stuart said. He was one of the people who saw the . . . ghost."

"How did he know it was a bowie knife?" Dallas demanded.

"How do I know? Maybe he saw *The Alamo* a zillion times!" she snapped back, her irritation showing.

"He doesn't have a knife now," Dallas pointed out.

"No. He wasn't holding it when I found him," she said. "I looked around, and I didn't see a knife anywhere. But if you looked at his hand . . ."

"Yes," Dallas said. "It does look as if he'd been holding something. You touched the body. Are you sure you didn't move his hand? Even by accident?"

"No, I definitely didn't move his hand. I was kneeling on his other side, and I was still there when Officer Mann got here and told me to move away carefully so I didn't contaminate the crime scene. I did *not* touch his hand."

Dirk Mendini, the medical examiner down from the coroner's office in Marathon, rose and walked over to them just then. He indicated his wish to speak with the detectives by angling his head.

"Excuse us, Hannah, will you?" Liam asked gently.

She nodded. "Okay if I go inside and clean up?" she asked.

She had the dead man's blood on her, and Dallas found himself wondering if she was compassionate or just stupid. She'd heard the man had been wielding a bowie knife, but still she'd approached him before she was sure he was dead and not a threat.

He realized he was feeling bitter toward her, and he knew he was wrong. He wanted to blame her for the death, even though he knew he had no right to do so. He was frustrated and wanted to lash out, but he had to get himself under control.

Apparently *he* took too long to speak that time.

She stared at him and said, "I've already been photographed and swabbed for blood. Poked and prodded and questioned. The technician said he had everything he needed."

Dallas nodded curtly. He looked beyond her. It was just after seven in the morning—ridiculously early for a Key West morning—but even so, a few onlookers had gathered in the narrow alley. He let his eyes sweep over them. A tall, bald man who looked as if he had been a prizefighter at one time seemed to be watching Hannah with concern. A young woman with the light coloring and facial features of one of the Eastern European immi-grants who made up so much of the Key West workforce was watching the bald man. A slim older woman was staring past the crime tape. A bike messenger was gaping, wide-eyed.

Naturally, the local news had somehow heard all about it already. A Barbie doll of a blonde with a microphone was trying to get something—anything—from the stoic officers guarding the scene, a cameraman following her. When the police refused to cooperate she turned to the onlookers, but none of them seemed to want their fifteen minutes of fame. They replied to her with annoyance, as if she were a fly in the way of the television screen.

"Hang on, Dirk," Dallas said to the M.E.

He walked over to the newswoman, who was trying to speak to the bald guy. "Miss, so far we have nothing but a dead man. Out of respect, perhaps you could hold off until there's some-thing to report? When the police have enough information to make a statement, they will."

"And you are?"

"Not the police spokesman," Dallas said. "I repeat. When they *can* give a statement, they *will*."

"Wrap it up, Jake," she told the cameraman. "They're blocking the body, anyway. We'll get footage of the house from the street, show the proximity to Duval. . . ." She turned and glared at Dallas. "And we'll make sure our viewers know that the police are being extremely unhelpful."

Liam joined Dallas. "Sunny Smith, right?" he asked the blonde politely. When she nodded, he went on, "Look, Sunny, we don't know anything yet. We found a body in an alley. That's it."

"Who found the body?" Sunny Smith demanded.

"We found a body," Liam repeated firmly. "When there's news, we'll get it to you."

"Who is the dead man?" Sunny asked.

"We don't know yet," Liam said.

"How was he killed?" Sunny demanded.

"I didn't say that he was killed, Sunny," Liam told her.

"Which one of these people found the body? The woman you were talking to?" Sunny demanded.

"Hey, Sunny, please, as soon as I have something, you'll get it," Liam promised.

"And right now you're taking up our time and hindering an investigation," Dallas said.

"We'll question the pretty woman with the blood on her," Sunny said, turning and speaking to her cameraman and then looking around for Hannah.

But Dallas was suddenly grateful to Hannah O'Brien, who had taken advantage of the reporter's intrusion and disappeared.

Frustrated, Sunny went on to the bike messenger.

"You don't want to let any info out, see if it pulls anyone out of the woodwork?" Liam asked him. "Because we're going to have to make a statement soon. Too many people know this has happened and have seen the body."

Dallas shook his head. "We can give a statement—just carefully. I'll explain later."

He turned and rejoined Dirk near the body, and Liam went with him.

"Dallas, what are you doing on a Key West murder?" Dirk asked immediately, then turned to Liam. "Is he taking the lead?"

"We're not sure what's up yet, Dirk," Liam said, then shifted his attention to Dallas. "But I'm assuming this has something to do with a Federal case."

Dallas shrugged. "Yes, well, a Federal lead on a combined case."

He hadn't been assigned to the Key West FBI unit long. It was a small office, just as the U.S. Marshals' office was small here. His headquarters were on the mainland, in Miami.

Oddly, though, despite the small size of the office—or perhaps because of it—his was in an interesting position. Agents here worked closely with the Coast Guard, the city police, the county sheriff's office and the U.S. Marshals Service— all because of Key West's location, accessibility and . . . unique nature, its strange atmosphere. It was a crazy place to call home, but it was *his* crazy place. The island had a long and checkered history. It had provided a stop for pirates, a haven for wreckers, a hard passage for Confederate blockade runners and now it offered access for smugglers bringing everything from illegal drugs to refugees into the country.

He'd grown up here—grown up most of the way, anyway. In his heart, it had always been home.

And now he was back.

"I'm taking on just about anything, Dirk," Dallas said. He glanced over at Liam. He was here now, and so quickly, thanks to Liam. When they'd been kids here on the island, they'd been best friends. Then Dallas's father had been offered a civilian position with the FBI, and Dallas had only been back for a few nostalgic vacations now and then since those long-ago years.

But, he decided, for a pair of kids who had spent a few evil days torturing tourists on ghost tours and stealing beers from the unwary in a multitude of local bars, they'd turned out okay. And they were still friends who respected and trusted each other, something that was all-important right now.

"We may have the best liaison system going just about anywhere," Liam said to Dirk. "We have to. The island's so small that every agency is understaffed, so we've got to work with each other. No other choice," he said.

"If you ask me, the Key West cops do a damned good job," Dirk said.

"They do," Dallas agreed. "But sometimes cases overlap."

"Sure. I get it," Dirk said, nodding. "The murder happened in Key West, but the victim could be from another state. He might have been smuggling drugs, or . . . hell, the U.S. Marshals Service might have had a warrant out on him."

Or, Dallas thought—because he knew—*he might have been an officer of the law. Either way, I intend to get his murderer.*

He didn't say so, though. Not yet. "So, are we looking at the obvious cause of death?" he asked.

"Throat slit. But the killer only nicked the major bleeder," Dirk told them. "That's why he didn't bleed out immediately. I'm thinking that since he made an appearance in a yard at about 3:00 a.m. he must have been attacked a few minutes earlier. Body temp and rigor mortis agree with that timing. The blood loss would have disoriented him. I have tissue and blood samples out now for toxicology tests, so I'll be able to tell you more."

"Damn idiot. Why was he stumbling around in that yard?" Dallas asked, speaking to himself as much as to Liam and the M.E. "If he'd gotten help . . ."

He immediately regretted the passion he'd allowed to enter his voice. The M.E. looked at him strangely, as if aware there was more here than met the eye.

"I don't think he could have been saved unless the damage had been done right smack in the middle of an emergency room," Dirk told him, setting a hand on his shoulder. For an M.E., he seemed to have a decent sense about the living. He asked quietly, "You know him? The local boys were really good about protecting the crime scene, and they checked for identification first thing but came up empty. We'll take fingerprints, of course, and run them through the system. If he's got a sheet of any kind, anywhere, we'll find him."

"You'll match them," Dallas said, looking over at the body. The dead man was Jose Miguel Rodriguez. Dallas had met him briefly once or twice; he'd been an extraordinary agent. Working undercover, he'd done a great deal to stop drug traffic into the South Florida area. Dallas had been due to meet up with Rodriguez the next day on the beach by Fort Zachary Taylor. "But not because of a rap sheet. And when you do ID him, make sure to keep his name and affiliation confidential among law enforcement agencies— the truth can't leak to the news. This man was an agent working undercover—Jose Rodriguez. You

can't release anything I'm telling you now—
and nothing can get out at all except that an
unidentified body was found in an alley, with all
other information pending the medical examiner's
report. Some things the public can't get for a
while, all right, Dirk?"

"Gotcha," Dirk said.

"So he's one of ours?" Liam asked, frowning.

"FBI," Dallas said. "He was working the Los
Lobos case."

"The wolves," Dirk said.

Dallas nodded. "We're all working it, Dirk. I'm
not divulging any secrets—you've obviously
heard about the Los Lobos gang, and everyone
from the cops to the military has been alerted to
keep an eye out for the members and their
activities."

Dirk nodded. "Who hasn't? When they started
up, I had a few corpses up for autopsy at the
morgue in Marathon. Seems they're run by some
big shot out of Colombia—supposedly an
American expat. The members come in all colors
and nationalities—the one thing is they have to
swear absolute loyalty. The smallest betrayal
means death—execution style."

"That's why they're doing so well," Dallas said
grimly. "No one knows who they are, and they're
all too scared to turn on the others. They know the
islands. They slip in and out at night, moving
from the Caribbean to the Keys."

"But from what I understand, they're not drug dealers, they're smugglers, right?" Dirk asked.

Dallas nodded. "Museum pieces, looted artifacts. They've gotten into and out of a number of places here in the Keys, as well as in South America, Cuba, Jamaica—they've pilfered Mayan artifacts from Mexico. They also smuggle people in and out of the country. Anyway," he added quietly, "Jose had infiltrated them, he was the first man on the inside ever. He was just getting in deep with the 'field workers,' who are at the beck and call of the headman. The thing about this gang is that many of them aren't what you'd expect. They aren't tattooed, and they don't wear motorcycle jackets or lounge around like barflies. A lot of them look like upright and ordinary citizens— businessmen, churchgoers, even cops and politicians."

"They work like veins and arteries from a heart," Liam said. "A very peculiar pyramid scheme." He glanced at Dallas. "How many people do they think are involved all across the country?"

"Our best intelligence officers—CIA, FBI, Homeland Security—estimate about a hundred and fifty scattered across the United States."

Dirk nodded, taking in their words. He was silent for a moment and then said, "Odd."

"What's odd?" Dallas asked.

"Los Lobos . . . the bodies I've had that the county officers think were members were done in true execution style—bullet to the back of the head. This is different," Dirk said. "I'm not an investigator, of course. I can only tell you what . . . what the dead can tell. But it's something to think about, right?"

Yes, it was.

Dallas hesitated before speaking. "Different crimes call for different punishments." He hunkered down by the dead man. "Look at his hand, Dirk. He was holding something, right? Something somebody pried out of his hand."

"So it appears," Dirk agreed.

"Like a knife," Dallas murmured.

"Hard to tell. I'll have more for you after the autopsy. Traffic is going to be bad, so it'll be an hour or so before we even have him on a table." He hesitated. "I'm sorry, Dallas."

"I didn't know him well. I just know that he was one of the good guys," Dallas said. At least Dirk had done Rodriguez the mercy of closing his eyes.

Dallas set his fingers lightly on the dead man's shoulders as he studied him. For a moment he felt the fierce grip of pain and sorrow.

This scene was too familiar. Not that long ago they'd lost another agent. Not that long ago he'd come upon a dead woman—that same agent—in the same position, lying in the street on her back. He had been close to what was going on . . . close to finding the truth, to rounding up a bunch of greedy bastards who didn't care who they killed in their quest to amass more and more wealth.

They had made arrests. But he had suspected then, and he suspected now, that the real killer—the man giving the orders—had eluded him.

Jose Rodriguez had died on his back. His left hand was still curved and slightly twisted. His right hand lay in a puddle of blood.

Frowning, Dallas studied the puddle.

Jose had been trying to write something in his own blood.

Dallas took a moment to envision the scene and figure out how Rodriguez had managed to write something while lying on his back. Only one scenario made sense.

Jose had fallen forward, dying. He'd started to write something, but the killer had come up behind him before he finished, and wrenched him around so that he had landed on his back—his hand still in the pool of blood he had been using as ink.

Dallas looked over at Liam. "Can you make that out?"

"Make what out? It's a pool of blood—oh! I see what you're saying."

They both bent closer, trying to read the dead man's message. "That first letter's a *C*," Liam murmured.

"Yeah. I think you're right. Then . . . a *U?*" Dallas asked.

"Yeah, *C-U-R,*" Liam agreed. "Cur? Like a dog?"

"I don't think so. Can you get one of the photographers over here?" Dallas asked.

Liam rose and motioned for a crime scene tech. The man hurried over, took pictures as Dallas indicated, and then moved back to the fence where he'd been working.

"Whoever he was," Dallas told the dead man quietly, "we'll find him."

Two of Dirk's assistants came for the body, and another tech walked up to Liam. "Sir? Anything specific you want us to look for?" he asked.

"Inspect the alley and all the nearby streets, and the yard, too. Our vic was seen with a knife—a big knife, like a bowie knife. Try to find it. Search everywhere our victim could have been."

"Do we need a permit for the yard?" the tech asked.

"Hannah is a friend. We have her blessing for anything that's necessary. Do your jobs, but don't be careless. Try not to leave the place looking like a war zone," Liam said.

The tech nodded and moved away.

Dallas shook his head, looking from the yard to the house. "How the hell could anyone think that a dying man was a ghost?" he demanded.

"The power of suggestion, probably," Liam said. "People love ghost tours. They go on them all the time. They want to be scared. They don't want real danger, but they want to be scared. Hell, Dallas, nothing's changed since we were kids. This place survives on tourism. Tourists like stories. We're full of them."

"But this guy was stumbling around your friend's yard and she didn't wake up until some tourist screamed, and then she was all, 'Wow, you saw a bloody ghost in my yard? Okay.'"

"Hannah is a good kid, Dallas. Lay off. She was dealing with screaming tourists who told her they saw a ghost, not a man."

Dallas nodded. "Yeah, all right."

"Come in and talk to her. Talk. Don't yell."

"I was never yelling."

"You basically accused her of causing his death."

"The hell I did. I merely suggested that an intelligent and rational human being might have thought from the get-go that there was something more than a ghost in her yard."

Liam lowered his head, a slight grin on his face. "I'm going in for coffee. If you can be nice for a few minutes, you're invited, too." He looked up at Dallas, and his smile faded. "You heard the doc. He couldn't have been saved unless he'd been in an emergency room when it happened. It's not Hannah's fault your man is dead."

"I know. I just . . . I just feel like something is escaping me and that I should be able to grasp it, and I can't. I'll be pleasant. I promise."

"No sarcasm?"

"No sarcasm."

They took the path from the gate past the pool, where the techs were busy stringing tape to try to salvage what they could of the victim's route from the yard to his death.

There were no blood trails to the yard, which seemed impossible, but unless the techs could find something with their equipment that neither Liam nor Dallas had seen, Jose Rodriguez might as well have appeared in the yard like the ghost those kids had thought he was, because there was no sign of where he had been before he showed up by the pool.

How could that be? He must have been bleeding steadily by that point.

There was a crime scene marker at every spot where Hannah O'Brien had seen blood as she'd followed the trail through her yard to the alley.

Dallas couldn't help himself. He paused, looking at the lawn chairs beside the pool. He imagined the couple lying there. . . .

Opening their eyes.

Seeing Rodriguez bleeding, holding a knife, then screaming in terror at what they thought was a ghost.

They had still been out there freaking out when Hannah came out to see what was going on, so why hadn't Rodriguez stayed there with them and asked for help?

The pool was surrounded by attractive tile

work, which gave way to lawn. It appeared that Rodriguez had stumbled past the chairs, then across the grass, past the bushes edging the yard and through the gate into the alley. It hadn't rained recently, so the foliage was dry and brittle. He had to assume there would be evidence if Rodriguez had gone through it. Since there wasn't, he had to assume Rodriguez had taken almost a straight line out to the alley.

Had the gate already been open?

He closed his eyes and tried to picture what had happened.

Sliced, bleeding, dying . . . but he hadn't headed to the house?

Why?

There could be only one reason.

Rodriguez had come from the alley, trying to escape through the yard, and the killer had been behind him. But he'd seen the kids by the pool and hadn't wanted anyone else to die, so he'd sacrificed his own life and turned around, back toward danger.

So where was the killer now?

And where was the knife the couple had seen Rodriguez waving?

The answer was obvious.

The killer had followed him until he had fallen, then wrested the knife—which might well have been dripping with the killer's blood—from Rodriguez's dying grasp.

2

Hannah had hurried past the pool area and inside without looking back. Once there, she leaned against the door, just breathing.

She still felt as though, even if she were pinched, she wouldn't feel anything.

He'd been real. The "ghost" in her yard had not been a ghost at all. At least, he hadn't been a ghost when her guests had seen him. He had been real—he'd been flesh and blood and . . .

Alive.

But according to the medical examiner, nothing could have saved him at that point.

And still, in her mind, she kept replaying everything about finding his corpse as clearly as if it were happening all over again. First the blood . . .

And then the body.

She'd rushed to his side, fallen to her knees while fumbling to get her phone from her pocket. She'd touched him, ready to do whatever necessary to help him.

And then she'd seen his eyes.

Dead eyes.

Every corpse she'd ever seen had been laid out tenderly in a casket at a wake or a viewing.

The dead never look right, never, no matter how good the mortician is, Melody had told her once.

But they didn't look like the dead man in the alley. Lying there as if he'd known death was coming, as if . . .

As if he had tried to speak, tried to say something before succumbing to the darkness.

If only she'd gotten there sooner.

No. She couldn't have gotten there sooner; she hadn't had any idea of what was going on when Shelly and Stuart had started screaming, and it had seemed so cut-and-dried. Shelly, already on edge after the ghost tour, had thought she'd seen a ghost and Stuart had gotten carried away on the wave of her hysteria. And then she'd had to deal with all the other guests shrieking and shouting and just generally going nuts.

There was nothing she could have done. Even if she'd run right out to look for a bleeding man with a huge knife in his hand, it would have been too late. He'd already been dying.

"Keep telling yourself that," she muttered drily to herself. She realized she felt incredibly guilty, which was ridiculous, because she hadn't done anything wrong.

But the man had been alive. . . .

And now he was dead.

She pushed away from the door. She didn't just feel guilty about the dead man, she realized. She felt guilty for suspecting her resident ghosts of being up to no good, which had been entirely stupid of her. They always looked exactly the same. Melody was always beautiful in her Victorian gown, and Hagen always looked like a handsome swashbuckler in his fawn breeches, boots and muslin poet's shirt. They didn't change clothing—and they didn't run around with weapons, much less bleeding.

She needed to do something, get busy. She couldn't just stand there all day feeling guilty. But she'd already stripped all the beds in a fury and cleaned the house, powered by the adrenalin that had raced through her after the scare and the effort of getting all her guests settled elsewhere. By the time the sun came up, the Siren was ready for business. Too bad she didn't have that much energy every day.

In the kitchen she poured herself another cup of coffee and took out her scheduling book. Stuart and Shelly and their friends had been due to stay another three days. There were prospective guests who had wanted to come, but she'd had to turn them away. Several had left their numbers, though. Maybe she could call them and . . .

And tell them that a dying man had walked through her yard before his death and scared everyone else away?

The pages seemed to swim before her eyes.

She thought she heard someone knocking at the back door. She rose and went to check.

No one.

She moved back through the house, looking out the windows as she went. There were people walking along the sidewalk out front, but no one was at her door or trying to get her attention.

She headed back to the kitchen, but once she got there she felt a strange sensation creep along her spine as if she wasn't alone.

"Melody? Hagen?" she said. Her words were soft—and hopeful.

But neither of her resident ghosts replied. They were angry—they had a right to be.

But, despite their silence, were they here, watching her? Watching everything that was going on?

"Guys, please, I'm really, really sorry," she said.

No one answered her. She decided she must be feeling off because of the bad night she'd had and all the people crawling around her yard, not to mention that she'd stumbled on a body this morning. She let out a soft sigh and tried to imagine her bank accounts in her mind's eye, then decided on a course of action. She asked herself again whether she should call the potential guests who'd left their numbers or not. Maybe it was too soon.

Too soon after discovering a dead man.

Hannah drummed her fingers on the table. She was glad that Liam had come when her emergency call had gone through; he had been her friend for as long as she could remember. As for the FBI agent . . .

She didn't have anything against FBI agents. Her cousin Kelsey was an FBI agent. She wished fiercely at that moment that Kelsey was still in Key West, but she was in the D.C. area, part of a special unit. Hannah hadn't gotten to see a lot of Kelsey since she'd moved.

Hannah missed her.

Missed her now more than ever.

She pulled her phone from her pocket, suddenly overcome by the urge to speak with her cousin.

She stopped herself before opening speed dial. She would call Kelsey soon and spill everything that had happened. Kelsey was tough but compassionate. She would put everything in perspective.

Hannah just wasn't going to call her now, while she was in a panic. She would wait until she was calm, when she wouldn't sound as hysterical as Shelly had sounded that morning.

Her best course of action right now was to try to come to grips with what had happened. She winced.

She hadn't even known the man.

But she had held him in death.

She gave herself a mental shake. She needed to be busy so she could take her mind off things.

Hard to do, of course, when her guests had fled.

So she would sit down, breathe, check out her

bank accounts and assure herself that she could weather this storm. Yes, a man had died and that was tragic. But she hadn't known him, and she had done what she could. She had to move forward now.

Liam was obviously good friends with Hannah O'Brien, Dallas thought when his friend went straight to the back door, opened it without knocking and walked right in.

The house was old—probably one of the island's oldest. Tongue-and-groove paneling was evident in a rear room that had been set up as a social area, with a large flat-screen television surrounded by old bookshelves that also held a stereo system. The furniture seemed to be what was locally called Victorian Keys—rattan and wicker decorated with cushions covered in period-design fabrics. The drapes back here were sheer and floated through large open windows that looked out over the patio and pool.

"Hannah?" Liam called.

"In the kitchen!" came the reply.

"You should lock your door," Liam told her.

"I usually do," she replied. "Honestly."

By then they were walking through the formal dining room. If it had been 1839, Dallas thought, the room wouldn't have looked any different. The table was large enough to seat at least twelve and was highly polished. Intricately carved legs each ended in a dragon's head. Lace doilies, along with a handsome silver service, covered the tabletop. Liam didn't pause but walked on through to the kitchen. Dallas followed him.

There was another table in the kitchen—this one smaller and far more casually set. It sat six, tops. The kitchen itself was large and in keeping with the rest of the house. The sink had reproduction faucets that resembled old pumps, the counters were butcher block, with marble tops by the stove and sink. Copper pots and pans hung from the rafters, and there was a huge fireplace with a large kettle hanging over carefully stacked wood. Dallas was pretty sure it was just for show.

Hannah was seated at the table. She had changed into a sundress and was no longer covered in blood. Her hair was wet; she had apparently washed it. Her cheekbones were high, her eyes were wide. She was, he thought, very much a beauty, like a classical statue in her near perfection.

She was sipping from a mug as she studied a record book in front of her.

"I'm debating whether to call the people I had to turn away," she told Liam drily. "My bottom line could certainly use the help."

"Don't know how to help you there, I'm afraid," Liam told her as he pulled out the chair to her right and helped himself to coffee.

"There's quiche and croissants if you'd like,"

she said. "Obviously I'm not serving a dozen guests this morning."

"How sad. Your guests are gone," Dallas snapped before he could stop himself.

She stared at him, obviously stung by his tone. "I *found* that poor man. I saw his face. It was . . ." She shuddered. "Anyway, think whatever you want of me, but we're still here and so is the food, so help yourself if you're hungry."

He *was* hungry; the call from Liam had dragged him out of bed early in the morning, and he hadn't had a break since. But he felt like an ass. No way in hell could he accept her food after he'd just been so rude to her.

"I'm pretty sure you both know I didn't kill that man," she said quietly. "But the clothes I was wearing are in that paper bag if you need them for anything."

"The lab might want them," Liam said.

"Interesting," Dallas said. "That's a good call, but it's interesting that you thought ahead like that."

She gave him a smile that wasn't a smile at all. "The techs outside asked me to bag up the clothing I was wearing in case they could find trace evidence from the killer on it."

Dallas kept his mouth shut and took a drink of the coffee Liam had already poured for him, but inside he was thinking, *You ass* all over again.

"Hannah, by any chance did your guests tell

you what direction the 'ghost' came from?" Liam asked her.

She shook her head. "I wish I could tell you more, Liam, but no, they didn't say anything. I assume you'll want to talk to them yourself, though. I arranged for them to stay at the Westin. None of the B and Bs would have had room, even if I'd been able to reach someone at that hour of the morning."

"I'm assuming you have cell numbers for them so we can track them down if they're out?" Dallas asked.

She nodded and reached for the guest register on the table. "Of course."

Liam rose, pulling out a small pad and a pen. "What are their names?"

"Stuart Bell and Shelly Nicholson saw him and thought he was a ghost," Hannah said, and gave him their numbers. "Their friends are Pete and Judy Atkinson, and Mark Riordan and Yerby Catalano. And then there were the Hardwickes. They're regulars, and much too elderly to be your murderer, if that's what you're thinking. They woke up with all the screaming and came rushing down, just like I did. They were just as confused and disoriented as I was. Everyone but the Hardwickes was on my ghost tour earlier. I start off here, and I always end at the Hard Rock—part of their ticket price gets them a drink. I left them there, came home and went to sleep. I didn't hear them come in. I didn't hear anything until the screaming started. Just call over to the hotel. I'm sure you'll reach them there."

"Thanks," Liam told her, then got up and walked away from the table as he started making his calls.

"They really thought a dying man was a ghost?" Dallas asked, shaking his head.

"I guess you don't really understand this island," Hannah said.

He smiled grimly. "Oh, I think I do."

"You're new here, right?"

"I haven't been assigned here long, no. But I know the island. I was born here, Miss O'Brien."

"Ah," she said, studying him. "Really? I'm going to guess that you've been away awhile. Because you should know that people like to come here and steep themselves in ghost stories, then party at the bars on Duval Street."

"They were drunk?" he asked.

That seemed to give her pause. She shook her head. "No, actually, I don't think they were."

"There's a big difference between a supposed ghost and a dying man," Dallas said. He took another drink of his coffee. It was good. Strong. Exactly what he liked and needed.

"I might remind you, Mr. Samson, that I'm not the one who saw him. My guests told me that they'd seen a ghost, and since they were clearly terrified I did what I thought was the right thing—I gave them their money back and sent them where they'd feel safe."

He leaned forward, looking at her. "It's Agent Samson, Ms. O'Brien. And while you were busy doing the right thing, weren't you afraid yourself?"

"Of a ghost? A *supposed* ghost? No."

He leaned closer to her. "What about the knife?"

She shrugged. "They said he had a knife—and no, I don't know why they thought a ghost was able to carry a real knife—and that he was about to do them in. *I* never saw the knife."

Liam returned to the table and told them, "They're still at the hotel. I spoke to a friend at the desk. She's slipping a note beneath the door, because they have their phones off—probably trying to get some sleep. We can stop on by when we leave here or wait to speak to them when they wake up. Hannah, the crime scene techs will probably be around for a few more hours. There's a lot of foliage around the property, and they're trying to find any clues—blood, broken branches, a scrap of fabric . . . whatever. Trying to figure out where he came from before he wound up in your yard and where the killer might have hidden."

She nodded thoughtfully. "We're just a block off Duval," she said. "I imagine . . . well, the backstreets here are pretty quiet once the bars close."

Liam nodded. "I'm going to take you up on breakfast before we go."

"Please do," she said, rising. "Let me nuke it for you." She turned to look at Dallas. "Agent Samson?"

What the hell. He was hungry.

"Sure," he said. "Thank you."

She put the food in the microwave to heat, then set plates before the two of them.

"Did you know who he was?" she asked. "Was he a criminal—or just a good guy who happened to be walking around carrying a bowie knife?"

Dallas looked at her. She could also have an acid tongue when she chose.

Liam said, "It's a closed investigation, so I'm sorry, but I can't tell you anything."

Hannah turned from Liam to stare at Dallas. "I see. I'm not sure how you're going to keep a lid on things, but I guess I don't really need an answer."

"Yes," Dallas said quietly, making the decision to let her into the zone of trust. "He *was* a good guy walking around with a bowie knife. He was one of ours, an agent named Jose Rodriguez. Luckily he doesn't have a wife or kids, and his parents died a long time ago in a South American coup. When the Bureau spins what happens, they'll probably let the media think that he was a criminal—and he would have approved of that. It took him forever to get undercover.

They won't want that information getting out."

"I'm really sorry," she said quietly. "And I won't say a thing."

"Thanks," he told her.

An awkward silence reigned. Liam broke it. "Great quiche, Hannah. There's a reason you're known for having one of the best breakfasts in town."

"Glad you liked it, Liam."

"Very good," Dallas agreed.

She nodded. "Thanks."

"Was anyone else here?" Dallas asked suddenly.

Hannah frowned. "What do you mean?"

He thought she sounded a little defensive. "Exactly what I said. Was anyone else here? Do you run this place by yourself?"

She let out a breath. "Valeriya Dimitri helps out with housekeeping, but she goes home at night. Bentley Holloway takes care of the grounds and does repairs. He works for a few other people, too, and lives in the little shotgun house next door. Neither of them is here in the middle of the night, and I called Valeriya this morning and told her to take today off because of what happened. She emigrated here from Russia about ten years ago, and she's a lovely young woman who's just happy to be living with her family here in Key West. And Bentley is almost as much an island icon as Fort Zachary Taylor. Neither of them would ever hurt anyone. Actually, you probably saw both of them earlier. They were out back in the alley. Valeriya was already on her way in to work when I reached her, and Bentley—well, like I said, he lives next door. The commotion probably brought him out."

"Bentley was the bald guy standing in the back," Liam said to Dallas. "And Valeriya is a pretty blonde, so I doubt you missed her." He grinned.

"But they weren't there when you found the body?" Dallas pressed.

"No. I guess Valeriya decided to come see what was going on. I did tell her the cops were here and that I'd found a dead man. You can't think her being there means anything," Hannah said.

"People do stop and stare at accidents," Liam added.

Maybe. But she and the handyman would both be worth talking to, Dallas thought. Liam caught his gaze. He was thinking the same thing.

Just as they were swallowing their last bites, Liam's phone rang. He answered it quickly and listened. "We'll be right there," he said, looking over at Dallas. "That was Shelly Nicholson. She and Stuart are up and anxious to speak with us. They've decided to cut their vacation short and head back to Miami."

"Then we need to get over to see them," Dallas said, and stood. "Ms. O'Brien . . ."

"Don't worry, Agent Samson. I don't intend to leave town," she said drily.

"Actually, I was going to say thank-you for breakfast."

"Oh." A slight flush suffused her cheeks. "My pleasure," she murmured.

He nodded, still studying her. He hadn't known her when he'd been a kid; he would have remembered her. Her eyes were unforgettable.

"Please remember, don't say anything about Jose," he told her.

"I don't know anything, do I?" she asked innocently.

He smiled. "Thanks."

Liam gave her a quick hug as she rose. "See you later," he told her.

Dallas followed him through the front of the house. The entry and parlor were large with a check-in counter created from an old telephone desk. The place was Victorian to a T and beautifully kept.

He found himself pausing to look back. He knew that Hannah had stayed in the kitchen, but despite that, he had the feeling that he was being watched.

"What is it?" Liam asked him.

He shook his head and looked at his friend. "What the hell happened to the knife?" he asked.

"Dallas, the crime scene techs are good. Really. This may be an island paradise and we may only be a small department, but we're up to par. If there's a knife out there to be found, they'll find it."

"That's just it . . . it should be out there to be found, but I'll bet you it isn't."

"You think the killer hung around to see him die, then took it?" Liam asked.

"Have you got another answer?"

"Let them do their work," Liam said quietly, then opened the front door and stepped outside.

Dallas nodded and followed.

He still felt as if the house—or someone *in* the house—was watching him.

Had Hannah O'Brien really been alone?

Hannah rose when they left and looked outside. From the kitchen window she could see that her yard was still crawling with cops and crime scene techs.

She headed to the front and bolted the door, feeling suddenly nervous in her own house. She generally kept the house locked, and guests were given keys. But she'd never been particularly worried before about making sure that it was locked, especially during the day.

She headed to the back of the house and made sure that door was locked, too. She found herself looking out at her usually peaceful yard. It really was beautiful. She paid for someone to come frequently to clear the pool of leaves from the foliage that surrounded it, because she just couldn't make herself screen it in. There was something too pretty about the crotons and palms and old banyans. But today her normally serene view felt disturbing.

She couldn't stop herself from thinking about the dead man. His face was burned into her brain; she had knelt by his side, ready to administer help, until his wide, sightless eyes had assured her it was too late.

Undercover agent.

She hadn't suspected. He'd been perhaps thirty or so, nice looking, dark haired, with a slightly scruffy jawline. He'd been wearing jeans and a T-shirt.

He'd looked like any tourist, or even a local.

Good thing Agent Dallas Samson wasn't trying to go undercover. The man reeked of law enforcement. He was tall, with exceptionally broad shoulders and a lean, muscled physique that probably came from hours at a gym. His sandy hair was cut short, and his gray eyes looked as predatory as an eagle's. He'd worn jeans and a short-sleeved tailored shirt, not a suit, but even so, she'd pegged him as some kind of a cop even before he flashed his badge. He'd said that he was from Key West. She sure as hell didn't remember him. And if she'd known him, she didn't think she would have forgotten him. But then, he was a friend of Liam's. Liam been a few years ahead of her in school, and they hadn't really become friends until they'd both come back to the island after college, though she'd been close to Katie O'Hara, now Liam's sister-in-law. The island could seem small, with everyone knowing everyone else, and then you'd find yourself surprised when you met someone new who turned out to have lived there all his life. It was also the kind of place where some people stayed forever and would never leave, while others were just passing through.

She winced as she looked out the window. It wasn't as if Key West didn't have crime. Any place that dealt with that much tourism—hundreds or even thousands of people coming and going daily—was going to have crime. Paradise could be a great place for a thief.

But murder was a rarity.

And she had never—never!—discovered the victim before.

She jumped back suddenly as she realized that someone was looking in.

It must be one of the crime scene techs standing at the back door.

But as she stared out, she froze.

Her eyes met those of the man staring in. They were dark and brown and expressive. She knew those eyes. She knew that face.

Jose Rodriguez—a dead man—was standing at her back door.

3

Stuart Bell and Shelly Nicholson seemed to be an intelligent young couple.

They'd taken a small suite, so it was easy just to speak with them in their room. The couple was seated on the sofa, and Liam and Dallas had chairs facing them.

"You're saying that was a real man—and now he's dead?" Stuart asked, staring at the two of them blankly.

"Oh, God," Shelly said, her eyes fixed. "Oh, God. He was *alive.*"

Liam wasn't sure why, but he felt compelled to ease their guilt. "You couldn't have saved him. The M.E. said that unless he'd literally been in an emergency room when it happened, there was nothing anyone could have done."

"We'll never know, will we?" Stuart asked, wincing. "We screamed. We panicked. We were just so . . ."

"I was terrified already," Shelly said. "We'd been on the ghost tour. And there's something about the way Hannah tells the stories. . . . She doesn't get dramatic or anything, but all that history, it gets to you. We were down at the pool because I was too scared to sleep."

Stuart cleared his throat. "And we'd been drinking," he admitted as if they'd committed a horrible sin.

"It's okay. This is Key West. Everybody drinks here," Dallas said, glancing over at Liam. "But . . . it never occurred to you that he was real?"

The two looked at each other. Shelly lifted her hands. "No."

Stuart said, "When Shelly screamed, I opened my eyes. I saw him and screamed, too. And then I blinked and he was gone."

"Okay, this is important," Dallas said. "Think back. Do you have any idea where he came from? We think he was out back in the alley before he came into the yard. Did you see anyone else?"

"Like I said, my eyes were closed," Stuart said.

"So were mine," Shelly said. "When I opened them, he was just . . . there."

"Did you see or hear anyone before he appeared?" Liam asked.

Stuart shrugged. "We heard someone when we were upstairs, but they were gone by the time we went down."

"No," Shelly said. "I didn't see anyone because no one was around. I mean, even when we came in things were pretty quiet." She stopped to think for a moment, then said, "Wait! Stuart, remember when we were walking back? There was a group of people ahead of us. They were crashing into each other as if they were *really* drunk."

"They probably were," Stuart said. "But, yeah, I remember them."

"Maybe the dead man was with them," Shelly said.

"How many were there?" Dallas asked.

"Four," Stuart said.

"Five," Shelly corrected. "I remember counting them. I was a little nervous, but I was thinking that there were six of us, so at least we had one more in our group in case they caused some kind of trouble. Of course, they were all guys and we only had three guys."

"I don't know," Stuart said. "That short one might have been a woman. Hard to tell. They were all wearing hoodies. Pretty weird, considering it was about fifty."

Interesting, Dallas thought. Someone else might remember a group like that, because most tourists didn't bundle up when it turned sixty. Time to go and follow up on this first lead.

He and Liam seemed to be of one mind. They rose together. Dallas handed them his card. "If you think of anything else—anything at all—please call me."

"Are you going to speak with the others? They might remember something," Stuart said. "I mean, not about the—the dead man, but maybe about the group we saw when we were walking home."

"Yes, we're just waiting for them to wake up," Liam told them.

Shelly looked over at Stuart. "That may be awhile."

Stuart nodded. "They're going to be really hungover."

"We'll be gentle," Dallas promised.

Hannah blinked. The dead man was still there, looking at her beseechingly.

He could—though he apparently wasn't aware of it yet—just walk in through the door if he wanted to. Should she let him in?

According to Agent Samson, Jose Rodriguez had been one of the good guys. Florida—especially South Florida and Key West—had a long history of Spanish settlement and Cuban immigration. His family might have been in the area for centuries. But wherever he had grown up, it seemed someone had taught him manners.

He was knocking. Hoping she would let him in.

She lowered her head for a minute. *No, go away, please,* she thought fervently. *I don't want to be ghost central. I don't want to get involved with your murder.*

She felt immediately embarrassed, because she knew that attitude was wrong. She had to help if she could.

She opened the door, swallowing hard. "Hello, Jose."

At least his apparition wasn't as bloody in the afterlife as his body had been in death. He looked as he must have soon before death, wearing a typical Cuban guayabera shirt and khaki pants. His hair was sleek, dark and combed back. He was clean shaven, with dark eyes and handsome features.

"You—you know me?" he asked her.

His voice was brittle, a little like sandpaper, as if he was just learning to speak.

She nodded. "I found you."

He nodded. "I remember. You tried to help me, but it was too late."

"Yes." She studied him for a minute. "I'm sorry I couldn't help. I hear that you were an undercover agent, one of the good guys."

"Yes."

"I guess you know you were murdered. My friend Liam Beckett, a police detective, has had some experience with . . . the dead. He doesn't see as easily as I do, though—lucky me," she couldn't help but add a little bitterly. "But if you tell me who did it, I can tell him."

A grim smile curved his lips. "If only it were that easy."

"Your throat was slit. You really don't know who did it? And you were carrying a knife—a big bowie knife—with blood on it. Of course, it's gone now. The crime scene techs are still out there looking for it," Hannah said.

"Yes, I see them. But they won't find it," he said.

Hannah realized that the techs in the yard could see her through the back window; they probably thought she was standing there talking to herself.

Maybe she was.

"May I come in?" Rodriguez asked politely.

She nodded. "Oh, of course. Please. Let's move into the parlor."

She led the way through to the front, taking an armchair by the fire and curling her legs beneath her. The ghost took a seat across from her on the sofa.

"I'm so sorry," she said aloud. It seemed lame. He should have had a lifetime ahead of him. She took a breath. "I want to help you. But . . . how can you not know what happened?"

"Because whoever got me came up behind me. We—I was with a bunch of guys—had just turned the corner from Duval and I heard someone behind us. He grabbed me, and the other guys saw. One of them screamed 'Run!' and we all took off. I think the other guys had to be in on it—either that or they're running scared, thinking they're about to get the same," Rodriguez told her. He stared at her for a moment. She thought he was assessing her. Perhaps he was deciding if she could be of any help.

"Anyway, like I said, we all took off," Jose went on. "I threw the guy off me and crashed through the yard next to yours. That's when he caught up with me. I didn't have a gun on me, only my knife. I got a slice of him, but since I couldn't see anything, I don't even know where I cut him, but I know he . . . he got me. Slit my throat. I kept running, and that's when I scared your guests. But I heard him coming after me. I knew I didn't have a chance, and I didn't want him to kill anyone else, so I kept running. I ended up in the alley, tried to write . . ." He trailed to a stop. "And then I . . . died. He followed me—must have, if the knife is gone. But he couldn't leave it. They would have gotten his blood off it."

Hannah found herself suddenly fighting tears. Even as he was dying, he had thought to save others.

"You've heard of Los Lobos?" he asked her.

She nodded. "I think most of the country has heard of them. Every once in a while there's something in the paper about a body popping up somewhere and they're suspected of the murder, or a treasure goes missing and they're the only suspects. They're like the mafia, or that's what it sounds like, anyway."

Rodriguez nodded. "More or less. Every agency from the FBI to the Coast Guard has been trying to turn one of the members. The problem is, they'd rather die or go to prison than take what they'll get if the organization turns against them. Case in point," he said, indicating his throat.

Hannah exhaled. "But . . . this isn't so much a Key West thing as it is a national one, right?"

"It's at least partly a Key West thing, because Los Lobos specializes in treasures from the New World." He paused. "I'm not sure where to begin. Do you remember hearing anything around a year ago about a small research-slash-salvage operation at a recently discovered shipwreck? The crew disappeared in the midst of a storm."

"Yes. It was on the news and in the paper. The *Discovery* went out with a captain, a mate and three scientists. They were all lost in the storm," Hannah said.

"I don't believe the crew was lost in that storm at all."

"You think Los Lobos killed them?" Hannah asked, horrified. "The storm wasn't that bad on land, but a lot of other ships were caught in it, too, and barely made it out. The remains of the *Discovery* eventually turned up, but none of the crew's bodies were ever found, although that's not uncommon when someone is lost at sea. And now you're telling me that—"

"The storm didn't kill them."

"So someone went out in that storm and—and murdered them?" Hannah asked, appalled. The loss of the crew had been a local tragedy. To think that they might have survived Mother Nature only to be murdered made the situation all the more terrible.

"There was a rumor that the treasure chest from the *Santa Elinora* was aboard the *Discovery*."

"What?" Hannah demanded. "That treasure has been the subject of rumors for years! It was supposedly on the *Wind and the Sea* when *she* went down."

"Supposedly," Rodriguez said. "Key word—*supposedly*. Where it is now, no one knows. A historian wrote a piece on the *Santa Elinora* and the treasure about a year and a half ago, which started people speculating that it was still off Key West somewhere. Legend always had it that the chest was aboard Ian Chandler's *Wind and the Sea* when she went down in the 1850s, but no one really knows if that's true, and since the wreck was never found, no one's been able to confirm that it was there."

"So how did it end up on the *Discovery*?" Hannah asked, confused.

"There are thousands of undiscovered ship-wrecks out there—the ocean along the coast was once like a marine I-95. And since no one could predict storms, over hundreds of years, thousands of ships went down. And those looking for them are often cutthroat and are perfectly happy to commit murder over even the hint of something valuable turning up. Honestly, I don't believe the treasure chest was ever aboard the *Discovery*. What I *do* believe is that members of Los Lobos heard the rumors that it was there, and that they caught up with the *Discovery* right before the storm and killed the crew—for nothing. Since they didn't find it, they're searching in Key West again, because at this point no one really knows where the treasure is—on land or underwater. The items in the treasure chest are supposed to be so rare and historic that it's impossible to estimate their value—jewels set in the purest gold ever mined in South America."

"I've heard about the treasure my whole life," Hannah said. "According to legend, the *Santa Elinora* was discovered and salvaged when David Porter and his Mosquito Squadron came down in the 1820s, back when Florida was still a territory, to clean out the pirates. But Porter didn't keep any documents because officially they were supposed to be stopping pirates, not salvaging wrecks. But lack of proof didn't stop people from claiming that Porter found the chest and kept it in Key West until he tried to send it up to D.C. on the *Wind and the Sea.* Most of the people on the island at the time believed that the treasure went down with the *Wind and the Sea* when she sank, and to this day most people think it's still there."

Jose nodded and smiled slowly. "You would know. Your home is part of the legend of the treasure, and that makes you involved. Are you a descendant of the original owners? Not many left these days who go that far back."

"In a roundabout way. I'm a descendant of the original owner's first cousin."

"And you give ghost tours."

Hannah lifted her hands helplessly.

He laughed. "Not to worry—it's a legitimate business. And people like to be remembered. They like to have their stories told. I'd like my story to be told, one day."

Hannah hesitated and then said, "I know that you were working undercover. My friend Detective Beckett was here, along with a Federal agent."

"Dallas Samson," Rodriguez said, nodding.

"They said you were a good guy."

Jose knitted his fingers together and then released them, looking at her with a grim smile. "I've been with the FBI about five years. I made a point of getting this case. I've spent the past six months trying to get in with Los Lobos. I just made it in, but evidently I did something suspicious, or someone in the gang had seen me when I wasn't undercover. Or someone betrayed me. I have some ideas. But this case meant more to me than just bringing down the gang."

"Oh?"

"Los Lobos concentrates on 'priceless' treasures they can sell on the black market. But when their cash flow is down they deal in anything. Drugs. Human cargo."

"Human cargo? Are you talking about slavery? Today?"

He nodded. "Trust me, it still goes on." He shook his head. "One case—which at least had a happy ending—involved a young girl in Texas who was set up by a wealthy *friend*. A man in Eastern Europe offered a multimillion-dollar sum for a blue-eyed redhead under twenty-five. Los Lobos got wind of the offer and acted fast. The young woman went to a party at her friend's mansion, where she was drugged. Luckily we already had a man watching the friend and she was rescued. As for her millionaire friend, he mysteriously killed himself in lockup while waiting to be taken in for arraignment."

"You mean the millionaire was part of Los Lobos?"

"There are very rich people out there who covet things—and they know that Los Lobos can get whatever will make their collection complete."

"How horrible."

He nodded. "And we still don't know who the leader is or the gang's exact hierarchy. I'd hoped I would figure that out, but so far all I had discovered was that they only communicate with prepaid phones that they use once and toss. But," he said, "I never reported the real truth of my involvement to my superiors. They won't let you work a case when you have a personal interest in it." He seemed to inhale deeply, as if unaware that ghostly lungs didn't need oxygen. "My sister disappeared almost a year ago. I have reason to believe she fell into the hands of a Los Lobos general."

"You mean she was kidnapped?" Hannah asked.

"Yes. And either she's being held for the highest bidder or she's already been murdered, or . . ."

"There's another 'or'?" Hannah asked.

He nodded. "I was likely killed because the leader, a man they call the Wolf, discovered that I was FBI. And it's possible my sister . . . might have joined them—and that's why I'm dead."

Dallas and Liam met Mark, Yerby and the Atkinsons at a little coffee and ice cream shop on Duval. All four looked as if they'd had a long night. Judy and Pete Atkinson were in their late twenties, possibly early thirties. Pete was already balding, but he was slim and fit—even if he was looking haggard right now. Judy was tiny, maybe a full five feet in height, and a little round. Her eyes were a red-rimmed bright blue, making Dallas think of the American flag. Yerby Catalano was pretty, about twenty-two, with dark eyes and long dark hair, while Mark Riordan was probably a year or two older, tall and broad and muscled, as if he played sports. All four were more than willing to talk, they just didn't seem sure what to say.

They sat huddled over triple lattes, as if that could drive away the memory of the previous night.

"Shelly and Stuart are already packing up to head home, you know," Yerby told them. She shook her head. "Shelly was so freaked out."

"I wanted to kill her this morning," Pete said. He winced. "Bad choice of words. But . . . we thought that she and Stuart were just freaking out over something imaginary."

"Yeah, but I've never seen her so upset," Judy offered. "And Stuart was just as freaked out."

Yerby laughed. "We were all thrown—you should have seen us stumbling around like idiots."

"Maybe *you* were stumbling," Mark said.

"Hey, you were no better," Yerby said.

"None of us was any better," Judy said apologetically. "We were just . . . well, for Pete and me, this was our big weekend out. My folks have the kids. We have a four-year-old girl and a six-year-old boy, and we're both teaching and getting our doctorates. We came down to go a little wild."

"Hannah was great, though—you know, Miss O'Brien, the owner," Mark said. "She calmed them down, and who the hell else is going to give you your money back and send you to a nice hotel in the middle of the night just because you got scared?"

Yerby lifted her sunglasses to stare at him. "Sounds like you've got a crush on her."

Dallas could understand that. There was something unique about Hannah. She could snap back with precision, but she was also careful and wary—older than her years.

"Yerby!" Mark protested.

She smiled. "Just kidding. I almost have a crush on her and I'm straight," she said with a grin. "She was pretty cool. But we were wrong—all of us except for Stuart and Shelly. They *did* see something. A dying man."

"And I thank God we didn't," Judy breathed.

"Yeah, that's why I can't figure out how we can help you," Pete said.

"Shelly and Stuart remember a group leaving Duval about when you did. Do you remember anything about them?"

"I don't remember anything about anything," Yerby said.

"I do!" Judy said, perking up. "Shelly was kind of unnerved all night. She took all those ghost stories to heart. Anyway, Shelly was walking with me, and she grabbed my arm. Said we should slow down and let that group get ahead of us. Just in case. They looked like trouble, you know? They were all wearing hoodies, so we couldn't see their faces." She hesitated for a moment. "It was almost like they were trying to look stoned or drunk when they really weren't."

"Did you see them anywhere else earlier in the night?" Dallas asked.

"We didn't really go anywhere except for the tour and the Hard Rock," Pete said.

"I didn't notice them until Shelly pointed them out," Judy said.

"Do you remember seeing anyone else that night who stood out?" Liam asked.

They looked at each other, then shook their heads.

"Okay," Dallas said. "What do you remember after you were woken up? Did you hear anything from outside?"

"Except for Shelly screaming? Because I don't know if we *could* have heard anything from outside besides that," Judy said.

"Shelly screamed really loudly," Yerby said, nodding.

"And, by then, even Stuart was pretty hysterical," Mark added.

"Wait a minute," Pete said, frowning. "I do remember hearing some kind of . . . thrashing. I went to the window in the back to look out, but I didn't see anything. Although I didn't look long. Shelly was hysterical, and we all ran out to see what was going on. But you have to remember— they were convinced they'd seen a ghost. None of us even began to imagine she might have seen a real man."

"Back to the drunks in the hoodies. Did you notice any of them earlier?" Dallas asked. "Think about it. You notice people in hoodies down here. This is a vacation city. You mostly see shorts, halter dresses, tank tops, swim trunks."

Pete frowned thoughtfully. "You know, earlier in the evening—before the tour—we were having a drink, and I do remember seeing at least one hoodie hanging over the back of a barstool."

"Where were you? Do you remember?" Dallas asked.

"Yeah. A really cool Irish bar toward the south end of Duval. O'Hara's," Pete said.

Liam groaned.

Dallas turned to look at him. "Someone should be able to help us out there, don't you think?"

"Oh, yeah, I think so," Liam said.

"Yeah?" Pete asked. "How come?"

"My sister-in-law's family owns the place," Liam said.

4

"I've been watching the news all day. They still aren't letting out much information," Katie O'Hara said. She indicated the television above the bar and the wide-screen in the main room. "They went over the same few facts so many times it was ridiculous."

"What exactly have they said?" Hannah asked.

"That an as-yet-unidentified man was found in an alley, his throat slit. That even once he's identified his name will be withheld pending notification of next of kin. They're warning people to stay in groups and stick to well-lit streets."

"Hmm," Hannah murmured. She'd told Katie about what had happened, and she didn't feel she was violating anyone's trust. She hadn't revealed anything Agent Samson had told her, only confided in Katie regarding the ghost of the dead man. Besides, Katie was married to David Beckett, Liam Beckett's brother, and she was sure to know what had happened through the family.

And, like Liam, Katie and her brother, Sean, had their own strange and unearthly Key West experiences. They all shared a strange bond because of that.

Hannah had desperately needed to talk to someone, and Katie was not just a good friend, she was a friend who knew all about souls who hung around after death because something was keeping them from moving on.

"What about Melody and Hagen?" Katie asked.

"I haven't seen them since early this morning," Hannah said, and winced. "I accused them of playing tricks. I think they're mad at me."

"They'll come back. They love you—and the house," Katie said drily. "But you say this Agent Samson is a hard case?"

"Rude. Obnoxious. And suspicious of me, for whatever reason."

"I don't think I know him," Katie said.

"He said he grew up here."

"It's an island, but people come and go. Did he leave the Keys when he was young?"

"He's supposedly friends with your husband."

"Really? Well, he might have been. But he hasn't been back here long, right?"

"I don't really know. He and Liam seem to work well together, but I'm in a difficult situation."

"Because he's on your case and you have information that can help him, but you can't tell him what you know because a ghost told you," Katie said.

"Something like that. Except, of course, I *can* tell Liam."

"I say you call Kelsey," Katie told her. "Your cousin Kelsey O'Brien, not Liam's wife."

"I thought about that. I mean, she's FBI, too—with a special unit that handles this kind of thing." Hannah paused, then said decisively, "All right. I'll call her."

"No, I mean, like, *now*," Katie said.

"I just hate to bother her," Hannah said.

"Let's see—dead FBI agent in your alley and another one thinking maybe you had something to do with it. And she's not only an agent, too, she's part of the Krewe of Hunters and specializes in paranormal cases. I don't think calling her in these circumstances counts as bothering any-one," Katie said.

Even as she spoke, Hannah's phone—sitting on the table by her coffee cup—began to ring, and the screen identified the caller as Kelsey O'Brien.

Katie stared at Hannah. "You two have telepathy now?"

"No," Hannah said with a dry smile. "She probably heard about what happened."

She picked up the phone, and Kelsey started off by asking her how she was. Hannah lied and said she was fine. "But I was about to call you," she added. "Have you guys up there heard about the murder in the Keys?"

"We always hear when something like that goes down. This is . . . bad. I've spoken with Logan, and we're coming down."

Logan Raintree was the head of Kelsey's special unit. They were also a couple. Hannah was pretty sure they had either gotten married already in secret or were planning on a quiet wedding soon. She would have expected their relationship to be taboo, but apparently they really *were* very special agents and the tight-knit community in which they worked didn't discourage close—even intimate—relationships between agents.

"That's great," Hannah said. "I can't wait to see you."

Katie, watching her, nodded enthusiastically in agreement.

"But until I get there, hang with Liam and Katie, okay? Just to be safe."

"Because this has to do with Los Lobos?"

Kelsey was quiet for a minute and then she said, "Yes. So you *do* know."

"Yes, I know it's all related. But, why would I be in any danger? I didn't see what happened," Hannah said, surprised.

"There were cops, agents and crime scene techs stomping all over your yard today, right?" Kelsey asked.

"Yes, but . . . the only two people who saw any part of what happened are headed back to Miami—or there already, depending on who was driving," Hannah said.

"Los Lobos has a long reach. I wouldn't count on them being safe," Kelsey said.

"They didn't see the killer, just the dead man."

"I'm sure the police are doing everything they can," Kelsey said. "And there's always the possibility that Jose Rodriguez can help us himself."

"He can't."

"You've seen him already?" Kelsey asked, surprised.

"Yes, and he gave me the names of the people he was with, but he's not sure whether they were involved or not. And he has no idea who came up behind him."

"What else did he say?" Kelsey asked. "Did he tell you he was going to be working with Dallas Samson? You met him, right?"

"Yeah, I met him. You know him?"

"Uh-huh. I took a class from him when I was at the academy."

"In?"

"Self-defense. Good class. The guy looks like he's made out of iron, and he was teaching a class to show female agents how to deal with that kind of strength. Mind and balance over brawn. It was an excellent class. I loved the man."

"Wonderful," Hannah said.

"Anyway, I'm not sure how many of us will be coming. Logan needs clearance from Adam Harrison for a big operation, so I'll tell you as soon as possible. Do you have any rooms free?"

Hannah laughed drily. "All of them. In fact,

when word gets out, I may have all of them free for a very long time."

"Don't kid yourself—haunted rooms are always in demand," Kelsey told her. "Okay, stay safe. I'll be in touch."

Hannah's phone rang again the minute she and Kelsey hung up. She picked it up and saw that it was her reservation service. She winced and answered. A recorded message came on. "Good evening. This call is to inform you that your tour reservation cap for this evening has been reached. Guests have been told to arrive no later than seven-thirty this evening. All credit cards have been applied and have cleared. Thank you so much for using Zoom Reservation Services."

She hung up the phone and looked at Katie morosely. "I have a tour tonight. It's filled."

"It *is* a Saturday night," Katie pointed out.

"Right. And what do you want to bet that people expect me to show them where a man was killed last night?"

"Want me to get this place covered and come with you?" Katie asked.

"No, don't be silly. I'm not afraid of tourists."

Katie laughed. "Be afraid—be very afraid," she teased. "Seriously, I can go with you."

"And seriously, I'm okay. And when I get back, since I don't have a single guest, the night will be all mine."

"You'll get guests back, I promise you."

Katie would know. Her husband, David, had once been accused of killing his high school sweetheart. In proving his innocence, he'd caught the real killer. And the museum where the killings had taken place belonged to Katie now—and it was thriving.

"Hey," Katie said. "There's Liam."

Hannah jerked around quickly. Liam was blinking against the darkness of the pub in contrast to the brilliance of a Key West summer afternoon.

Katie jumped up to greet her brother-in-law. Hannah followed and then stopped. Liam wasn't alone. Agent Samson was with him.

There was no way to miss him when he walked into a room. He was tall—six-three or -four—but it wasn't just his height. It was the way he carried himself. She couldn't help but note that every female in the pub was staring at him. The men were watching him, as well—wary, perhaps.

"Hey, Katie," Liam said, greeting her with a kiss on the cheek. "I guess Hannah's brought you up to speed."

"Yes, she told me she found a dead man in her alley," Katie said, giving nothing away. She looked inquiringly at Agent Samson.

"Katie, this is Dallas Samson. We were best friends until his dad got himself a top job in Washington. He's down here again, and we're working on this case together."

"Hey," Katie said, studying the man, then glancing at Hannah with a little grin. "Nice to meet you, Agent Samson. I heard you were here."

"And we need your help," Samson said. He, too, looked at Hannah—suspicious, probably, that she was there.

"I need to head back home," Hannah said. "I'll see you soon, Katie."

"Don't leave," Samson said.

It sounded like an order given by a drill sergeant. Hannah instantly felt her temperature rise.

Then he added, "Please."

It still sounded like a command.

"You want me to stay?" she asked, her skepticism clear.

"For a few minutes. Liam and I can talk to the Hardwickes later, but for now I'd like you to take me back to your place after I talk to Katie."

"Oh?" She knew her one word had attitude, but she couldn't help it. He was obnoxious.

"I was hoping you would come with me to meet your handyman neighbor, Mr. Holloway."

Hannah nodded slowly. "All right. If it will help, if you think it's necessary."

"Katie, the group that was staying at the Siren of the Sea noticed a group wearing hoodies who might have been in here earlier in the evening. Do you remember seeing a bunch of guys like that?" Liam asked.

"Let's see, it was Friday and pretty busy. You know I'm not here all the time, right? I just run the karaoke and help out Uncle Jamie when needed," Katie said.

"Were you here around seven, by any chance?"

"Yes, I was," she said, frowning. "Let me think. Hoodies?"

"Dark hoodies," Liam said.

"I don't remember anybody wearing one, but I do remember seeing one on the back of a barstool," Katie said. "I saw some guy pick it up, and it looked like he was with three or four friends. They were young—early twenties, I'd say. One looked a little older. They looked like they were in town for a bachelor party or a frat weekend, something like that."

"Would you recognize any of them if you saw them again?" Liam asked her.

"I might," Katie said.

"Can you come with me to the station?" he asked her.

Katie looked at Hannah worriedly. "Yes, I guess so. Karaoke doesn't start until eight."

"Hannah, you can take me to meet your neighbor and see what he can tell us," Agent Samson said. "If you don't mind?"

She shook her head. As soon as Katie gave the staff some instructions, the two of them left with Liam and Dallas Samson.

Liam drove the few blocks south down Duval

and then around the corner to drop off Hannah and Dallas.

"Do you want me to call Bentley and see if he'll come over here?" Hannah asked.

"No, let's just see if he's home. I'd like to see his place."

Holloway's property was separated from Hannah's by tall cherry hedges. Hannah looked at Dallas for a moment, shrugged and started up the old coral pathway to the house. They climbed the two steps to a small porch.

"Do we let him know that you're a Federal agent?" Hannah asked.

"I think he's figured that out already, since you said he was in the alley this morning," Dallas said.

"Probably. But the body is still officially unidentified, right?"

"Yes, until we say otherwise. You can handle that, can't you?"

"Oh, yes, I can handle that." She knew that her voice had attitude again. She couldn't seem to help herself, but then he couldn't seem to help being obnoxious.

Hannah knocked on the door. Dallas had a feeling that Bentley Holloway had been watching them from inside, because the door opened almost immediately.

The man was wearing khakis and a Doors T-shirt. His bald head gleamed in the sunlight, and his eyes were sharp as he studied them. He appeared to be about forty-five or fifty, bronzed deeply with features lined by years in the sun. He was leanly muscled, and his arms bore a number of tattoos. He looked like a seaman, as so many Key Westers did.

There didn't appear to be any defensive wounds on his arms, neither did he appear to be in any pain, as if he'd been in a fight.

There really was no reason to suspect the man. Still, Dallas studied him carefully.

"Hey, Hannah. And . . . ?" Holloway asked, looking at Dallas.

Dallas offered Bentley Holloway his hand. "Dallas Samson."

"You're a cop, huh?" Holloway asked.

"Agent—Federal," Dallas said.

"Oh. I saw you out in the alley this morning. How come the Feds are on a local murder case?"

"Oh, there aren't many of us in the office down here," Dallas said. "We step in wherever we might be needed."

"Liam is a good detective," Holloway said defensively.

"The best. He's a friend," Dallas said. "Okay if we come in and ask you for some help?"

"Help? Hell, I wish I could," Holloway said. "But sure, come on in."

The door opened right into the living room. Dallas quickly noted that it was filled with plain furniture that looked as if it had come from the mix and match department at the Salvation Army, but he'd spruced it up nicely. The walls were decorated with watercolors of various scenes of Key life: sailboats in the harbor, kids playing on a beach and also an arresting picture of the local lighthouse. At first glance, it sure as hell didn't appear that he was living the high life.

"Sit down, sit down," Holloway said. "You want lemonade? Iced tea? Something stronger?"

"Sure, I'd love iced tea or lemonade—anything you have handy," Dallas told him.

He sensed that Hannah was surprised that he'd accepted the offer, but he wanted to see as much of the house as he could without a warrant. There was no reason in particular to be suspicious of Holloway. He was just suspicious of everyone, and he was pretty sure Rodriguez had cut through Holloway's yard after he was attacked.

Which meant the killer had probably come through, too.

"Make yourself at home—have a seat," Holloway said, heading toward the kitchen.

But Dallas didn't sit; he followed Holloway, with Hannah at his heels.

"Great place," Dallas said.

The house wasn't as old as Hannah's. Originally built in the shotgun style, you could see straight through from front door to back door as one room opened straight into the next. It was obvious that over the years—and with the advent of electricity and air-conditioning—the house had been enlarged. Now additional rooms branched off to either side.

They walked through the dining room to get to the kitchen, but Dallas noticed that there were doors leading off both sides of the dining room.

"Yeah, thanks. I inherited it. Property values down here are killer now. I've had a lot of friends sell out, move up to the center of the state then wish they were back here, only they can't afford it. Key West kind of gets in your blood. I'll never let this place go," Holloway said. "It was originally built by my however-many-greats grandfather around 1875."

"Nice," Dallas said. "Really nice."

The dining room, furnished with a table that sat eight, a cupboard and a buffet, had seascapes on the walls.

The kitchen had been remodeled. There was a granite island in the center, with four stools around it, pots and pans hanging from the overhead rafters and brand-new appliances.

Holloway stopped when he got there and looked around as if surprised he had been followed. Dallas stopped so short that Hannah crashed into him.

She steadied herself with her hands on his back.

He was startled to discover that he liked her touch.

"I love old houses," he told Holloway.

"Yeah? Well, then Key West is the place to be. People tend to think of South Florida as a twentieth-century invention. Not down here. We've got some of the richest history in the nation—and one of the largest concentrations of old Victorians anywhere," Holloway said proudly.

Dallas nodded. "I actually grew up here."

"No kidding?" Holloway asked.

"No kidding. I left when I was sixteen. I've gotten back every chance I could since, though."

"You living here now?" Holloway asked.

"I'm assigned here for now, yes." Dallas nodded.

"Oh, right. You're a Fed. You could wind up anywhere," Holloway said.

He took lemonade from the refrigerator and glasses from the cupboard. When the glasses were filled, he indicated that they might as well take a seat at the granite island.

"So what can I do for you?" he asked. He looked at Hannah with a frown, as if wondering what she was doing there.

"I wanted to ask you what you saw this morning, Mr. Holloway," Dallas said.

"Bentley—just call me Bentley. We're still casual down here," Holloway said with a smile. "What did I see? A bunch of crime scene tape."

"You didn't see or hear anything before you

came out and the police were already on the scene?" Dallas asked.

"Sorry. I was sleeping. I woke up when I heard the ruckus out back. Went on out to watch. I wish I could help. I really do," Holloway said.

"Bentley, you *can* help," Hannah said, speaking up with a smile. "I'm pretty sure after the man was attacked he stumbled through your yard into mine. They've searched my property and the alley. Would you mind if they searched your yard, too?"

Before the man could answer, Hannah touched his arm. "I know it's an intrusion. But I'd be grateful. I found him, Bentley. I can't tell you how that felt . . . to bend down and see him there, dead. Please?"

Holloway stared down into Hannah's beseeching turquoise eyes.

Dallas was sure *he* couldn't have refused her or remained unmoved.

Holloway shook his head ruefully and looked at Dallas. "Since Hannah asked . . . go ahead. Look wherever you need to look."

"Thank you," Dallas said. He wondered how she'd known the scenario the cops had settled on. It was almost as if she'd known what happened when Rodriguez was killed.

"Thank you, Bentley," she said, smiling. "You'll help put my mind to rest."

Dallas swallowed the last of his lemonade. "I'll

step outside, then, and let the techs know to get started."

Leaving the two of them in the kitchen, he went outside and walked half a block toward Duval, then turned around and retraced his steps. He tried to envision what had happened—and where.

He moved slowly, checking for signs of blood on both the sidewalk and the grass.

He knew he wasn't going to find anything like the kind of high velocity spatter a bullet created. According to Dirk, Rodriguez's jugular had been nicked, leading to a fatal loss of blood.

But Rodriguez had cut his attacker, as well.

He gave up searching for blood drops and walked through the yard. If Rodriguez had crashed through the hedge, he should be able to see where.

The door to the house opened, and Hannah came out. He paused. He should thank her. She had gotten him the clearance he needed to examine Holloway's property without a warrant. If there was evidence he had to find it now, and getting a warrant would take time.

"Here's my theory. I think he came from the street . . . that way," she said, and pointed to the right. She wasn't looking at him as she approached. "He heard his attacker coming up behind him. He was with a group of new . . . friends, but they took off when he was attacked from behind. He got away and ended up here.

Somewhere along the way he drew his knife and fought back, managing to slice his attacker, which gave him time to get away. He gripped his throat and staggered through the hedge and into my yard."

Hannah walked to what had to be the exact spot where the dying man had gone through the hedge. As he followed her, Dallas could see the trail.

"Here," she said softly, coming to a stop by a lounge chair near the pool. "Here's where he scared Shelly and Stuart half to death. But he must have heard the killer coming, so he staggered out to the alley. He needed to lure the killer away. But I think the killer saw where he went and never even came through my yard, so Shelly and Stuart never saw him."

Dallas stared at her. She didn't appear to be in a trance, hadn't claimed to be a psychic, but somehow she seemed to know exactly what had happened.

Of course, any good detective would have figured out the course of events; the evidence was clear.

She wasn't a detective, yet she had homed in so exactly on the truth. . . .

She walked from the pool through the yard, her footsteps faltering. She wasn't staggering the way a dying man might have done, she was just following the path Dallas knew he had taken.

Dallas followed her out to the alley. She stopped just outside the crime scene tape.

She met his eyes at last.

Dallas was very still, watching her.

"Anyone would think you'd been with Agent Rodriguez."

"It's just . . . apparent."

"Apparent, yes. But . . ."

"But?" she asked.

"It's as if you know something," he said.

She flushed. "Are you accusing me of—?"

"I'm not accusing you of anything," he said. "Let's go inside."

"The house? The killer was nowhere near the house."

"I want to rent a room," he told her.

"What?"

"You operate a bed-and-breakfast, right?"

"You have a home here. You work here," she said.

"I want to rent a room."

It was obvious she didn't want him staying in her house.

"My cousin is coming soon, maybe as early as tomorrow. I'm not sure how many people are coming with her, but they'll probably need all my rooms."

"Not a problem. I only need a room for tonight," he said.

"Why?" she asked him.

"Do you have a guard dog?" he asked.

"A guard dog? No."

"Do you have an alarm system?"

"Oh, please. Didn't you listen to me? Jose led the killer away. There's no reason for him to come here looking for me or anyone else."

He turned and walked back through her yard, then waited at the rear door. She followed him, still confused and a little belligerent. "I don't understand—"

"You were thinking about calling people you'd turned away to see if anyone still needed a room, so I know you have space. How do you work things? Do guests get two keys? One for the door to the house and another for the door to their rooms?" he asked her.

"Why the third degree? Are you still suspicious of me for some reason?"

He let out an impatient groan. "No, I'm not suspicious. I'm worried, and I'm thinking like a cop. The killer was, to all intents and purposes, right here. He almost certainly saw you and knows that you found the body."

"How?" she demanded.

Dallas hesitated. "It might be a cliché, but killers do sometimes return to the scene of the crime. Sometimes, they're sick bastards who come back to enjoy the kill all over again. Sometimes they come back to watch the cops and see what they've discovered. There's every chance the killer was in that alley this morning. But say he wasn't. That newswoman shot a lot of footage, and you're bound to be in it. Just as a precaution, rent me a room."

She stared at him, but he couldn't tell what she was thinking. She was too damn good at keeping her face expressionless.

"I have good locks."

"You could have the best locks ever invented," he told her, "and if someone wants to get in, they'll get in."

She moved ahead of him and unlocked the door. She went inside without looking back to see if he followed, but she didn't slam the door on him, either. He followed her to the reception desk, where she opened a drawer and produced a set of keys.

"The whole house is empty, right?" he asked her.

"At this moment? Yes."

"Then I'd like the Melody Chandler room, please."

"What?" she asked.

He let out a sigh that he hoped didn't sound as impatient as he felt. His start with Hannah had not been a good one, and it didn't seem as if they were going to get along any better now.

"I told you," he said quietly, "I'm from here. This was Melody Chandler's home. She lived here when the man she loved, Hagen Dundee, died trying to save passengers off the *Wind and the Sea* when she went down. When I was a kid, I took a ghost tour and the guide pointed out her window. I'd like to stay in her room."

"*I* sleep in Melody Chandler's room," she told him.

"Ah," he murmured. "Then give me her father's room, the Ian Chandler room."

For a long moment she stared at him.

"Please," he said. His tone was gruff, and he realized that even when he was trying to be polite, he sounded like an ass. And he didn't know why. What was it about her that brought out this side of him?

He couldn't help it. He pictured Jose Rodriguez. Dead.

And he pictured Adrian Hall where she, too, had lain dead in a pool of her own blood.

He pulled out his wallet to produce a credit card.

"Don't be ridiculous," she said. "You're staying here for one night to make sure I don't get killed. I'm not going to charge you."

"Don't be silly. I'll put it on an expense report."

"You want to stay here—stay here. If not, leave. I won't charge an officer of the law for doing what he sees as his duty."

"Fine. Keys, please."

She slammed a set of keys down on the desk. "I give a ghost tour at eight. I never take more than sixteen people out. They start arriving around 7:30 p.m. We're here for about thirty minutes, starting from eight. I'm back at about 10:30."

"Great. Sign me up."

"I'm fully booked for tonight."

"Consider me a special guest."

"I only take sixteen."

"Then think of me as an annoying fly following you wherever you go."

She looked at him, her face giving everything away this time. She was tense and exasperated.

"Don't you have some investigating to do? You're not going to find Jose's murderer by following me around."

"Jose?" he asked. "You're talking as if you knew him. As if you two were on a first-name basis."

"Why shouldn't I use his name? It *was* Jose, right?" she demanded, her voice as tight as her jaw.

"Yes. His name was Jose," Dallas said. He pointed at the desk. "Are those my keys?"

She nodded, still staring at him.

He took the keys. "Keep the doors locked at all times, at least until this guy is caught."

"What about people coming for the tour, or, eventually, guests, who arrive at all times during the day?"

"Let them ring the bell." Unwilling to argue anymore, he started upstairs before he remembered he didn't know where he was going.

He started back down.

"Turn left at the landing. Ian Chandler's room is the first one on the left. You'll find it easily enough. All the rooms have plaques by the doors that identify them."

"Thanks," he said gruffly, but he didn't move. He didn't know why he was hesitating.

"Hey," she said.

"Yeah?"

"Why did you want Melody Chandler's room?"

"I heard the legend growing up. She's still supposed to haunt the room."

"And you want to see a ghost?" she asked.

"You never know. Maybe her ghost could be helpful. Maybe she saw something no one else did." He turned then and hurried up to his room. When he reached it, he found that the door was open. He walked in and looked around. The decor was masculine and nautical. A heavy wooden cabinet complemented the antique captain's bed. A ship's wheel decorated one wall, along with various flags and paintings of sailing ships at sea.

He checked out the bathroom. It was small but had been updated in the not too distant past. Returning to the bedroom, he sat on the bed.

He wasn't really sure what he was doing. He hadn't intended to take a room here when he had headed with her to visit her next-door neighbor.

But watching her . . .

She knew too much. He didn't know how, but

she did. And that meant she might put everything together and come up with answers that were too close to home.

And someone else—like a killer—just might realize that.

Machete hid in the hedges and carefully watched the Siren of the Sea.

The house was quiet. He'd seen the man and the woman enter the house. He knew them, of course. Well, knew that the tall sandy-haired man was an agent. And Hannah was a local; everyone knew her. So pretty and blonde. So full of life— at least for now.

He felt his phone vibrate and answered it. He'd been expecting the call. It was the Wolf.

"So?" came a single sharp word.

"The Fed went inside with her. He didn't come back out."

"When he leaves, make your move."

Machete said, "Her tour customers will start arriving in a few hours."

"Get in there when they're gone. Find the key."

Find the key? Search an entire house in a few hours and find something as small as a key?

"It's not going to be easy."

"Of course it won't. Someone would have found it by now if it were obvious. Check the attic. It's probably up there somewhere."

"I can't promise—"

"Oh, yes, you can. The place is empty. No guests. Stay in there until you get me that key."

"But she could catch me!"

"I doubt she wanders around her attic at night, but if she *does* catch you," the Wolf said softly, "you know what to do."

Machete had never argued with the Wolf before. Never questioned him. Until now.

"I think going in now is a mistake. The key will still be there, and she's not a threat to us. She knows nothing. She saw nothing. She came out when it was over. But if something happens to this woman now, when the police are already looking for a killer, they will rip the city apart—and we'll never get in there to find the key."

There was silence at the other end of the line. Machete didn't dare breathe. The Wolf had eyes everywhere, and he had assassins everywhere, too. Machete didn't know who the Wolf was—no one did. And no one who didn't need to know had any idea of Machete's real name, either. Everything in Los Lobos was on a need-to-know basis.

Most of all, no one argued with the Wolf.

But the thought of killing her . . .

For a moment, Machete thought his infatuation with Hannah O'Brien might have been his undoing. He wished he could take back his words. The silence from the other end of the line stretched for what seemed like hours.

"I just don't want to lose this opportunity," he finally said quickly—desperately. "It could take time for me to find the key, and if something happens to her before I do, it would draw attention to the house. The Siren of the Sea could be closed down, and it would certainly be swarming with police. I would never be able to get inside then. I need to be able to go in and out safely until I find what we're looking for."

Again his words were met with silence. He felt sweat bead his brow and drench his shirt.

At last the Wolf spoke.

"Get in and get out, then. But remember, you're on your own. And remember, too, if that woman finds you and you don't do what's necessary, I will."

The phone went dead.

Machete stood there shaking and hot with sweat.

Finally the breeze began to cool his skin as he waited for the Fed to leave.

Except . . .

He didn't leave.

The sweat on Machete's skin began to turn to ice. He didn't want to make another call.

What the hell was he going to do if the agent never left?

Or, worse, if Hannah O'Brien didn't leave, either?

5

Great, Hannah thought. Broad-shouldered and bossy was staying at the Siren of the Sea.

Just what she needed.

But . . . she *didn't* have an alarm system. It was complicated enough to keep track of her keys—and no way was she destroying the Siren's period charm by using those little plastic cards the big hotels had all switched to. Guests got one key to the front door and then a key to whatever room they were renting.

Tourists tended to imbibe in Key West. Heavily. Some of her friends who also ran B and Bs had alarm systems, and they were constantly having them reset because their drunken guests couldn't get the code right. And the codes had to be changed constantly, since after a few months dozens of people had the same one.

Besides, in all her years of running the Siren of the Sea, she'd never had a problem.

She had never once been afraid. But now that Agent Samson had put the idea into her mind that she might be a target, she couldn't escape the fear.

It didn't matter. Tomorrow Kelsey and the Krewe would be arriving, and they would figure things out and everything would be okay.

No, it wouldn't be okay. It would never be okay. A dying man had come into her yard looking for help, then breathed his last in the alley behind her house, and now his ghost had come to her for help.

She'd really wanted to speak with Liam earlier. But then tall, dark and annoying had wanted her to come with him so that she could introduce him to Bentley.

Meanwhile, the dead man was no doubt off retracing his own steps, trying to figure out who his killer was, trying to repeat the last day of his life, trying to comprehend how he had been taken so quickly and unaware.

And her angry resident ghosts were still AWOL.

"So, here we are," she murmured aloud. "Me and Mr. Shoulders. And sixteen people coming far too soon so we can all go off on a ghost tour."

Dallas was probably all the more suspicious of her after she had retraced the dying man's route. But something had come over her when they had stepped out of Bentley's house. She had felt the pain of the man she had found dead and come to know as a ghost. He was determined to stop Los Lobos, and that meant he needed to know the identity of his killer.

He needed to know the truth.

"Would you like dinner?"

The question startled her so badly that she jumped up from her desk, nearly knocking over a nineteenth-century vase. She steadied it as she stared at Agent Samson.

"Uh, sorry. What?" she asked.

"I'm going out for dinner. Would you care to join me?"

"I, uh, no. That's okay," she said awkwardly. "But . . . thank you."

"You don't eat?"

"Of course I eat."

"Do you have previous plans?"

"No . . . I have a tour starting at eight."

"It's six."

She didn't know why it seemed churlish to refuse him. She wasn't obliged to eat with him. But damn. She wasn't even sure she entirely disliked him now.

"It's really okay. I can fix myself something here."

"I'm sure you can. But would you like to go out, anyway?"

No!

"I . . . sure."

He smiled at that. It was, she realized, a nice smile. And while he could come on like a bull bursting into a rodeo arena, he could also be . . . appealing.

"I don't want to force you if it will be a problem for you."

"No, no, it's fine," she said. "I mean . . . there's no one here."

He walked through to the back. She knew he was checking the lock, and she decided that was a good thing. Then he rejoined her, and they walked to the front door together.

"So, have you always lived here?" he asked.

"Not always. Just mostly." She locked the door behind them. "My father taught for two years up in St. Augustine. I think I was eleven or twelve. Then we lived here, and then I went up to New Orleans for college at Tulane. And then I came back."

"Ah. Where are your folks now?"

She smiled. "They're on a world tour."

"Oh, yeah? Alive and well and traveling the world. That's great."

They had reached the street. "Yeah, it is," she murmured, looking at him. Again she felt awkward. "Does that mean that . . . ?"

"Yeah, mine are gone. My mom had cancer. My dad died of a heart attack a few weeks after she passed."

"I'm so sorry."

He nodded. "It's been a while."

"You're an only child?"

"I have a great older sister living in Biloxi. She has three obnoxious but wonderful children. And my brother-in-law is a good guy, so all is well. You're an only child, though, aren't you?"

She smiled, lowering her head. "You can tell?"

He laughed. "No. I just had a feeling. You've turned the family home into a business."

"Actually, I didn't live here with my parents. My great-uncle left it to me. He said I had the good sense to love Key West and I should have the house."

"Did that fit with your dreams?"

She shrugged. "History major. So, yes, I guess. More or less."

"You're happy, running a bed-and-breakfast and telling the same ghost stories night after night?"

She would have been offended except that he winced so quickly. "Sorry—I didn't mean that the way it sounded."

"Oh? And how *did* you mean it?"

"Just that . . . there's a lot more history out there in the world."

She was secretly glad to see that he was actually uncomfortable. In fact, that made her smile. "I write, too. I've written what I hope is a good book on local ghosts and legends, with real history. I mean, a ghost isn't very interesting if you don't know why he—or she—is there, right?"

"True," he agreed. "I'll have to read it. Is it—is it published?"

She nodded, trying to hide another smile of amusement. "Yes."

"Title?"

"*Key West: Truth or Dare.*"

"I look forward to reading it."

"You don't have to."

"But I'd like to."

"Then I'll give you a copy."

"I'm happy to buy it."

"I've actually sold enough copies that I can afford to give you one. Honest."

He let out a breath, lowered his head and shook it. When he looked up, his eyes were filled with humor and he was smiling. She was startled to realize just how good-looking he was.

Personality. It was in the eyes, she thought.

And he had a lot of other assets to go with that personality.

"Miss O'Brien, may I start over? I'm Dallas Samson. Pleased to make your acquaintance. And I'll try not to be so obnoxiously rude in the future."

He offered her his hand. She took it. Naturally, his hand was large, and his fingers were very long. She could sense real power in his handshake.

"Lovely to meet you, Mr.—sorry, *Agent*—Samson. I'm sure the pleasure is mine. And I'll try not to—"

She broke off, suddenly feeling guilty for being so cavalier when a man had died so close to her home.

I'll try not to stumble on any more bodies, she thought.

"Hey," he said, and to her surprise he touched her chin lightly. "It's all right. Jose would want us to get along—and he'd want you to be safe."

How had he known what she was thinking?

She felt oddly as if they were talking about someone who had been a friend to them both. Maybe, in a way, he had been.

Or still was.

She suddenly felt as if they were sharing a moment that was almost intimate. How ridiculous! She stepped back.

"So, where shall we eat?" she asked.

"You choose."

"I've been here forever, you've just come back, so what would you like to have?" she asked.

They turned the corner and decided on a restaurant in a beautiful Victorian house on Duval just down from Caroline Street. Neither of them knew their waitress, a pretty young girl who told them she was from Russia. They ordered drinks and the house special, mahimahi almandine.

When their drinks were served and the waitress had gone on to place their orders, Hannah realized she still hadn't spoken to Liam and she really needed to. He wasn't quite as adept at seeing the dead as she was, but in both his personal life and his work he'd experienced enough to believe what she told him—or to at least accept that she might really have received reliable information from a source that most people couldn't see or hear.

She excused herself and went to the ladies' room where she put a call through to him, but she only reached his voice mail. She left him a message and returned to the table.

Dallas stood to pull out her chair for her.

She thanked him and asked, "So what's your next move?"

"Liam had Katie work with a police artist, so we'll get those sketches out and look for the people Jose was with last night before he was killed."

"They didn't kill him," Hannah said.

"What?"

"Uh, I . . . I don't believe one of them killed him," she said hastily. "I think they ran like rats when he was attacked. Maybe they knew someone was coming, though. They might have set him up."

"Well, it's important for us to find them, no matter what. Even if they didn't kill him, maybe they can lead us to the person who did."

"Do you think that will happen?" Hannah asked. "I thought the fate of a rat within Los Lobos was far worse than anything the law could deal out."

"We have witness protection, and we have ways to threaten, bribe and interrogate that can be quite effective," he told her. "Maybe others have failed, but we won't. We're also waiting on lab reports. We're testing every tiny drop we could find. We could be extraordinarily lucky and discover we have the killer's blood and his DNA is in the system."

"I suppose I know all that, it's just that . . ."

"That what?" he asked.

She shrugged. "You were so . . . geared to move," she said. "And now we're just sitting here having dinner."

He didn't reply for a moment. She felt a sense of unease trickle down her spine.

"You *are* working, aren't you?" she asked. "You really do think I'm in danger."

He raised his shoulders slightly in a non-committal manner. "We just don't know," he said.

"You sure know how to make a girl feel safe, Agent Samson," she murmured.

"I'm not sure you *should* feel safe right now."

"Hey, haven't you heard? I have an FBI agent staying in my house."

"There you go."

He fell quiet as their waitress brought their food. When she'd left he asked Hannah, "Does the word *cur* mean anything to you?"

"Cur?" she repeated.

"Cur, yes. *C-U-R.*"

"Well, it's a nasty dog, as far as I know," she said.

"Yes. I just wonder what else it might mean or refer to."

"Why?"

His eyes were level and unfathomable as he stared at her across the table. "He wrote it," he

113

told her. "Jose wrote it on the ground—in his own blood."

"Oh." Hannah had been about to taste her fish, but now she set her fork down. "Oh," she repeated.

"I'm sorry," he said. "I should have waited and not upset you while you were eating."

She shook her head. "I'm just so sorry. He was—he sounds like he was a fine man."

He nodded. "If it occurs to you later that it might mean something, let me know."

"Of course. I'll ask hi—" she began, then quickly cut herself off.

"Pardon?" He frowned fiercely.

"What?"

"You'll ask who?"

"Oh, around. You know. See if the word means anything to any of the old-timers. Or anyone else, for that matter," she said quickly. She looked down at her plate, picked up her fork again and began to eat. He was still watching her, and she knew it. "The fish is really delicious." She made a point of looking at her watch. "We should hurry a little. People sometimes show up kind of early, and when they do, I let them sit out on the patio."

"People," he murmured.

"Well, yes, *people*. They *are* the ones who take ghost tours," she said.

"And you just let them all into your house?"

"It's a bed-and-breakfast. I *have* to let people into my house."

"That's one thing. I'm assuming you get their names, addresses, a form of ID? Those are guests —and at least you have something to identify them. Anyone can take a ghost tour, right? And you just let them all in?" He sounded incredulous, as if he couldn't believe how foolish she was.

She set her fork down again. Dinner was over. She glanced at her plate. In fact, it *was* over. She'd been so hungry that she'd finished the fish without even realizing it.

"I'm in the tourist industry. Nothing is going to happen to me when sixteen people are following me through town. You've seen too much of the worst of humanity. I usually get to see the good," she told him.

He leaned across the table. She was ready to hop up, then realized that he wasn't trying to insult her. He was trying to convince her.

"You don't know who might be on that tour. Who might have signed up to check you out, find a way to get to you. I can understand you wanting to see the best in people, and that's a commendable quality. Except for now. And even after this is over, you might want to be a little more careful. You don't know who might see something they like when they're looking around the Siren of the Sea. Something they'd come back for."

"Oh, great." Distracted by that depressing thought, she stood. "This was actually a nice time. Thank you." She suddenly realized how that sounded. "Oh, sorry. That was presumptuous. Are we splitting the check?"

His mouth twitched. "It's my pleasure to get the bill."

They left the restaurant. When they returned to the house, there were already four people waiting out front. Hannah quickly introduced herself and opened the door, inviting them in. She turned to introduce Dallas Samson and faltered, not sure how much to say.

He stepped forward and took care of that himself. "Dallas Samson, hello. I'm staying here at the Siren of the Sea."

The foursome was the Taylor family, George and Ivy and their two grown sons, Trevor and Blaine. Ivy oohed and aahed over the house when they took seats in the parlor. Hannah excused herself to get them some bottled water as they waited for the rest of the tour to arrive.

In the kitchen, she paused. She didn't know why; it just felt as if something wasn't quite right. "Melody?" she said quietly. "Hagen?"

Neither of the ghosts replied. Looking around, she tried to find something that was different, but nothing stood out.

Had Jose Rodriguez been back in spirit form?

She was still, well, *haunted* by the sense that something just wasn't right, but she still couldn't place it, and now her house was filling up with people for her ghost tour. Reaching into the refrigerator, she grabbed three six-packs of water to take out to the parlor.

The Taylor family had been joined by Maddie, Belinda, Tobie and Josiah, the Rosewoods. The newcomers asked about the Siren's history, and Hannah assured them that she would talk about the house when the others arrived. Agent Samson, she saw, seemed comfortable with everyone. He was capable of casual, friendly conversation—just not so much with her.

Two couples, a lone college student and a family of three arrived, completing the group of sixteen.

"It happened out back, right? Really close to the house?" George Taylor asked.

Hannah felt a cold chill seep over her. It was natural, she supposed. The murder had taken place practically in her yard. Tourists whose interests ran to a ghost tour were bound to ask about it.

Once again, she didn't have to say anything, because Dallas stepped in. "In the alley that runs behind the house," he said. "But the police are still working the scene, plus it's cordoned off, so it will help if we just steer clear of the area for now."

"You a cop?" someone asked him.

"No," he said, and smiled at Hannah. "But we're all here for the history and legends that Miss O'Brien is about to disclose, so why don't we give her our attention and let the authorities handle the information about the murder?"

"Of course," George said, clearly sorry and slightly ashamed he had spoken.

"I'll start out with the house we're in," Hannah said quickly. "Please, take a bottle of water from the table over there and grab a seat." Her guests obeyed; those who didn't find room on the sofa or nab one of the armchairs—mostly the younger members of the party—simply found comfortable spots on the floor. "The Siren of the Sea is named in tribute to the original owner—a merchant who followed the siren call of the sea, at least until the tragedy that befell his ship, which went down in the early 1850s. I'm sure you've already heard some Key West history, but this house figures in that history—as will a lot more of the places we visit tonight—so I'll briefly recap. The Spanish were the first to arrive on this island, which they called Cayo Hueso, or Island of Bones. That's because the bones of the indigenous people lay everywhere. When the English arrived, they bastardized the name to Key West. In 1763 Key West passed into the hands of the British for a mere twenty years before it was returned to Spanish control.

"By the early 1820s, when Key West became an American territory, piracy was raging on the high seas. Commodore David Porter planted the American flag here on the island, complained about the pirates and was ordered to subdue them. He immediately instituted martial law, something that didn't go over well with the citizens, mainly fishermen and divers who either called the island home or made use of its resources. The pirates were pretty quickly expunged by the Mosquito Squadron, a fleet of small ships that Porter commanded. After that, salvage became the order of the day.

"There are many stories about so-called wreckers setting up lights to lure ships onto the reefs, but most of those stories are fiction. The wreckers of Key West didn't need to create any maritime disasters. The shoals and reefs off the shore were deadly all on their own.

"When Ian Chandler arrived in the early 1840s he built this house, and in its day it was considered an appropriate residence for a prosperous businessman. Mr. Chandler wasn't a wrecker, of course. He was, as I said, a merchant, one in possession of a number of ships. His *Wind and the Sea* was a three-masted schooner, a beautiful ship—as you can see by the painting above the fireplace. In September of 1857 the *Wind and the Sea* sailed from her berth in Key West carrying all kinds of goods, cigars from Cuba, sponges from the local waters and jewelry from workshops in Colombia. She'd barely left home when a vicious storm came tearing across the Florida Straits. The ship was tossed back on the reef, where it struck a coral shelf and began to sink. Ian Chandler was on the ship himself, but his beautiful young daughter was still at home.

"When word came that the ship had foundered and was sinking, the cry went up. Now, here's the thing about wreckers. The first man or company to get out to the wreck lays claim. Others who help with the salvage are entitled to a share of the goods and/or what they brought in. But the first wrecker on the site is the one to call the shots and divvy up the haul.

"As it happened, Ian's daughter, Melody, was in love with a young wrecker, Hagen Dundee. Ian— a widower by then—frowned on their relationship, despite the fact that Hagen was well liked and respected in the community. The two were planning on marrying but were still hoping for Ian's blessing. Diaries and letters left by those who lived in the area at the time suggest that Ian Chandler would have disliked anyone who won his daughter's love, because Melody was the light of his life.

"At any rate, when the ship went down, Hagen was quick to assemble his men and get out to the wreck. His plan was to return everything to Ian Chandler and thereby win Ian's approval to wed his daughter. And so, in the midst of horrendous weather, Hagen and his crew set out. But Hagen was a decent man. Lives had to be saved before material goods. And he knew Ian Chandler was sailing on the *Wind and the Sea* that night.

"Hagen was the first to reach the site—the salvage claim was his. But there was something far more important, and that was saving the life of the man he hoped was his future father-in-law. So imagine Hagen fighting the wicked battering of the wind and the tempest of white-capped seas, trying first to pluck survivors from the waves. Many had made it into the lifeboats, but those were being tossed about like volleyballs on the high seas. Bold, dashing and daring, eyewitnesses attest to the fact that Hagen dove into the churning waters himself to save his prospective father-in-law. Success was within his reach when one of his rivals, Valmont LaBruge—a man who wanted to ruin Hagen Dundee, because he also had his heart set on winning the hand of Melody Chandler *and* taking over her father's empire—reached the wreck. He maneuvered his ship *Mademoiselle* into position close to Hagen's *Saint Elizabeth*.

"Just as Hagen saved Ian Chandler, Valmont dove into the water himself, throwing both Ian and Hagen from the lifeboat Hagen's men had maneuvered into place. To the astonishment of those watching, in the midst of the raging storm Valmont swore he'd see Hagen dead before allowing him to claim the salvage from the *Wind and the Sea*—or the hand of Melody Chandler. In the fighting that followed, both Ian and Hagen disappeared below the surface.

"But before he was swallowed by the black

depths, Hagen shouted out a curse. He cursed Valmont LaBruge, the seed of his loins and whatever treasure he might claim. The curse may have had some effect, because Valmont didn't make it back to shore. Despite the storm, despite the wisdom that the salvaging of goods was best left until the storm abated, Valmont was determined to find something he believed was aboard the *Wind and the Sea.* He forced his men to create a safety line so he could board the quickly sinking ship. The line broke, and Valmont LaBruge died that night, victim of a curse spoken by a good man, so they say. Many lives were lost that night, but many others were saved due to the courage and determination of Hagen Dundee."

"But poor Melody!" Belinda said. "She lost her father and her lover the same night."

Hannah nodded. "The body of Ian Chandler washed ashore on what's now Stock Island about three days later. Crushed and disconsolate, Melody buried her father. You can find his grave in the Key West Cemetery. But Hagen was not to be found. So, night after night, Melody went to the beach to stare out at the sea. Some think she walked out into the water. I believe she saw a light out at sea and simply tried to get a closer look. At any rate, she didn't believe Hagen had drowned. She was certain he was out there somewhere. And, in searching for him, she was drowned herself. Neither her body nor Hagen's was ever discovered. And because they weren't given a good Christian burial, they are said to have remained behind in spirit form, together at last for all eternity."

"What a sad story," Maddie said.

"Hagen's and Melody's spirits can sometimes be seen right here in this house. Melody often walks the widow's walk on the roof, searching the sea for her missing lover. Hagen comes to the door seeking Melody, or he stands looking up at her window, singing to her. Local records show he often came to serenade her. Hagen and Melody were tragic lovers and, some say, are now doomed to haunt Key West until they come to peace with themselves—or the world. Anyway, everyone have their water? We'll head on down the street, and I'll tell you the story of the poor woman I consider Key West's most tragic haunt, Elena de Hoyos."

"We've already heard something about Elena," Tobie said excitedly.

"And Robert the Doll," someone else said.

Hannah said, "We'll go by Artist House, too." She looked across the room and caught Agent Samson watching her with a gleam of amusement in his eyes.

Fine, be a skeptic, she thought.

But, of course, he probably knew all the Key West legends, seeing as he was from here. Still, she thought, it did seem as if he'd enjoyed her rendition of this one and its connection to her house.

Hannah led her crowd down toward Simonton Street and stopped across from the Dean Lopez Funeral Home.

"This," she began, "is another story of love gone awry—and the strangest thing about this story is that it's fairly recent history, and everything I have to tell you is true and documented. It all began over eighty years ago.

"Maria Elena Milagro de Hoyos, a lovely Cuban-American, was born in 1910. In 1930, she came down with tuberculosis. At the time, it was still an incurable disease. She received her diagnosis when she came to the United States Marine Hospital in Key West. Elena was dark haired, vivacious, filled with life—loved by her family, but perhaps not so much by her husband, who left her almost immediately after the diagnosis. There was a German-born radiologist at the hospital named Carl Tanzler, who went by the name Count Von Cosel. He was thirty-three years older than Elena, but he saw her and he was in love."

"Yuck!" someone said.

Everyone turned to look. It was one of the young girls in the group—Belinda, Hannah thought.

Belinda cleared her throat awkwardly. "He was . . . what? Fifty-three? And she was *twenty*? That's gross."

Hannah laughed. "I never said that Elena fell in love with Carl Tanzler, just that Carl Tanzler fell in love with Elena. But that was how things stood. Elena had a husband, but he wasn't about to stick around as his lovely young wife sickened and died. And in fact Tanzler had a wife, but she lived up in Zephyr Hills. So he convinced the family that he could treat Elena with all his radiology equipment and save her. He visited her house and ingratiated himself with the family. But poor Elena died despite his best efforts. Her wake was held right here at the Dean Lopez Funeral Home, which, as you can see, remains in business today. Tanzler offered to buy Elena a beautiful mausoleum at the Key West Cemetery, and she was laid to rest. But here's where it starts to get really creepy. Tanzler visited her nearly every day, playing music for her, reading to her, speaking to her constantly of his undying love. This went on for two years, and then Tanzler suddenly stopped visiting."

"I know!" Tobie Rosewood said. "He stole her body!"

"Yes. He stole her body from the grave in the dead of night," Hannah agreed. "Now, Key West is known for having residents who are a bit eccentric. So when Carl Tanzler began buying piano wire, mortician's wax, women's lingerie and perfumes, no one really seemed to notice.

"And then one day, in 1940, Elena's sister,

Florida, heard rumors about Tanzler, so she confronted him. He was living in a broken-down plane on the beach, because he wanted to fix it and fly away to the heavens. She saw that he had her sister's body, and that was the end of Tanzler's 'romance.' The authorities came, and he was arrested. He claimed that although Elena never so much as agreed to date him in life, she had married him in death. He was given a psychological examination and deemed mentally competent to stand trial.

"And here's where it got tricky. He hadn't murdered Elena, and the statute of limitations on grave robbing meant that it was too late to charge him with stealing her body.

"Newspapers around the country hailed Tanzler as a great romantic. But back in those days, the press didn't reveal every salacious detail the way it does now." She paused, looking from person to person before revealing the next detail. "In his efforts to preserve Elena's body he used wire and plastic and whatever else he could find. And he maintained a relationship with her as if she were alive, as if they were truly man and wife.

"After her body was found, poor Elena was given another viewing here at the Dean Lopez Funeral Home. This time thousands of people came, some to pay their last respects but most, I'm sure, to stare at what remained of her corpse. She was buried once again at the Key West

Cemetery, but only the sheriff and a few other people knew where. Rumor says she was actually buried in several pieces in several places. Carl Tanzler's last words to the judge were a question. He wanted to know when he could get his Elena back. He never would, of course.

"Soon after his release, the mausoleum he'd had built for her exploded and Carl Tanzler left town. But the story gets even stranger. He moved up to Zephyr Hills, where his estranged wife *helped him* find a place to live and get on his feet. He died on July 3, 1952, and some say he was found in a coffin with what must have been an effigy of his Elena. Or was it? I personally believe our medical examiners would have known the difference between an effigy and a corpse. All I can say is that if anyone deserves to haunt Key West as a ghost seeking something better, that person is Elena de Hoyos."

Next she led the group to Artist House to tell the story of Robert the Doll, encouraging them to check out the East Martello Museum to see the doll and many other artifacts of Key West history. She followed that with the story of the children who'd died at the old theater and several other local legends, then led them to the haunted Hard Rock Cafe, where she told them the story of the Curry family and the tragic suicide by hanging of one member of the family in the building that now housed the restaurant.

She waited until everyone had ordered something to drink, sodas or one of Key West's famous libations, then left the group happily talking about the ghosts of the past rather than the present.

"Good job," Dallas told her as they started back toward the Siren of the Sea.

"You think?" she asked him.

He shrugged. "Absolutely. Just the right amount of history, and no ridiculous emoting, but enough drama and enthusiasm to keep the crowd riveted."

She laughed. "Well, thanks."

They walked through milling crowds of shoppers, partyers and lovers until they turned the corner. Moments later Hannah opened the door and stepped inside, where she was immediately assailed with the notion that someone had been in her home.

"What?" Dallas asked her, apparently sensing her unease.

"Nothing," she said.

"We'll do a walk around," he told her.

It was more than evident then that the man was an agent. He moved through her house as if he knew it inside and out. She followed a little nervously. "Anything out of order?" he asked a few times.

"No, nothing—I don't think," she told him.

They wound up back in the parlor.

"Would you, uh, like something? A drink? Tea . . . water. Anything?"

"Sure, tea sounds good," he said.

She fled to the kitchen. Setting water on to boil, she looked around. "Melody? Hagen? Come on, please. I need you to forgive me and get back here."

There was no answer. When the water had boiled, she set out a tray with cups and tea bags, milk and sugar.

When she walked back into the parlor, she nearly dropped everything.

Melody was elegantly perched on the sofa. Hagen was standing by the mantel. And Agent Dallas Samson was seated across from Melody, looking as if they had just been deep in conversation.

Dallas turned to Hannah. "I've just met your charming residents," he told her, then continued with a slight rebuke in his voice. "It would have been polite to introduce us."

6

Machete was watching the house again. He'd left it fifteen minutes ago, even though he hadn't found what he was looking for. Still, he'd known what time she was due back, and he hadn't wanted to take a chance of being caught.

So he left.

And he watched.

She didn't come back alone.

Damn. He sure as hell couldn't go back in again tonight.

Not when she had a Fed in the house. He realized it wouldn't bother him a bit to kill the Fed—he'd killed before, and he would kill again.

He just didn't want to kill *her.*

And it was more than the fact that he had a crush on her. Every man had his ethics. Machete killed those who were in the game. Those who knew what they were risking—like the Fed, who knew he was putting his life on the line every day—or other criminals. He didn't kill children, and he didn't kill women. Although the Wolf always told him that women wanted equal treatment and therefore they should be murdered just as often as men.

Machete was too old school. He just didn't see it.

Not that his feelings mattered at the moment. There was a Fed in the house, which meant that what he had told Wolf was even truer now. They had to hold off. They needed safe access to the house until they found what they were looking for. He was close—he knew he'd been close.

The lights remained on in the parlor. Maybe the Fed would be leaving soon. Maybe she would go to sleep. Maybe he could slip back in tonight, after all.

But the Fed didn't leave, and it finally occurred to Machete that Hannah O'Brien ran a bed-and-breakfast. The Fed wasn't leaving. He was staying.

As a guest, of course.

Then Machete began to wonder.

Was he just staying as a guest? Or was something else going on?

The thought made his stomach churn. Buff stud, beautiful woman.

He told himself that meant nothing. She couldn't be falling for that agent. She loved music and art and books, and he . . .

He probably loved steroids and boxing matches and punching bags.

They couldn't possibly be together. In truth, Machete would rather have her dead than with the Fed.

Than with anyone.

His phone vibrated, and he quickly answered.

It could only be one person, and he braced himself.

"Do you have it?"

"Not yet. I told you it wouldn't be easy."

"Are you still in the house?"

"No. I had to get out. She was on her way back."

"Go back in. One good thing—the guests are gone."

"No, there's a new one."

Wolf was silent for a long moment. Machete could almost feel the other man's anger.

"The Fed?"

"Yes."

Machete was afraid the Wolf was going to tell him to go back inside anyway. He imagined himself waiting until they went to bed, then quietly entering the house, slipping up the stairs and then up to the attic. But it was an old house, and old houses creaked. The Fed would hear him.

New scenario number one.

Kill the Fed before he could wake up.

New scenario number two. Hannah woke up first, went to the attic to investigate the noise, opened her mouth to scream . . .

And he had to kill her to silence her. By then the Fed might have heard anyway, and he would follow her up. Machete would have to try to kill the Fed before the Fed could kill him.

Back to scenario number one. Just kill the Fed first.

No matter what he did, chances were that he would have to kill someone, and that would blow everything all to hell. Crime scene tape would cover the whole house. They wouldn't get back in for weeks.

"Watch them. They'll have to leave again at some point. The second they're out of that house, get your ass back in there. Keep searching. If the attic doesn't pan out, try her room. I want that key—and I want the *Santa Elinora* treasure. They're both in that house somewhere—they have to be—and you're going to find them."

Machete let out a sigh he hoped the Wolf didn't hear.

Reprieved! Tonight, he wouldn't have to kill.

Or be killed.

7

Somehow Hannah managed to set the tray on the table without spilling or breaking anything. Somehow she managed to sit before her knees buckled and she fell flat.

He saw them! Agent Hardass saw ghosts.

"I'm so sorry," she managed to murmur after a moment. "I, uh, hadn't seen you all at the same time yet. There was no way to introduce you."

Melody looked at Hannah. "Agent Samson is quite gifted. He spoke to us when we had no idea he could even see us—caught us a bit unaware."

"Really?" Hannah said. She stared at Dallas Samson. "I must say, he's caught me a bit unaware, too."

"Hmm, I don't think I was surprised by any of you," Dallas said, but there was something warm in his eyes when he looked at her.

She still felt stunned. Although she wasn't at all sure why. Her cousin Kelsey was one of the most dedicated law-enforcement officers she'd ever met. Kelsey had the intelligence to be scared at times—but she was steadfast when she was solving a case. And though Hannah hadn't met Kelsey's team members yet, she'd talked to her cousin often enough to know they were intelligent, savvy people—who also happened to see ghosts . . . like Dallas, apparently.

"What disturbs me," Hagen said, looking gravely at Dallas and Melody from where he stood by the mantel, "is that Melody and I cannot help you. We were not here when it happened. We did not see anything."

"You're wrong. You can be of tremendous help," Dallas told them.

"How?" Melody asked.

"You can watch over the house," Dallas said.

Melody looked at Hagen. "We should have thought of that and returned earlier. I am so sorry. We were just very . . . upset, you know."

"I deserved it," Hannah admitted. "I know you two, and I should have realized you would never play such a cruel joke."

Dallas stared at Hannah incredulously. "Seriously, you accused these two of playing a trick? Still . . ." He turned to Hagen and Melody. "She was upset and obviously not thinking clearly. So how about you all just forgive each other now, okay?"

"Absolutely," Hagen said. "And we will do everything we can to help now."

"I am so, so sorry," Hannah said to the ghostly couple. She felt a soft touch on the back of her hand, as if a breeze were passing over her skin. Melody was trying to pat Hannah's hand in comfort.

"We love you, Hannah. You know that," Melody said.

"Good, then. We're all settled," Dallas said. "I'll have that cup of tea now."

"I so wish I could join you," Melody said, and she sighed wistfully. "I used to love tea."

"And I used to love a good whiskey," Hagen said with a grin.

Hannah wasn't surprised that Dallas took his tea clear. She topped off her own cup with milk and two teaspoons of sugar. As she sipped, Hagen asked Dallas, "What else? There has to be more that we can do. We are always overhearing people, and we have heard vague rumors about this Los Lobos organization you were telling us about, but honestly, we have not seen anything."

"You don't know how important it is for you to keep an eye on this house," Dallas said. "And on Hannah," he added quietly.

Hannah wanted to protest. She had a hard time believing she was really in danger. But he was giving Melody and Hagen a chance to feel needed, so she kept quiet.

"Of course we will keep an eye on the house," Hagen said. "We would never have left you if we had thought you were in danger."

"I know, and I appreciate that," Hannah said. She was suddenly exhausted. She'd been up since the wee hours, and it had been a day of extremes. It had begun with screaming and chaos, and segued into the pain of finding the dead man, followed by the shock of meeting his ghost, and now she had a Federal agent staying in her house.

And at that moment, she realized, she was glad he was there.

She stood up abruptly. "Thank you all, but I'm about to keel over, so I'm going to bed."

"Sounds like a plan," Dallas said. "I'll be up a bit later, if that's all right with you."

"Make yourself at home," she told him. As she walked toward the stairs, she realized with renewed astonishment that he was going to spend more time talking with Melody and Hagen.

She wanted to turn around and demand to know how the hell he was able to see and speak with the dead so easily. She knew other people—especially in her small, tight circle of friends—who could do it. But to most of the world it would seem bizarre.

So where and how the hell and why had he come to be one of the few people in the world who had the strange ability?

She could still hear the low drone of voices downstairs when she reached her door. She wanted to know what they were saying.

But she was falling asleep standing up. She headed into her bedroom, washed her face and brushed her teeth, then donned a large nightshirt, fell into bed and, before she knew it, was asleep.

"So you believe this killer thinks Hannah knows something?" Hagen asked. "If that is true, I understand why you are worried. From the little I have heard about Los Lobos, crossing them can be dangerous."

"I don't know exactly why I'm worried, I just am. There are too many little things that the killer could put together and come up with the wrong answer. A couple who were staying here saw Jose Rodriguez just before he died," Dallas told him. "Hannah herself found the body. And there's no alarm system here, so it would be easy for anyone to get in and hurt her. One bright spot is that she has family coming tomorrow. A cousin, I think."

"I hope it is Kelsey," Melody said, pleased.

"We know her. She sees us, too," Hagen told him.

"That's excellent," Dallas said, then hesitated. He wondered how many other people in Hannah's circle could communicate with ghosts and whether they'd been born with the ability. He hadn't learned to see the dead until he'd been older and no longer living in Key West. "Forgive me for asking, but, I'd like to hear it in your own words. Melody, how did . . . ?"

"How did I die?" she asked, then glanced at Hagen with pain in her eyes. Even so many years later, the memory clearly still hurt.

"I kept going down to the sea," she said. "Just

as the legends say. One day I walked out into the water, because I could have sworn I saw a boat."

"And if you *had* seen a boat and I had been on it . . . well, there would have been real irony. You would have been dead before I ever could have reached the shore," Hagen said roughly.

She nodded. "But," she reminded him, "you cannot imagine how I felt. Losing my father and you in one night . . . life was unbearable."

"We think that might be why we are still here," Hagen said.

"You think God sees what Melody did as suicide?" Dallas asked.

Hagen shrugged.

Dallas leaned forward. "I don't believe that for a minute," he said. "God, however one defines him, isn't cruel. *Life* is what can be cruel. What we do to one another can be cruel. Perhaps you're here to have a chance to be together now as you couldn't be in life. Or to help right a wrong or save a life when the time comes."

Melody rose and sat by him. He didn't feel cold, as he would have expected. Instead, he felt a surprising warmth. She touched his knee, and he felt it like a shift in the air.

"Thank you," she said, then looked over at Hagen. "I was foolish, heartbroken, and inconsolable. My poor Hagen. He might have saved my father and himself—if not for Valmont LaBruge."

"So that part of the story is true," Dallas said.

"People do not have all the details right, but yes," Hagen said, and there was bitterness in his voice. "I had Ian—I *had* him! We had just reached the lifeboat my men were in and were climbing aboard when LaBruge actually rammed it and plunged into the water himself. I do not suppose the dead like me should be spiteful, but I was glad I got to see him go down. I think he wanted Ian dead so he could have both Melody and Ian's fortune, but . . . I think he wanted something more that night, too. Maybe the treasure that was rumored to be on board the *Wind and the Sea.* I did not know then, and I still do not."

"You know, you may be right," Melody said. "My father was not happy that I was in love with Hagen, but I was his only child and he doted on me after my mother's death—afraid he'd lose me, too, I imagine. I do not think he would have liked to see me fall in love with anyone. LaBruge had spoken to my father about a match, but my father had never agreed to it."

"And you've never seen his spirit?" Dallas asked.

"No, and I do not expect to," Hagen said. "I saw him when he went down. I grant you, the storm was still raging. But the water turned black and created a whirlpool beneath him, and the wind howled. It was as if . . ." He paused and shrugged, as if feeling a little silly. Like a living person explaining a ghostly interaction. "It was as if hell-hounds were baying. I was dying myself, of course. But still, something of that stays with me. I do not expect to see him ever again."

"There is another piece to the story," Melody said. "Before the ship set sail, a soldier was killed, one of the men guarding the room at the fort where they kept important papers and other things. Some people suspected Valmont LaBruge. But he was a rich man—a very rich man. And he had a lot of power in the town back then. But he died that night and, I firmly believe, went straight to hell, and the truth died with him."

Dallas frowned. "I guess LaBruge really was after that treasure chest. When he didn't find it in the fort, he must have assumed it was on the ship."

"I will never understand how any *thing* could have been worth the lives of others," Hagen said.

"Sadly, history has shown that many men value *things* above human life," Dallas told him. Then he rose and said, "It's been a true pleasure to meet you. And you have my most sincere thanks for all the help I know you'll give."

"We would do anything for Hannah," Hagen said passionately. "We would die for her."

"Except that we are already dead," Melody reminded him.

"There is that," Hagen admitted.

"I understand the sentiment," Dallas said. "Thank you."

He bade them good-night and headed up the stairs. As he entered Ian Chandler's room, he wondered why the old merchant had never made an appearance. Then again, his body had been found, and he'd been given a Christian burial. Maybe that had made the difference.

There was certainly no sense of the man or any other presence in the room. Dallas stripped down to his briefs and found that the bathroom was nicely supplied with travel-sized toiletries. His own place—a rental for now—wasn't far away, just over in the Truman Annex, but he hadn't wanted to leave Hannah. There was something about her and this house, though he couldn't lay his finger on it. He was going to have to leave her at some point, of course, but he could ask Liam to keep an eye on her. And her cousin was coming, of course, though what good another young woman was going to do, he wasn't sure.

Safety in numbers, maybe?

And yet, Jose Rodriguez had been with other people just before he was assaulted.

Maybe the sketches made from Katie O'Hara's descriptions would help them find the men who'd been with Jose the night of his murder.

Dallas stared into the night. "I won't let this go, buddy," he said quietly. "I won't drop it until I find the man who took your life."

He lay staring at the ceiling for a while. The drapes were closed, but light from the street still filtered in. He could even hear—faintly—the revelry going on down on Duval Street.

There was something appealing about the room. The heavy furniture had sat in the house for years and years. It befit a wealthy merchant with a fleet of ships at his command.

He began to drift off to sleep. As he did, he thought about the last time he'd lost a colleague in the field.

Adrian Hall had been a good agent. Smart and talented, the best in her class at Quantico. Eventually they wound up being best friends with benefits, filling holes in each other's lives without making difficult emotional demands. The relationship worked because they were both convinced they weren't cut out for a long-term relationship, and they shared a desire to, silly as it sounded, save the world, or at least as many innocents as they could.

They'd been trying to capture a serial rapist/murderer in Alabama. Adrian had gone undercover as a prostitute who was so desperate for money that she was willing to solicit tricks despite the fear pervading the streets. They'd been prepared. He'd been key man on the team, she'd been wearing a wire and carrying a tiny handgun in her garter belt, and they'd done everything right.

And yet, in the blink of an eye, the killer had

taken her. She'd never even had a chance to use the gun.

Dallas had been barely a block away, hiding with backup in the bushes. He'd gone running the second he heard the killer curse at finding the wire and call her a bitch cop. And he had found her, dead as Jose Rodriguez had been dead. She had bled out, her throat slit so savagely that she'd nearly been decapitated.

He'd held her—held her dead body. There had been no goodbyes.

But in the end he'd caught the bastard.

Because she'd managed to leave a clue in her own blood, just as Jose had done.

She had written three letters, too. *W-I-L.*

There had been a William on their suspect list. Dallas had caught him two nights later, about to slit the throat of another woman.

There was no trial. Dallas followed the rule book to the letter. He gave the guy a warning. But when the bastard started moving his knife, Dallas fired. The intended victim had nearly died; she would have the scar for life to prove it. And William Warwich *had* died, just as he deserved to.

Everyone said that Adrian would have been glad that they'd brought down the bastard who'd killed twelve women, that they had saved the next one—because of her.

He didn't care. She shouldn't have died. She should have lived.

But she *had* died. And she hadn't come back.

He lay in the darkness thinking about those who had been lost. He knew that loss came with the territory, but it was still hard to take. He knew he had signed on that line, as well, that he was willing to risk his own life. Somehow, that seemed different.

He heard it the second his doorknob turned. He hadn't bothered to lock it, since there were only the two of them in the house, and he'd gone over every possible point of entry with a fine-tooth comb to make sure it was as secure as possible. Still, he reached over to the night table for the regulation Glock he carried. He kept his Smith & Wesson—his backup weapon of choice—tucked in his briefcase at night.

The door opened, and for a moment he saw Hannah O'Brien only as a dark silhouette created by the night lights in the hallway. Even in shadow, her hair seemed to shimmer. As his eyes adjusted and she came into focus, he found her somehow both appealing and vulnerable in bare feet and a long cotton T-shirt.

His hand relaxed, and he let go of the gun. He realized she was hesitating, presumably thinking he might be asleep.

"Hey," he said.

"Oh, you're still awake," she said with relief.

"Yes, come on in." His shorts were almost as

146

good as bathing trunks. And he was covered with a sheet.

She turned the light on as she entered. The sudden blaze hurt his eyes for a second, and he blinked.

"Oh, sorry," she said.

"It's okay. What is it? Did you hear something?" he asked, frowning.

"No, I just woke up because . . . there's something important I haven't told you."

"Oh?" he asked. There was that sharp tone in his voice again. He knew better than to use it with civilians. He winced. "Sorry. Please, sit," he said, indicating the foot of the bed. "Tell me."

"The thing is, it wouldn't have made a difference before tonight. I mean, I wouldn't have told you before tonight. Because I didn't know you . . . well, you must know what it's like to tell someone you've been chatting with a ghost. Anyway . . . he's here. Not right now. But Jose Rodriguez came back. He was here this afternoon, and he wanted help. I told him I'd talk to Liam. He doesn't have as easy a time as you seem to, talking with the dead, but he has seen and communicated with them. He wouldn't have thought I was crazy. I left him a message, but he never got back to me. And then tonight . . . you don't just see them, you can talk to them like I can. I was so surprised that . . . well, I didn't think to tell you about Jose until now."

"He's back—and he talked to you," Dallas said. And why not? The woman was open to the spirit world. Jose had felt her touch in death. He'd known.

Dallas inhaled and looked at her, and was both surprised and dismayed by the undeniable effect she had on him. That long blond hair, the deep color of her eyes . . . the warmth of her body. Somehow that T-shirt was sexier than any silk lingerie could ever be.

He couldn't have gotten out of bed then, even if he'd wanted to.

Neither could he shake her and tell her how important the information was that she'd just given him, and how frustrated he was that she hadn't told him earlier.

He nodded slowly, trying to remember his manners. "Hannah, that's great," he finally said. "And I can't begin to tell you how important it is. If you see him, sense him—if you have any idea he's near—it's imperative that you tell me right away. Okay?"

"Of course," she said. "That's why . . . I guess it doesn't make any difference. I could have told you in the morning. But . . . I didn't want to wait."

"Thank you."

"Of course. I should have said something earlier, I just . . ."

"Trust me, I know," he said.

"Really?" she asked. "You've really tried to tell people you can speak to the dead?"

He grinned at that. "Oh, yeah. First time? We'd moved to D.C. I was about sixteen, and I told the priest that my grandmother, who'd been dead for five years, had spoken to me. Next thing I know, my mom had me seeing a shrink. I quickly learned to say the right thing to him. Next time, still in D.C., I was working as a cop. I was smart enough not to say anything overt, but the ghost had given me the killer's name. He wasn't even on our radar, but when I arrested the guy he still had the weapon on him. People started looking at me funny, but what could they do? By the time I joined the Bureau, I'd pretty much learned how to use the information I got without arousing suspicion. It's hard, though. I mean, you *know* something, but sometimes your superiors think it's a faulty theory, so then you have to prove everything or—or make it work, somehow."

She smiled, listening to him. He realized for the first time just how beautiful she was.

And he wished she would go away.

"Got to get some sleep," he said abruptly.

She jumped up. "Of course, sorry."

"Don't be sorry," he said. "Come anytime. It *is* your house, after all."

Machete was startled and more than a little alarmed when his phone vibrated. He knew there was only one person it could be, and he felt his body tighten.

He thought about not answering.

Of course, if he ignored the summons, he might as well put a bullet through his brain.

"I'm watching," he said, answering the phone. "The Fed is still in there. Not a good time for me to get back in."

"I've got something else for you," the Wolf said.

"Oh. But you told me—"

"I need my best man on this, and you're an expert. This has to look like an accident."

Don't let it be a woman. Please, God, don't let it be a woman.

But if there was a God, He wasn't listening, Machete thought. Or maybe long ago—too long ago—he had forgotten God, and now God had forgotten him.

Wolf kept talking.

"What about the Siren of the Sea?" Machete asked dully.

"Covered. I've got Hammer on it," the Wolf said.

Machete felt sick. It wasn't that he'd ever been one of the good guys. But even criminals had their codes. He'd done what he'd needed to do when he needed to do it, and he didn't hurt people unless it was necessary.

As if reading his mind, the Wolf said, "This is

necessary. I need to shake things up here, create a distraction. And to make certain all my people are on their toes."

"All your people," Machete said dully.

"Insurance, if you like."

Machete was silent.

"You're not going soft on me, are you? You signed a solemn pledge. In blood."

There was something about the way the Wolf said *blood*. He gave it a nuance of evil. The truth he had in mind hid behind the word.

If you fail, you will pay—with your blood, Machete thought.

"Start now, so you can get the logistics right. And remember, I want this to look like a tragic accident."

"I'm on it," Machete said wearily.

Criminals, he decided, didn't get to have a code of honor.

Hannah returned to her room, absurdly glad she had spoken to him. She was shivering, for some reason. The house felt unusually cold, probably because it was nearly empty. She usually kept the central air at an even seventy-five. All her life she had hated it when it was a zillion degrees outside and then she walked inside and needed a coat. She kept the Siren comfortably cool but didn't freeze anyone out.

Her thoughts drifted to Dallas, who'd looked

pretty damn irresistible lying there in bed. Maybe it wasn't so bad having him around. She wondered if she would see him after tomorrow morning. Once Kelsey was here with her fellow agents, they would offer her whatever protection she needed. Not that she believed she needed protection at all, not locked inside her house at night. So it was just her bad luck that she was beginning to like the guy who had raised her hackles when they first met.

Of course, it didn't hurt that he was gorgeous.

She'd been alone too long, she told herself drily. And that was true, but it was also what happened when you lived in such a small community. She knew pretty much everyone in town, and none of the guys were *the* guy. And she just wasn't attracted to the idea of a one-nighter with a tipsy tourist.

It had been nearly a year since she had broken it off with Lars Nicholson. Luckily, he'd gone on to join a dive expedition in the Mediterranean, so they never ran into each other. She was glad. He'd insisted they could make it work if they got back together, but she'd known that was an impossibility, even though she'd been devastated. He'd cheated. And it wasn't that she couldn't forgive. She just couldn't understand how easy it had been for him, and she would never be able to forget or trust him again. That was no way to build a relationship. If she took him back, she would become someone she didn't want to be.

Still, it had been a dry year, although she'd barely thought about it until . . .

Damn him. There was no way out of it. He was extremely sexually appealing.

"Enough. Time to sleep," she whispered to herself.

Though how possible that would be with him just a few doors away, she didn't know.

She gave herself a mental shake and walked to the window. She pulled the drapes slightly open and froze.

There was someone out there. Someone standing in the shadow of the streetlight. Staring up.

Without intending to, she had looked right at him.

And, cloaked by the night, he might have looked right at her.

She dropped the curtain and stepped back. Then, carefully, she tugged at the drape again.

Too late. Whoever he was, he had gone.

Or she had imagined him.

She thought about running down the hall and waking Agent Samson.

To say what? Besides, what could he do? There was no one out there now.

She pulled the drape a little farther open and looked up and down the street. Arm in arm, two frat-boy types were ambling toward another bed-and-breakfast. Another man—probably a bartender, done at last for the night—was moving swiftly and with purpose.

Hannah hesitated and then wondered if what she'd seen had meant anything at all. This was Key West. People were out and about all night long. Maybe the man she'd seen had just stopped to light a cigarette or answer his cell, and he'd simply been looking around, the way people do.

She lay down, but by the time she finally drifted to sleep it was almost morning.

The colors of the reef and the water were beautiful, Yerby Catalano thought. There was a feeling about diving—being down dozens of feet below the surface—that was like nothing else in the world.

She loved to dive. She'd gotten her certificate just last year, and now she went every chance she could get.

This wasn't the happiest dive of her life, though. The other three had begged off, still shaken by the effects of the day before. She didn't quite get it. It's not as if any of them had known the dead man. Even Shelly and Stuart, who'd had the worst of it, had only seen him for a few seconds, and even then they had thought they were seeing a ghost.

To Yerby, this was the reason to come to the Keys, and it was ridiculous that the others were going to skip it. She wouldn't have missed it for the world.

The dive boat hadn't been crowded, maybe because she'd chosen the early dive. Most of Key West wasn't even awake yet. The *Minnow* made three trips a day, plus there were night dives for people with more advanced credentials. She made a mental note to go pursue her diving further. A night dive would be cool.

But this 8:00 a.m. dive was splendid, too. They went first to Joe's Tug, which had sunk mysteriously in sixty-five feet of water, and she made up a trio with a young couple from Maine, since no one was allowed to dive alone. As the odd person out, she had to admit to being pissed that Mark hadn't joined her.

But that was all right. Don and Lottie were nice, and she took pictures of yellow tangs and a giant grouper, along with a barracuda drifting a few feet below her and even a nurse shark.

The second dive was to an artificial reef growing up around a deliberately sunk small World War II gunship.

The ship rose from the sand like an eerie steel-gray ghost. Yerby wished Mark was with her. He would have loved it.

The divemaster paused, indicating that they weren't to disappear into the ship. Yerby silently rebelled at that. Why dive to a ship at all if you couldn't go inside her?

The divemaster led them around the port side. A tiny ray shook free of the sand as it rose from the seabed. Yerby snapped it with her camera.

She felt a tap on her shoulder. It was one of the other divers. She turned and saw the couple from Maine just ahead. Don was taking pictures of Lottie, who was doing a lot of posing.

Yerby didn't recognize the diver who'd joined her. Even if she had seen him on the boat, she wouldn't have known him now. He was wearing a full wet suit—a bit much for Florida, she thought. But a lot of people who came down had learned to dive in the Great Lakes or the Pacific, so they were used to diving with a suit.

He motioned toward the ship, smiling.

She looked around. No one was watching. She'd wanted to look inside the ship, and she wasn't going to get a better opportunity. She would just take a peek inside. She would be careful not to get lost. She wanted to live.

She automatically checked her air gauge. She would be fine; she had another twenty minutes of air. This was the deepest dive of the day, and they were only fifty feet down. She was breathing slowly and easily, just as she had been taught.

The mystery diver disappeared inside the wreck. Vaguely wondering where his partner was, she cautiously followed him.

She felt it the second she passed into the dark interior, a vicious grip on her shoulders, whirling her around. Her hose was wrenched from her mouth.

She struggled fiercely in a blind panic. The arms holding her were like iron bars. She tried to scream, but the sound was swallowed by the water rushing into her lungs.

The amazing thing was that, as she weakened, she felt a strange sense of peace. She was being murdered; she knew that. She didn't know by who—or why. But she knew that she couldn't fight. Stars burst in front of her eyes and cold surrounded her. Cold. In Florida. It was ironic.

Darkness claimed her.

Hannah woke early. When she saw that it was only six-thirty, she ordered herself to close her eyes.

She drifted off again into a restless sleep.

She didn't really dream. She simply saw faces, as if they were emerging from a fog. She saw Stuart and Shelly, then Liam and Bentley Holloway. He was watching gravely, as he had been in the alley yesterday morning. Then Valeriya Dimitri's face appeared before her, pale and haggard. She saw Katie O'Hara, her eyes serious and her head cocked as if she were listening. And then . . .

Then she saw the dead man. Jose Rodriguez. Saw his eyes as he stared at her.

And she remembered the things he had said.

She woke with a start, thinking she had just

drifted off for a few minutes. She was shocked to see that the bedside clock read 10:35 a.m.

She leaped out of bed and flew toward the shower. Within a few minutes she was dressed in a cool halter dress and sandals, and hurrying down the stairs. There was no sign of Dallas in her parlor or the entertainment room in the back, but when she reached the kitchen, she found him.

He'd made coffee, and apparently he'd put breakfast together, too. She saw a plate sitting in the microwave.

He was sitting at the butcher block table and watching the television intently. His expression warned her something was wrong.

"What's happened?" she asked.

She moved to stand beside him, her eyes on the TV screen. The newscaster was talking about the safety record of a certain divemaster, who had never been involved in so much as a minor accident before.

But one of their divers from earlier that morning was missing. Police divers were searching for her even now.

A chill settled over Hannah as she asked, "Who . . . ?"

"Yerby Catalano," he said, turning to meet her eyes. "And I guarantee you that what happened wasn't an accident. And they aren't going to find Yerby—at least, not alive."

8

Dallas Samson was on his feet quickly. "Come on," he told Hannah.

"Where are we going?" she asked.

"I'm going to join the police dive. I'm dropping you at the station for your own protection."

"No, you're not," she said firmly. She was amazed at the strength in her voice. But if there was one thing she didn't want to do, it was sit around doing nothing and waiting.

Dallas stared at her, shocked. He drew a deep breath. "Yes, I am. Don't you get it? *Yerby is dead.* You have to stay where you'll be safe."

"Fine. Let me go with you. I'm an expert diver. I even fill in for friends as divemaster sometimes."

Dallas stared at her in wordless frustration.

"I can help. I'm willing to bet Liam is already out there. I'll stick with you like glue."

"Even if I were willing to take you with me, Hannah, it's not my call. You'd have to be cleared by the police, and let's face it, you may be a great diver but the police have a whole team of great divers who are trained to handle weapons and work in teams and—"

"Liam will okay me to dive. You'll see. And

he's in charge, not you. There's no way in hell they'll consider this a Federal situation."

She was right, and she could tell he knew it. Though whether Liam would concede to her demands or not, she didn't know.

"You must have a death wish," he told her.

"I'll be with you—how could I possibly be safer?"

"I never claimed to be Superman," he said. "You'd be safest sitting in a police station."

"But I want to help," she said.

"I'm out of here in two minutes," he warned her.

"I can get my gear in one and a half."

She raced upstairs, shed her dress, scrambled into a bathing suit and raced back down. He followed her as she headed outside to the old carriage house, now a garage, for her equipment. Her bag had wheels, and she rolled it out before he could even follow her in.

It took them less than three minutes to reach the wharf, where the officer on duty quickly informed them that Liam was already out on the reef. Hannah was afraid Dallas would consider that a victory and refuse to let her come. But apparently he wasn't going to argue anymore. There was a Coast Guard vessel on hand, and Dallas quickly commandeered it. Hannah had a feeling that the captain had been hovering, hoping to be of assistance.

They headed out to the site. Hannah could remember when they had sunk the *Jefferson* to create an artificial reef. She'd dived the site dozens of times; it wasn't even fifty feet down.

The Coast Guard radio operator put Dallas through to Liam, who was out of the water taking a break before heading back down, and he told them that the dive boat had been some distance from the wreck when the captain had done his count and discovered he was missing a diver. Yerby's dive partners had thought she was with them until they'd gotten out of the water, because one of the other divers was about her size and had her coloring. Dallas told Liam that they would start their search right at the ship.

A few minutes later they were above the wreck and putting on their tanks. Knowing that Dallas was watching her, Hannah was nervous for the first time in years. Ridiculous! She'd been diving most of her life and had gotten certified the second she was old enough.

She checked her gauges, adjusted her mask and slid backward into the water. A second later she heard the splash as Dallas joined her.

She moved smoothly down toward the *Jefferson*; having her own equipment meant that her weights were just right. She was glad that despite her nervousness at Dallas's presence, she wasn't behaving like a novice. A giant grouper swam by her, curious and close enough to stroke, and she was sorry this wasn't the time to stop and appreciate the sights along the way. She moved toward the steel hull of the World War II vessel, Dallas right by her side.

They reached the wreck, and he swam past her, following the line of the boat forward from the stern, searching to see if Yerby had somehow become snagged on the hull itself. When they had completed a circuit of the ship he paused by one of the openings—there were four, two on each side—the hull doors had been ripped away.

He signaled for her to follow and swam into the darkness of the wreck.

The ship hadn't been built for comfort, and the passages were narrow. This particular hallway ended in a closed door just twenty feet from where they'd entered. Dallas worked at it for a moment, then turned and shook his head. She looked more closely and saw that the door had been sealed.

She turned and headed out. Once they were back outside the ship she noticed the sound of her own breathing and rise of her air bubbles. She spotted a lemon shark as it swam toward them and then away. As she watched it, she thought she heard a mournful sobbing sound. It was impossible, of course. They were in the water. It wasn't that you couldn't hear someone—though they would be garbled and muffled—if you were close or if they were wearing the right gear, but no one was near them and on a dive like this, only the police divers might have the right gear.

Dallas entered the second doorway. Hannah followed, but she suddenly knew they weren't going to find Yerby there. She tugged at his leg. He turned to her, and she indicated that they needed to go to the other side of the ship. She saw the skepticism in his eyes through the glass of his mask, and he frowned and shook his head.

She nodded emphatically, so he looked at his air gauge and let her lead the way.

She let her intuition lead her to what she knew was the right doorway. As soon as they reached it he took the lead. As he shone a flashlight into the dark water ahead of them, she saw tiny reef fish swimming by and noticed barnacles and anemones taking hold on the walls.

Like the first hall they'd explored, this one also ended at a closed door. And, like that first door, it refused to yield. Hannah remembered something about a plan to seal off most of the ship so that divers wouldn't find themselves trapped.

But she had felt certain this was the place to look.

He started to turn away, so she swam past him, determined to try it herself. He looked at her and shrugged, then gave the door another tug.

It opened.

And the corpse of Yerby Catalano swung out at them.

Yerby's body hadn't been underwater long enough to bloat. Dallas was relieved, then wondered why he cared. She was dead. What she looked like now didn't matter to her.

But it might to those who loved her.

When they reached the surface, Dallas and Hannah were quickly relieved of the responsibility of the body. Yerby's drowning was a matter for the local police. Her body would be taken up to the coroner's office in Marathon for autopsy.

Dallas couldn't help but be grateful he didn't have to inform her friends that she was dead.

He was certain she had been murdered, though at the moment everyone else seemed to believe she was the victim of a tragic diving accident. But Yerby had been with Shelly and Stuart and the others when they'd seen Jose Rodriguez at O'Hara's Bar.

Why kill her, though? She hadn't known anything.

He was sorry Hannah had been with him. She hadn't gotten hysterical; in fact, she'd handled it very well.

When they'd gotten to the surface, the Coast Guard had radioed Liam, and they'd reached the dock at about the same time. While Dallas had described finding Yerby's body, Hannah had stood perfectly still on the dock, wrapped in a large beach towel, watching. Afterward Liam had walked over to ask her, "You okay?"

She had nodded.

"What the hell were you doing down there?" Liam asked.

"I hoped . . . I hoped I might find a clue, something to help," she said.

Then Liam had looked at Dallas. "You let her go down with you?"

"She threatened me with you," Dallas said, then turned to Hannah. "Now let's get you back to your place."

She didn't fight him.

In the car, she was quiet. "Do you mind if I swing by my place to get a few things?" he asked.

She shook her head. She didn't even fight the fact that he was coming home with her, although he had expected trouble since her cousin was coming in sometime that day.

He decided not to talk anymore and just drove into the Truman Annex and parked. She got out of the car and followed him, still saying nothing.

He had a town house with a small yard—with nothing in it. He hadn't really noticed that until now. As he opened the front door and ushered her in, he felt for the first time the coldness of his place. He had all the right things, even a leather sofa and chair in front of the electric fireplace that he'd never even used. Of course most people down here had to crank up the air-conditioning so they could use the fireplace and enjoy the ambiance.

There were no pictures anywhere, he realized.

He compared his apartment to the Siren of the Sea, which was everything this place wasn't.

She clearly didn't notice. She had tugged on the shorts and T-shirt that she'd brought with her but still had the towel wrapped around her as if she was cold.

"You all right?" he asked.

"Of course."

"I can get you something warmer."

"I'm fine."

"I'll only be a few seconds. I'm going to take a quick shower and change," he said.

"Okay."

He set his hands on her shoulders, trying to get her full attention.

"Stay inside. The door's locked, so leave it that way. Okay?"

"Of course," she said.

Dallas ran upstairs, stripping off his shirt as he went, and he was naked by the time he reached his bathroom. He was showered and dressed within five minutes. He threw together a bag just as quickly—one thing he excelled at was split-second packing.

When he came back downstairs, she was exactly where he had left her. Clearly he needn't have worried about her walking out. She had barely moved. She was staring at the fireplace as intently as if a fire were burning there, as if there was something to see.

"Ready?" he asked.

"Yes."

They walked back out, and as he locked the door to his place he thought how odd it was. He'd felt as if it was home before. He spent so much of his time working, it had been fine. A place to sleep. Now . . .

He might as well have been leaving a chain hotel.

The drive to her house was short—a matter of eight or so blocks. She got out of the car, walked up to her door and turned the key in the lock. He entered the Siren right behind her, wary and ready for anything.

There really was something enchanting about the house. It had pictures, flowers . . . life. But he could tell that she was waiting—as he was—to *feel* whether anything had changed.

"We're here," Melody Chandler said, materializing in the doorway to the kitchen. "And everything is fine. Oh, dear!" she added, seeing Hannah's face.

"We found the missing diver," Hannah said.

"I'm so sorry," Melody said. She apparently knew from Hannah's expression that they had found her dead. "She stayed here, right?"

Hannah nodded. She spoke to no one in

particular as she said, "I'm going to take a shower."

As she started for the stairs, Dallas reached out and touched her shoulder. She started, spinning around.

"I'm sorry. I just . . . are you okay?"

She was looking into his eyes. She almost smiled as she nodded.

"Want me to make coffee for when you come back down? Tea? Something stronger?"

She managed a weak smile. "Nothing like a drop or two of Jameson's in a cup of tea." Then she turned and ran up the stairs.

When she was gone, Dallas looked at Melody worriedly. "Do you think she's all right? She's hardly spoken."

"She's going to be fine. She cares about people—which is good—but it means she takes things hard," Melody said. "Can I help you in the kitchen? I can show you where to find the tea bags—and the Jameson's."

He had just set out cups and the teapot, and gotten the water almost to boiling, when he heard a car in the drive.

Melody, who had been perched by the table, and Hagen, who had been leaning in the doorway, disappeared into thin air.

Dallas, knowing Hannah's cousin was due to arrive, walked out the front door to see if this was her.

He was startled when he saw an attractive young woman with long red hair exit an SUV accompanied by a tall man who definitely had Native American blood in his background. They were an attractive couple, but there was something about them that he instantly recognized: they were some kind of law enforcement.

Why hadn't Hannah told him? He felt like a fool for worrying about her when her cousin was packing heat in a shoulder holster.

The redhead looked toward the door and looked momentarily surprised to see him. Then she waved and headed toward him, offering her hand. "Hi, I'm Kelsey O'Brien. Hannah and I are cousins. Are you a guest here? I didn't know she had people in the house right now."

Dallas found himself grinning wryly. "Ms. O'Brien—or, more accurately, Officer or Agent O'Brien—I'm Agent Dallas Samson, FBI."

"Samson?" said the man heading up the porch steps. He offered his hand, as well. "I'm Logan Raintree. I've heard of you."

"Oh?"

"I'll explain when we get inside," he said.

"Where's Hannah?" Kelsey asked.

"Upstairs. A woman died during a dive earlier today. Hannah and I helped with the search and found her. She was staying here the night our agent was killed, so I don't think her death was accidental. Maybe she saw more than she knew."

"I'm going to go up and see how she's feeling," Kelsey said.

"She's handling it pretty well," Dallas said. "For a civilian, anyway."

"She would, but still . . ." Kelsey trailed off and hurried up the stairs.

Logan walked into the house behind her. He was about Dallas's height, with striking features. The man belonged on a coin.

"I'm making tea, and I think I hear my water boiling," Dallas said, heading toward the kitchen. "You know the house?"

"No, first time here," Logan said, following him. "I feel like I know a lot about the city, though. Key West is Kelsey's home. She talks about it a lot, but I've never made it here with her. Our unit has been traveling pretty much nonstop."

"You're not assigned to a city?" Dallas asked.

"Well, we have a base. Offices not far from Quantico. But, no. We go wherever something comes up that fits our parameters. Ours is a different kind of unit. The Krewe of Hunters."

Dallas froze for a moment. He'd heard about the unit, of course, and he, like many people, had been skeptical, at least at the beginning.

Maybe he'd been more skeptical than most because he knew what was really out there, and few people were the real deal when it came to dealing with ghosts.

But Hannah was definitely the real thing.

And, he was willing to bet, so were Kelsey and Logan.

The Krewe—despite what others might think or what jokes they might make—had a great record, at least when it came to those of their cases that made it into the media.

He supposed it shouldn't be much of a surprise that Hannah's law enforcement cousin was part of the Krewe.

Dallas reached the stove and turned off the boiling water. Then he turned back to stare at Raintree. "So. You're with the Krewe of Hunters?" he asked.

"*Technically* we're the Special Sciences Unit," Logan said with a shrug. "We have equally 'special' offices in Arlington. I'm not sure if it's to keep the information we turn up as quiet as possible or to protect us from everyone who likes to call us the Ghostbusters and consider us the joke of the department."

"Except you have an amazing record for clearing your cases," Dallas said.

Logan smiled. "Yeah. Yeah, we do. And we have more history than most people know. The unit was formed by a man named Adam Harrison, who had been quietly called in by the powers that be a number of times over a decade or so. Adam is a brilliant man and a philanthropist who lost a child with special abilities. He started looking for people like him and pulled together a group to solve paranormal cases across the country. Eventually they became official. Our director, Jackson Crow, reports to Adam and heads up the original unit, the Krewe of Hunters. I head up a second unit, the Texas Krewe, so-called because we were first put together for a case in Texas."

Dallas nodded. "The local Bureau was invited in because one of our agents, Jose Rodriguez, was working undercover to bring down Los Lobos. He was murdered the other night. Our main state office is up in Miami, along with the U.S. Marshals' main office."

"Yeah, I know. Kelsey was a U.S. Marshal down here before she became Krewe," Logan said.

Interesting, Dallas thought. Both women were tall and gorgeous, but since both were able to converse with the dead they were similar in more ways than met the eye.

Logan grinned and went on. "Anyway, I know about you because Adam has an interest in you."

"I've heard of him, of course, but I don't actually know him."

"No, but he knows you. Even with two Krewes on call, we're always scrambling. This is a very big country. We have a number of agents now, but as you can imagine, we can't just look at each year's graduating class. You've been on his radar."

That was actually a little disconcerting, Dallas

thought. It was difficult explaining sometimes why he had certain information. Even so, he'd thought he'd kept the nature of his unique informants well hidden.

"Don't worry," Raintree told him. "Adam has a unique ability to assess people. I doubt anyone else has figured out what you can do."

Dallas didn't respond right away, instead turning away to make the tea. He was saved from answering at all when Hannah came into the kitchen with Kelsey right behind her.

Hannah seemed much better. The weight of the world seemed to have fallen from her shoulders. Dallas wished he could have made the past couple of days easier for her—he hadn't known her long, but the hours they'd shared had seemed incredibly intense. He was feeling things for her that he knew he shouldn't. He needed to back away—fast.

"You might have mentioned that your cousin was with the Bureau," he told her wryly.

"Sorry. It never came up. Kelsey is like me. Or I'm like her, I suppose, since she's a year older. She—well, she knows Melody and Hagen, if that tells you anything."

He nodded. He knew she hadn't withheld the information out of any malice, but it still bugged him.

"We're not here officially," Raintree said. "If that helps."

Dallas nodded and said, "Good to know. I'm the lead on the Jose Rodriguez case, since he was one of ours down here."

Hannah sank into a chair. "And he's all of ours, in a way," she said quietly. "I told Kelsey that I've seen him—except that I haven't seen him since that first time. And now . . ."

"Now there's been another death," Kelsey finished for her.

"That poor girl," Hannah said. "I can't help but feel . . ."

"Hannah, you had nothing to do with it," Dallas told her firmly. "Don't go blaming yourself."

"But I knew her. She was a guest here," Hannah said.

Dallas found himself walking over to her, hunkering down. "If you blame yourself, then Jose would have to blame *himself,* too, and he isn't at fault, either. Whoever runs Los Lobos is responsible, and everyone involved deserves the harshest punishment the law can dish out. Jose died in that alley trying to avoid putting anyone else at risk. It didn't work. But we can't know that whoever killed Yerby Catalano knew she'd stayed here. They might have seen her at O'Brien's or on the street, walking behind Jose and his group."

When her eyes met his, he was surprised at the gratitude in them.

"Katie!" she gasped suddenly. "Katie worked on those sketches with the police artist, and she was definitely at O'Hara's. She could be in serious danger."

"David Beckett is no man's fool," Kelsey assured her quickly. "Not to mention that Liam is Katie's brother-in-law."

"David is married to Katie O'Hara?" Dallas asked.

Hannah frowned. "You know David, too?"

He nodded. "Haven't seen him in ages, but of course I know him. Liam and I were friends for years."

"Small world," Raintree said.

"It's Key West," Dallas replied, his words echoed by Kelsey and Hannah at almost the same time. For a moment he was another Conch and not the outsider.

Conchs, as native Key Westers were called, were few and far between.

"We should still call and make sure they're aware," Hannah said.

Kelsey nodded. "I'll call Liam right now." She reached into her pocket for her cell phone and took a seat at the table.

Hannah suddenly went into hostess mode, rising and heading for the tea.

"I can do that," Dallas said.

"I'm fine," she assured him, smiling. "I'm not an invalid. You all may be the agents, but Jose came to me. I can't help but feel involved, but I'm okay."

"You still have to be careful," Dallas said.

"I intend to be," she promised as she took the teapot and put it on the table. He picked up cups and saucers.

"Can I do anything?" Logan asked.

"The Jameson's is in the corner cupboard over the sink," Hannah said.

She found a box of scones and put them on the table with a stack of plates. Everyone joined Kelsey around the table as she finished her phone conversation.

"I read the file, but there's not a lot there, so why don't you bring us up to speed on what you know about Los Lobos?" Raintree said to Dallas.

"If you read the file, you know pretty much everything I know. As far as we know, Los Lobos has been active for about a year. Because of their fierce code of silence, we've never had much to go on.

"The members of the group don't even know one another half the time. Everyone has a code name. The Wolf is the guy in charge, hence the name of the gang, and he seems to be the only one who knows who's who. By keeping dis-association going, he keeps control. And he keeps such tight control that everyone's afraid not to follow instructions to a T. He orders someone or maybe a couple of people to do something. If they don't follow orders, or if, God forbid, they fail, he calls in someone else, someone they don't know, to take care of the situation. He has members killed to warn other members. They're wary of one another all the time.

"Last October, an ancient Peruvian chalice was smuggled out of a museum in Lima and found here in an abandoned building. Apparently one of the gang members messed up and that's why it was discovered, because soon after, a man was found dead—shot execution style—on Stock Island.

"The Coast Guard found artwork from Venezuela when they ran down an unidentified boat close to shore last January. After that, two men—shot in the head—washed up in Miami. Jose Rodriguez was the first man we had who managed to get anywhere close to the Wolf. He had made contact through a cell phone given to him by a man he'd befriended at a bar while pretending to be a petty criminal with aspirations."

"And now the one man to get a toe into the operation is dead," Raintree mused. "As for the woman who drowned, is it possible it was an accident?"

"It's possible, just not likely. There will be an autopsy, of course. The body is already on its way up to the morgue in Marathon," Dallas said.

"If we only had more information," Kelsey murmured.

As she spoke, Dallas felt as if something in the

room had changed. He looked toward the kitchen doorway and stiffened.

No one had come in—they would have heard. And yet something had him on the alert, ready to draw his weapon.

Then, slowly, the form of a dead man began to materialize.

Jose Rodriguez had joined them.

9

Jose was leaning against the kitchen counter, looking thoughtful and a little tense, just as he would have when he was alive and attending any tactical meeting.

Except for Dallas's momentary reaction, no one else in the room appeared surprised to see him.

Of course, Hannah had always known that Kelsey saw what she saw; she'd assumed it was something that certain people in a family inherited—just like blue eyes or dark hair.

"I've been all over the city," Jose said. He looked at Hannah and smiled. "Since I left you, I've prowled every venue on the island—I haven't seen a single one of the men I was with the night I was attacked. Of course," he said, and hesitated, looking at them sheepishly, "I'm just getting used to this new way of life. No, not life. Death. I'm just learning how to exist on this different . . . plane. Time disappears on me sometimes. I try to appear to you, but I fade. I'll get there." He grinned at Dallas. "It's like going through a different kind of academy. Plus," he said apologetically, looking around the room, "I had to be sure of who you all were first."

"Of course," Hannah agreed.

"We're going to find your killer," Dallas said, a hard edge to his voice. "We'll take all the help you can give us."

"Thank you. So here's what I have. There are about five gangs here on the island, mostly teens, guys in their early twenties. I followed them all, tried hanging around every known drug-dealing site in the city, and I couldn't find the guys I was with that night."

"Do you remember *anything* that could help us?" Dallas asked.

"One of the guys goes by the name Blade. He's about five-eleven, dark-haired—from Colombia, I'm pretty sure. I was allowed to use his phone and talk to the Wolf, who told me the rules. Basically, absolute loyalty and obedience. I told him I was in, that I needed the money and wanted to rise up in the ranks, and I was willing to do anything. He told me I'd get my own phone and my orders as soon as I checked out." Jose paused.

"You never got the phone," Dallas said.

Jose looked over at him. "No. I thought I was getting it that night. I got it, all right," he said drily.

No one said a thing.

"Someone was onto you," Dallas said after a moment.

Jose nodded. He looked at Hannah. "I heard about that woman who was killed diving. I'm so sorry, but I never saw her. I don't know why she was killed."

"We don't know yet that she *was* killed," Logan said.

Jose offered a rueful smile. "Not that diving accidents don't happen," he said, "but I think we all know she was murdered."

Hannah plunged in. "Jose, would you mind telling us about your sister? Maybe we can go at this from that end."

"My sister," Jose said quietly. He looked at her earnestly. "My little sister—by about two minutes. We're twins. But while I always knew I wanted to go into law enforcement, Alicia never figured out what she wanted to do with her life. She was a wild child, sweet as could be, but rebellious. She made my parents crazy. Then she fell in love with a great guy, a GI, and everything seemed good. She was living in the Miami area when her husband was killed overseas.

"I worried about her, tried to figure out how to help her. Our parents were gone by then, so it was just the two of us. I was there for Alicia as much as I could be, given the job, and she told me she was doing okay. She said she'd decided to become a social worker, because she wanted to make life better for people. Then I had to go out of town on a case, and while I was away a friend texted me that he was afraid she'd gotten into drugs. I got myself assigned to the Keys and made plans to come see her, but by the time I got down here, Alicia was nowhere to be found. She hadn't paid her rent, had abandoned all her belongings."

"And you had no idea where she was, what she was doing?" Dallas asked.

"She called me once, just before I made the move down here. I didn't mention that I was worried about her, just said I was coming to the Keys to work an important case. I told her I'd see her soon. She said that she'd come down to see me as soon as I got here. But I never saw her, never heard from her again. Naturally I reported her disappearance, but no one's ever found anything. The case is still open up in Miami–Dade."

"What makes you think she disappeared from Key West? We're at least three hours away," Logan pointed out.

"When I came down for her husband's funeral, she was wearing an odd pendant. It looked like an ancient medallion. When I mentioned it, she laughed and said it was just a piece of costume jewelry. Said she'd tried to help an old friend of her husband's get back into civilian life. When she disappeared and Los Lobos started really gaining prominence, I kept thinking about that pendant. It wasn't cheap costume jewelry, even if she believed it was. I'm convinced that friend was—is—part of Los Lobos. And he was using my sister—possibly making her dependent on drugs again, but also making her think he cared by giving her such an expensive gift, an antique pendant that was part of his cut from the Wolf. That's speculation on my part, but it makes sense. All I know for sure is that somewhere along the way I lost my sister."

Hannah reached for him, but of course she couldn't touch him. She lowered her hand. "I don't believe she would have betrayed you," she said. "No matter who she was involved with."

"There's something I didn't tell you," he said, meeting her eyes.

"What?" she asked.

"The night I was killed . . . the group I was with . . . at least three of them were in Los Lobos, and they particularly wanted to come down your street," Jose said.

"So, they were setting you up," Hannah said.

"That's certainly one of the possibilities I considered at first. I knew a couple of the guys weren't 'in' yet. They might not even have known they were being scoped out for possible membership."

"So you *weren't* being set up?" Dallas asked.

"I don't think so—not anymore. I think they specifically wanted to be on this street to see something."

"You mean . . . this house?" Hannah asked, a chill ripping through her.

Jose nodded. "I think so. Do you have any idea why?"

"There's nothing here—nothing Los Lobos

would be after," Hannah said. "And if they *were* looking for something here, why were you killed here? That pretty much guaranteed a big police presence."

"I don't know," Jose said. "But you have something here. Something you don't realize. Something they want."

"The chest," Dallas said. "Do you think there's any possibility that they could be after the treasure—that they think it might be here?"

"But it isn't here! There was never even a story that it was kept in this house. And if it *were* here, I'd know it. Trust me."

"Maybe someone in Los Lobos doesn't believe that," Logan suggested.

"It doesn't matter what they believe. I know all these rooms—it's a bed-and-breakfast, for God's sake!" Hannah said. "The attic is as neat as a pin. The stairs to the widow's walk are right there, and people go up them all the time, especially at sunset. They want to catch a glimpse of Melody. Sometimes, when she's in the right mood, she obliges them."

"The truth doesn't matter," Dallas said. "People act based on what they believe to be true—whether they're right or wrong." He suddenly turned his attention to the ghost. "Jose, what were you writing in your blood?" he asked tensely.

"What?" Jose asked, clearly confused by the quick change of subject.

"In the alley. You were trying to leave a message in your blood," Dallas said. *"C-U-R."*

"Oh! I had forgotten. Imagine that," Jose said. "Curse. I was writing the word *curse.*"

"Curse," Dallas repeated.

"There's a curse on the chest from the *Santa Elinora*," Jose said. "I was planning to write 'cursed treasure,' so you'd know what Los Lobos were looking for and maybe you could stop them."

"The real curse is that evil men will always want treasure," Dallas said.

"Too true," Jose agreed. "And I think that if you find the treasure and set a trap, you can catch the Wolf. The problem is, the Wolf believes what he's seeking is here, in this house."

"What have I been telling you, Hannah?" Dallas asked gravely.

"I can't just leave. This is my home—my business. I can't just bail because someone might be looking for some nonexistent treasure here."

"No one is suggesting that," Kelsey assured her.

"We don't even know for a fact that any of this is true," Hannah said defensively. She knew that she didn't *want* it to be true. It was terrifying. And she couldn't expect Kelsey and Logan to stay here forever, protecting her. And Dallas Samson had his own place to get back to. Eventually he would leave, too.

"No, we don't know it for a fact," Jose said.

"But that doesn't mean it isn't true." His last words were faint. Hannah turned to look at him just as he faded into nothing.

"Jose!" she said.

"He's used up all the strength he has for the moment," Dallas told her.

She was silent for a moment. "There is the possibility that his sister betrayed him. I think he doesn't want to believe that it could be true—and I don't want to believe it, either. But it *is* possible."

"Yes," Dallas agreed.

She realized that he was resting a hand on her shoulder. He had been like a stone pillar today. She suddenly wanted to take his hand and hold it. She tried to draw on her own inner strength. She had to stop. She was finding him more and more attractive. There was something pathological about that, she knew. She was getting fixated on a man who was protecting her purely from a sense of duty. Not good. Not good at all. She needed to back away. It probably didn't help that she hadn't dated more than once or twice since she and Lars had split.

A little voice in the back of her head was whispering that she didn't have to have a *relationship* with someone to enjoy him. Other people did it all the time.

She very firmly told the voice to shut up.

"So where do we go from here?" she asked.

"We keep you safe," Dallas said.

Logan looked at Dallas. "We need to get the autopsy reports on Jose and the diving victim."

Dallas nodded. "The autopsy reports would definitely be helpful."

"I have a tour tonight. People will start showing up around seven-thirty," Hannah said.

"You need to cancel it," Kelsey said.

"No, I don't think we should cancel the tours," Dallas said. "I think we need to be on them."

"I think that's risky," Kelsey argued. "We don't know who will be on a tour."

"That's the point. We're hoping someone will show up who we can use," Dallas said.

"But how do we protect Hannah?" Kelsey asked.

"Hannah is sitting right here," she reminded her cousin sharply. "I may be afraid, but I refuse to imagine never having a normal life again."

"I intend to be so close no one will be able to get to her," Dallas said to Kelsey.

"Where's the M.E.'s office?" Logan asked.

"Up in Marathon, just over the Seven Mile Bridge," Kelsey said.

"We'll all go. We won't need long in there," Dallas said. "Then we'll all come back."

"What about the house?" Logan asked.

"The house will be watched by the best," Dallas said. "Melody Chandler and Hagen Dundee."

"The resident spirits—I told you about them on the plane," Kelsey explained to Logan.

"But they can't stop someone from coming in," Logan pointed out.

"Maybe we want to know who comes in," Dallas said. "And what they do while they're here."

Hannah was silent. Yesterday she'd *felt* as if the house had been invaded—as if someone had been there while she was out. But that might have been paranoia.

"I have a better idea," she said. "You two can go, and Kelsey can stay with me."

"We can go to the dolphin research center," Kelsey said. "We have friends who work there. I haven't been in ages, and you can drop us on your way up, then pick us up on your way back."

"It's not safe for Hannah to wander around," Dallas insisted.

"Who will know we're there?" Hannah demanded. "*I* didn't even know until two seconds ago."

"And I *am* an FBI agent—not to mention I used to be a U.S. Marshal," Kelsey reminded Dallas.

He still looked as if he wanted to protest, but he lowered his head for a moment and then nodded.

"Of course," he said. "I'm just going to talk to Liam quickly—see if he has anything. Tell him what we're doing."

Ten minutes later they were on their way. Dallas and Logan seemed to hit it off immediately, chatting while Logan drove and Kelsey sat with him.

Hannah sat in the back of the rental SUV with Dallas and wondered how she could feel that she already knew him so well and why she wished she knew him even better.

After dropping off the women, Dallas and Logan made good time up to Marathon, where Dirk Mendini met them in front of the coroner's office looking harried. After Dallas introduced him to Logan, Mendini said, "You know, two murders in two days. That's a lot when you're not looking at a big city."

"So she *was* murdered," Dallas said.

"Yes, that's what I'm putting in my report. Murder by person or persons unknown."

"What makes you think it was a homicide?" Dallas asked him.

"The bruises. Come on. See for yourselves," Mendini said. "You can grab a mask on the way in."

Dallas remembered talking to the young woman who was now lying naked on the stainless steel table, being sewn up. He was very glad that Hannah wasn't with them.

"See what I'm talking about?" Dirk asked them as he lifted her right arm. Bruises had formed on her flesh—bruises that clearly came from the grip of forceful fingers.

"She drowned?" Logan asked.

Dirk nodded. "I believe she was drawn into the wreck and held there. Based on bruising and the water in her lungs, her killer ripped the regulator from her mouth, held her—and watched her drown." He shuddered.

Dallas touched the body, his sympathy rising for Yerby Catalano. He was glad that Liam had been the one to tell her family she was gone.

He lingered by the body, hoping to get a sense that her spirit was lingering. He felt nothing, but that didn't mean she was really gone, not after such a horrible death.

Logan also touched the body, under the pretense of studying the bruises.

"We know, of course, almost exactly when she died, since she was on a dive," Dirk added. "It's like hell come to paradise."

"It has to be stopped," Logan said quietly.

"And it will be," Dallas vowed, then he turned to the M.E. "Did you get any trace evidence? Anything under her nails?"

"She tried. She fought," Dirk said. "We're a long way from any possible answers, though. She had a few fibers caught in her nails. They look like they belong to a run-of-the-mill dive skin."

Dallas shook his head. "Not many people go down in wet suits. Not at this time of year."

"Some do," Dirk said. "I know a lot of people who wear them year round. Helps if you brush against fire coral or run into a school of jellyfish."

That was true. But it was still going to be easier to ask witnesses about someone wearing a wet suit, because most people stuck to bathing suits in the summer.

"Liam is canvassing the dive boats in the area. Maybe he can find out something," Dallas said. "Any little detail can help."

"Of course. But you have to remember, she was under the water for at least an hour and a half before she was found. Seawater does a number on a corpse, even in a short period of time," Dirk reminded him.

"Her bathing suit and dive gear?" Dallas asked.

"Forensics is already working on them," Dirk said.

Yerby Catalano's eyes were mercifully closed. She looked small and frail, her once lovely body now scarred by a wicked Y-incision.

She was gone. And there was no way in hell they could have known that they needed to save her.

As they left the medical examiner's office, Dallas noted the breeze of the early evening. The sky was nearly crystal-blue, with light puffs of clouds riding across it. Even here, just off US 1, they weren't far from the water.

They got in the car to drive back to the dolphin research facility where they'd left Kelsey and Hannah. There were plenty of cars on the road.

The news was out about the deaths, but as far as the general public knew there was no connection between them, so people were still heading south, on their way to Key West. They would, Dallas knew, feel no connection to the victims. As far as they knew, Jose Rodriguez had been a drunk who hung around with the wrong crowd. And as for the tragic death of Yerby Catalano, well, it was sad, but some people insisted on trying dives that were too difficult for them or didn't follow their divemaster's rules.

"You know," Logan said, "it could be we'll find out they were killed by two different people."

"Maybe, but I can guarantee you they'll both be connected to Los Lobos. That gang is nothing but a bunch of snakes, like Medusa's head," Dallas said. "I want whoever killed these two—and I want them to pay. But more than anything I want to find the Wolf."

Logan nodded. "Which means we need the killer, or killers, alive," he said.

"I don't know what you're thinking, but I've only ever killed a man when it was to save another. I'm not a cowboy, Logan. I don't let my emotions rule, and I don't shoot unless I have to," Dallas said.

Logan glanced at him quickly. "Sorry. I wasn't implying anything. But I know how hard it is when you lose someone on your team."

Of course the guy knew about him. After all,

Adam Harrison had been watching him. "You're talking about William Warwich."

Logan shrugged and said, "I know you had no choice—I read the report. The victim came within split seconds of death. I know it was a justified shoot."

"Then . . . ?"

"I lost my wife," Logan said. "And I remember wanting to skin the killer alive, that's all."

They were both silent as they continued to drive. Then Dallas said, "We both know we need to take the killer—or killers—alive. But first we have to find them."

They hadn't gone far, not even ten miles, when Dallas saw the giant sculpture of a dolphin on the left side of the road that announced the presence of the research facility.

People were leaving. It was past five, and the place had closed. But they explained who they were to the employee manning the entrance, and a few minutes later the facility's friendly photographer led them out back.

Hannah and Kelsey had evidently borrowed bathing suits so they could swim with the dolphins. Now they were using the "splash zone" to rinse off.

Hannah was standing under the spray of a playful whale, smoothing back her wet hair. Her eyes were closed; her face was turned to the water. She appeared as graceful as the best swimmer in the sea, sleek and stunning. He found himself staring and gave himself a mental shake.

"Hey!" Kelsey called to Hannah. "The guys are here for us."

Hannah quickly turned and went for her towel. As she dried off, she waved to a tall woman with dark hair and equally dark flashing eyes. Hannah quickly introduced Dallas and Logan to her friend who ran the center, Stella Marsh. Stella greeted them warmly, urging them to return when they had time.

"You look good," Logan said, smiling at Kelsey.

"Stella got us in on the last swim," Kelsey said. "I love dolphins. They're such magnificent creatures."

"You should see them with Stella," Hannah said. "They're like puppies. They know her. They're affectionate with her."

"What can I tell you? They're smart," Stella said.

"Give us two seconds to get dressed," Hannah said, hurrying for the changing rooms. Kelsey followed on her heels.

Stella chatted to the two men while they waited. Of course the deaths in Key West came up. Logan and Dallas were careful in their replies. Investigations were under way. No one really knew anything yet.

As they talked, though, Dallas felt the tension

in him easing. It had been okay. Hannah had come here and enjoyed a break from the situation. And she was safe. Nothing had happened.

He almost felt calm as they got into the car for the return ride.

"Impressive place," he murmured as Logan pulled out onto the road.

"Oh, I love it there," Hannah said. She smiled at him, but her smile quickly faded and she looked at him somberly. "Well? What did you find out? Was she . . . ?"

He nodded. "Someone held her down there."

She didn't reply but looked out the window.

"Did the M.E. tell you anything? Was there any evidence on her body?" Kelsey asked.

"Whatever they found is with forensics. He'll tell us what they find as soon as he hears," Dallas said.

"I hope it's soon," Kelsey said, looking out the window. "I do miss this place. There's something wonderful about growing up on an island."

"And difficult sometimes, too," Hannah said. "I mean, it's only ninety miles to Cuba but about five hundred miles to the state line. Sometimes it felt like we weren't even part of the rest of the country."

The cousins talked comfortably as they went, pointing out places they loved along the way.

"We're being followed," Logan said quietly after about ten minutes of reminiscing.

Dallas turned slightly, discreetly, to look out the back window.

It was hard not to think you were being followed on the way to or from the Keys. The only through-route in either direction was US 1, but it was unlikely that a car would stay with them by coincidence through Marathon, where there were multiple lanes through both the business and residential districts.

Now, though, they had left the town behind and driven onto Seven Mile Bridge.

Dallas quickly caught Logan's eye in the rearview mirror, his own expression questioning.

"Same car that pulled in behind us right after we left the dolphin facility," Logan said. "It deliberately hung back through town, but now it's with us again."

"We sure as hell can't pull off," Kelsey murmured.

Dallas reached for the Glock in his shoulder holster.

He never had a chance to make a move.

The car behind them sped up and rammed them at eighty miles an hour.

Logan fought to regain control of their car as it leaped forward and began to spin.

10

Hannah had never been so grateful that, even in the backseat of a car, she automatically put on a seat belt. It was Florida state law, but not everyone obeyed, especially in the backseat. Even so, she could never have imagined anything as horrible as the uncontrolled motion of the car and the horrendous sound of metal screeching against metal. The soar and spin of the out-of-control vehicle made bright lights appear before her eyes—lights created by her blinding fear. She didn't see her life rush by behind her eyes in those seconds; instead, she felt an agony of dread. She was thrown against Dallas as the car smashed into the median, and just before the air bags sprang to life, she felt his hand grip hers.

She gasped for breath as the car came to a stop, amazed that she was in one piece, that the pressure of the air bag hadn't crushed her. They were alive! They'd made it.

She heard Dallas cursing as, somehow, he quickly cut away the remnants of the air bags. He must have been carrying a knife. She wasn't sure why it was so urgent that they rid themselves of the air bags so quickly. Then she knew.

It wasn't over.

The man who had hit them was still out there.

"Everyone all right?" Dallas called out quickly.

"Yes," everyone answered in unison

"Down! Get down and stay down!" Dallas told Hannah.

He didn't need to ask twice. Shaking, she hunkered low. She could hear steam coming from the front of the car and, peeking, realized they were slammed against the guardrail. Another violent impact would end them. Her door was crammed against the barrier.

"He's coming back at us!" she heard Logan shout.

"Stop!" Dallas roared, shoving his way out of the wrecked car to stand beside Logan on the road.

Hannah braced herself and peered out above the seat. The car *was* coming back toward them.

She heard a gunshot, then another and another. Each one seemed to rip through her, and she jerked in rhythm to the sounds.

"It's all right," Kelsey said, and Hannah realized that her cousin had her weapon out and steadied on the dash as she aimed at their attackers through the open driver's door. "They got the car."

Got the car?

She looked closer and realized what Kelsey meant. Dallas and Logan had shot out the tires of the car that had hit them. She watched as it skidded and crashed into the guardrail ahead of them.

"Who the hell is that?" Kelsey whispered intently.

Hannah saw the driver's side door of the big sedan that had struck them opening. A man emerged. He looked about forty, she thought, and he was wearing jeans, a T-shirt and a baseball cap.

And carrying something that looked like a very big gun.

It was her turn to scream "Get down!" at the two men outside the car.

"Drop it!" Dallas or Logan—or maybe both of them—shouted.

The man fired but, perhaps dazed by the crash, only hit the headlight of the rental car. She watched Dallas's gun go off. The other man squealed in pain—and drew a second gun from his waistband.

The two agents fired again.

This time the man went down. For a moment, the air seemed impossibly still. Time seemed to stop. Then it started up again, and she realized she could smell gas. She caught Kelsey's shoulder and said, "Out!"

Kelsey must have smelled the gas, as well, because she scooted across to the driver's side door as Hannah crawled out of the back.

Dallas and Logan were walking toward the

fallen man when Hannah shoved Dallas in the back with a single explanatory word. *"Gas!"*

They all ran toward the corpse. She realized cars were close behind them now and turned to run in the other direction to warn them. Waving her hands wildly, she tried to stop them from passing. Then she felt herself being lifted off the ground—not by an explosion but by Dallas. He fell to the pavement with her, taking the brunt of the impact. Two seconds later a car whizzed by, speeding when it shouldn't have been speeding, seeing her too late.

The rental car suddenly exploded. The bridge shook as if there had been an earthquake. Flames leaped to the sky. The car that had nearly clipped her crashed into their attacker's ruined vehicle and added to the chaos.

Time seemed to go crazy in a cacophony of smell and sound. Fire on the air, shouts and reverberations, heat from the flames . . .

As Hannah returned to the here and now she realized that Dallas was lying above her. He had rolled to use his body as a shield against the rain of debris.

Protect and serve. The man certainly had it down pat.

He rose, drawing her to her feet. "You okay?" he asked anxiously, and as soon as she nodded, he caught her hand.

The local police had arrived already—there

must have been a patrol car nearby—and the state cars were bound to follow.

Dallas drew her along with him as he hurried back toward Logan and Kelsey, who were already speaking with the cops.

They were standing by the body of the dead man, who lay in a pool of blood on the asphalt. One of the agents had caught him dead center in the forehead. His head had rolled to the side, and most of the back of it had been blown away. Only a gaping black hole remained, surrounded by bits of bloody dark hair. He had been in his mid-forties, Hannah thought dully.

"No," she said when asked. She'd never seen him before. Dallas used a handkerchief to search in the dead man's pocket for a wallet. His license identified him as Robert Brown of Fort Lauderdale; he'd been forty-seven.

The next thirty minutes were a blur as the road was blocked off, and the agents and police hunkered over the dead man, soon joined by Dirk Mendini. The local police, aware that she was the civilian in the mix, kept offering to make her comfortable in the backseat of a patrol car, but Dallas didn't want her out of his sight, not even in a police vehicle.

Somewhere in the chaos, she remembered that people would begin arriving at the Siren for the evening's ghost tour long before she could possibly get back.

Except there was a dead man on the road. Who had tried to kill them. What did a ghost tour matter?

Then again, in the greater scheme of whatever was going on, maybe it did.

While forms were filled out, while each new officer arrived and had to be briefed, she talked to Dallas about the situation. She realized she sounded like a robot. There was no rise and fall in her voice, no emotion. She wondered if she was in shock.

"You use a service," he said. "Call them and let them cancel. There's nothing else you can do. I wish there were. Oddly enough, I feel that tour should go out tonight."

"People get to the house early a lot of the time," she said. "I wonder if we can stop them before they get there." She hesitated, looking toward the dead man. "My tour and my bed-and-breakfast have always had top ratings. I know that's not a big deal when a man is dead, but they're still my livelihood."

He took her by the shoulders. "Hannah, I understand, and believe me, I wish it could be different. No one wants to use deadly force. But he tried to kill us, was probably ordered to kill us—or one of us. And I think that means you. I don't know if the Wolf *knows* you have inside knowledge about Jose's death or if he just thinks you might know something because of what your

202

guests saw. But I'm convinced he wants you dead."

"Do they know who he was? The man who hit us?"

"He had ID that said Robert Brown," Dallas said. "But fake IDs are easily acquired, and I have a strong feeling his was fake. They'll figure it out soon enough."

Kelsey was standing nearby. "You have every right to worry about your business, but first you need to worry about your life. And not only does the Wolf seem to be after you, he seems to think something he wants is hidden somewhere in your house."

"I know he seems to believe the treasure is in the Siren of the Sea somewhere, but why?" Hannah asked.

"Easy. If the treasure wasn't on Chandler's ship, it had to be hidden somewhere in town, and where better than Chandler's own home? And since no one knows where the wreck is but they do know the Siren's address . . ." Dallas said.

"But after all these years, wouldn't someone have been bound to find it if that was true?" Hannah asked.

"Here's where we're in trouble—the Wolf doesn't need proof. If he suspects something, he acts on it. He probably didn't have proof that Jose was an FBI agent. He just *suspected*. He didn't *know* that Yerby knew anything, he just *suspected* that she did, so he had her killed, too—maybe, as a warning to the others to keep their mouths shut."

"Well, he scared the hell out of me," Hannah said. "But he also . . . he's ruining my life and my business. He's making me mad, too."

"Katie could lead the tour," Kelsey suggested.

"But then I'd worry about *her*," Hannah said.

"David and Liam could go with her," Kelsey said. She turned to Dallas. "What do you think?"

Dallas looked at Kelsey and nodded. "That would be a good idea. I'll call Liam—see to it that a few of his plainclothes officers follow along, as well. I'll tell him we'll meet them back at the house afterward."

"Good plan," Kelsey said. "You okay with it?" she asked Hannah.

Hannah nodded slowly. "Except that I still don't want Katie involved."

"She'll be with Liam and David," Dallas said. "She'll be fine."

He took out his phone to make the call as Kelsey left to speak to one of the local police officers.

Hannah's mind raced. She didn't know how or why this had happened to ruin her life so quickly. And, she thought bleakly, there would be no end. Whoever the Wolf was, he would order killer after killer to come after her.

And the treasure he believed was hidden somewhere in the Siren of the Sea.

She felt suddenly anxious to get off the bridge, to reach the comfort of her home. But that wasn't going to happen anytime soon. The details of the attack and the ensuing accident had to be documented. Dallas, Kelsey and Logan had to be cleared of a wrongful shooting charge, which meant waiting for an agent to come down from Miami. Hours passed, then more hours.

Finally the corpse was gone. Tow trucks got rid of the wrecked cars. A Marathon officer was found to drive them back down to Key West.

They made it back to the Siren of the Sea just as Katie arrived, post-tour, with David and Liam. Katie rushed up to Hannah first, demanding to know if they were all right. The media had reported that a man had been killed, though not the details, and everyone in the Keys was talking about the accident, which had halted traffic in and out for hours.

Kelsey assured the others that they were all fine, having made it out with nothing but shattered nerves, and a few scratches and bruises.

Introductions were made as Hannah unlocked the door. She wanted to be a good hostess—offer tea or drinks all around. Instead she walked in, threw her keys on a side table and sank into a chair as the others filed in.

Katie took over, and in minutes the coffee was on and sandwiches were ready.

Hannah sipped at a cup of coffee—nothing was going to keep her awake now that her adrenalin level had dropped. She noticed that Dallas, Kelsey and Logan were hungry, though, and the sandwiches were quickly gone. But then, she thought, they were FBI agents. They were used to this kind of craziness.

They were accustomed to living—eating, breathing, going on with daily life—with the world in an uproar.

They were an odd assortment, she thought. She'd been friends with Katie all her life, and through her, she had become friends with the entire Beckett family. They all called Liam's wife Kels to avoid confusion, since they were all friends now and, Key West being Key West, they'd all spent a lot of time together before Kelsey's law-enforcement career took her away. It seemed odd to her that Dallas had also been friends with Liam forever, yet they'd never run into each other before.

The oddest thing, of course, that she was sitting in a room filled with people who spoke to the dead.

"So how did the tour go?" she asked as Katie took a seat opposite her.

"Fine," Katie said.

"Not a hitch," David assured her, studying her.

She could tell that he was concerned for her.

"It was filled," Liam said. "Everything from a bunch of college students to a couple in their seventies."

"Oh!" Katie said. "Guess what? At one point I was corrected by one of the college students."

"*You* were corrected?" Kelsey asked. "How could *you* be corrected? You know every single story there is to know about Key West."

"I guess I don't know them as well as I thought," Katie said drily. "This girl said she knew all about the treasure from the *Santa Elinora*. According to her, people *have* found it over the years. But if you find it, you're cursed. You'll die. I guess Hagen's curse had staying power."

A voice seemed to come out of thin air and Hagen himself appeared before them, leaning against the mantel. "What rubbish! I was angry with the man who killed me, but it was just talk, nothing but heated words spoken in a moment of desperation. I certainly didn't curse anyone who hadn't even been born yet."

"Well, that's not actually true," Hannah said softly. "You cursed the seed of Valmont's loins."

"I was angry—dying! Besides, I did not say anything about people who had nothing to do with my death."

"Please don't worry. No matter what that girl believes, I know you would never hurt an innocent person," Hannah said. "Now, I'd like to introduce you to Agent Logan Raintree of the FBI. I think you know my cousin Kelsey, and you've met or seen Katie and Liam and David, and of course you've spoken with Agent Samson."

Hagen nodded at the others in greeting.

"Let's think about this curse thing," Dallas said thoughtfully. "Over the years, the treasure of the *Santa Elinora* has become legendary. Things happen, they're exaggerated—legends grow. We know that whoever the Wolf is, he wants the treasure chest. Maybe *he* believes the treasure carries a curse, which would explain the size and anonymity of his operation. He wants the treasure, but he doesn't want to die, so he puts as many layers as possible between himself and whoever finds it."

Just then Petrie came into the room and jumped up on Hannah's lap. She stroked him, noting that he was staring straight at Hagen.

Cats, she thought, maybe all animals, could often see what most people couldn't.

"They work in groups, obviously," Liam said.

"Obviously?" Logan asked.

Liam nodded. "The night Jose Rodriguez was killed, he was with a group, and at least some of them were Los Lobos."

"And they'd been at the bar," Katie put in.

"You're sure?" Logan asked.

"Jose told us," Hannah said.

"You did sketches, right?" Dallas asked.

Katie smiled. "I didn't—the sketch artist did. I can't draw a stick figure. But yes, the police artist did a great job." She paused, frowning. "You know . . ."

"What?" Hannah asked her.

Katie shook her head. "No, no, he had short hair."

"Who had short hair?" David asked.

"One of the kids on the tour tonight," Katie said. "He was very clean-cut, but I remember when I was looking right at him, he reminded me of someone."

Hannah tensed. "And you think you remember him because he was at O'Hara's the night Jose was killed?"

"It never occurred to me until this minute," Katie said. "He looked like a guy who had dark curly hair, a band T-shirt and dingy jeans. The kid on the tour tonight had a short-sleeved tailored shirt. And a buzz cut. I didn't think of it until Dallas mentioned the sketches. You know how you feel like you've seen someone before, and then you figure they just look like someone else you know? I thought it was that, but it could have been the same guy."

Hannah saw Dallas and Liam exchange a meaningful glance.

"Hair can be cut. Katie, we'll need a new sketch in the morning," Liam told her.

Hannah shivered. "I'm starting to be really afraid—and not just for myself anymore. One of my guests is dead, and she hadn't seen anything but the group walking with Jose. We were nearly killed today. And this isn't the kind of case where you catch the killer and then you're safe. Katie can't be involved in this anymore."

"I'm not alone," Katie reminded her. "I have David."

"*And* we have an alarm system," David said.

"There you go. We're all in good shape," Logan told them. "No one goes anywhere alone. Agreed?" He fixed Hannah with a firm stare as he spoke.

"Hey," she said. "I'm all for living."

"You do have an early warning system," Hagen reminded her as Melody materialized at his side. "Us."

Hannah looked at the intangible spirits of the couple she knew watched over her very well. "And I'm very lucky in that, I know."

Hagen lowered his head in acknowledgment, pleased.

"There's something else we need to get going on," Dallas said.

"What's that?" Katie asked.

"Jose's sister. She disappeared before he went undercover, and Los Lobos are involved, but whether she's a victim or a member we don't know."

Logan looked at him. "And we know this because . . . ?"

"Because Jose told us," Hannah said.

"So she was here, in Key West?" Logan asked.

"Up in Miami," Dallas said.

"It would be nice if Jose would cruise on back here and fill us in," Kelsey said.

"I'm sure he will when he's ready." Hannah looked from Hagen to Melody. "You haven't seen him?"

Both shook their heads solemnly.

"I'll get on that right away—finding out about Jose's sister," Logan said. He looked at Dallas. "This is your call, since we're in your territory, but I'd suggest that, if Liam is willing, we get a police task force—local and state—going tomorrow."

"Agreed," Dallas said.

"I'll set it up," Liam said. "And now, if you all don't mind, I'm going to go home and see my wife. She needs to know what's going on." He met Hannah's eyes. "We're all going to be fine."

"If we can find the Wolf," Hannah murmured.

"We will," Dallas said. She was a little surprised by the passion in his voice. He sounded like a man who was becoming emotionally involved in his case, she thought.

"Liam, have you found out anything at all on Yerby Catalano's killer?" Dallas asked.

"We're sifting through, but none of the charter

boat captains were in the area with anyone unaccounted for at the time of death. The killer or killers must have had a private boat, and that's going to be hard to find," Liam said.

"It doesn't really matter," Hannah said, and realized that she sounded defeated. "I'm sorry. Of course it matters. Yerby deserves justice, and I'm sure you'll catch whoever killed her. And the man who attacked us today is dead. But there will be another and another and another."

"Until we catch the Wolf. And we *will* catch the Wolf," Dallas promised. There was a core of steel in his voice.

She was surprised to find herself feeling encouraged. He didn't say so, but she knew that Dallas would find the man—or die trying.

"On that cheery note," Liam said, "I'm going to go and get my wife."

"We're out of here," David said, reaching for Katie's hand.

Hannah stood to see them out, giving Katie a hug and thanking her again for handling the tour.

Once the others were gone, Hannah fed Petrie and cleaned his litter box. Logan and Dallas, meanwhile, fell into some kind of FBI-speak, saying words like, *Kitchen? Windows? Back?* and moving from place to place securing the house. Kelsey yawned and said she was going to bed, and finally Hannah, too, said thanks and good-night to the two men before climbing the stairs to her room.

By rote she went through the motions of preparing for bed. When she lay down at last, she realized that she was sore all over. She'd kept moving almost on autopilot until now, which had kept her from feeling the physical effects of the car accident.

There was a knock at her door. She sat up and said, "Yes?"

The door opened and she saw that Dallas was there. He didn't come in, though, only said, "I'm literally just steps away. If anything bothers you, if you hear anything . . . I'm here. Well, you know what I mean."

She nodded. She was tempted to tell him to come in. The world had been feeling a little lonely for her lately, and the man's looks were almost irresistibly tempting. But, she reminded herself, he was here only because she was under threat.

In fact, there was no guarantee that he was attracted to her at all.

"Thank you," she told him as coolly as she could.

He nodded, closed the door again and left.

Machete was watching the house. He realized he was becoming obsessed and that he had to fight it or his own life would be at stake.

He was grateful that he hadn't been asked to take her out earlier that day.

He would have done it right and they would all be dead.

He didn't understand the Wolf. The Wolf wanted the key that was somewhere in the house and the treasure that was linked to it. If she died—not to mention three FBI agents and her cousin—the house would be locked up tighter than a drum. How did the Wolf think *anyone* would get in at that point?

Or had he just decided he wanted Hannah O'Brien dead, no matter what the consequences?

It bothered Machete that he'd had to kill that young woman inside the sunken ship. He usually killed and still slept easily, but this was one death he couldn't shake. He couldn't sleep, because he kept seeing her eyes.

If he were forced to kill Hannah . . . would anything he'd done in life matter anymore? She didn't know how he felt, but that didn't matter, either. She was just *there*—and she made life good.

For the first time in his life, he felt regret. He wanted to quit, despite what he knew the consequences would be for his own continued existence.

His phone rang. He stared at it, loathing the sight of it. He didn't want to answer. He wanted to scream and hide under the earth.

He answered.

"Anything?" the Wolf asked.

"Nothing. The cop, and the bartender and her husband are gone. Everyone else has gone to bed."

"Just watch, then. Tonight, just watch."

"I'm watching," Machete said, and waited.

But the Wolf was gone.

His hands shook. Reprieved—for a night.

Dallas lay staring at the ceiling and listening to the house. He heard the breeze outside, and little noises that piqued his attention and kept him awake.

He knew the sounds of an old house, though. Knew the sounds of settling. He believed he would hear an attempt at a window or door. His Glock was at his bedside and his Smith & Wesson was in the small bag of belongings he'd brought with him. He could grab the Glock before a man could blink and reach the other nearly as quickly.

But he wished he was closer to Hannah.

She was certainly no coward, even if she was a civilian. Maybe she didn't even realize how her particular talents gave her an uncommon courage.

She knew what lay beyond the world that ordinary people saw.

He thought of her sitting up in bed when he'd poked his head in, eyes like the sea, hair tumbling around her like a sunburst.

Odd, he told himself drily. He usually preferred brunettes.

He winced. Getting close wasn't good.

He still saw Adrian, still heard her laughter. And he could still see her lying dead, could see the blood, the life and beauty and youth draining from her in a stream of red. . . .

And then Jose.

And Yerby, dead in the water.

He felt his muscles tighten and his jaw clench.

The Wolf had to be stopped.

He heard something. The whisper of a conversation. Women talking, but in hushed tones.

The voices were coming from Hannah's bedroom.

He bolted out of bed, telling himself it was just Hannah and Kelsey talking. They were cousins, hadn't seen each other in a while, were probably just catching up.

Still . . .

He picked up his Glock and raced the few steps down the hallway, bursting into Hannah's room.

He eased the gun down to his side.

Hannah was sitting up in bed again. And she *had* been talking.

To the ghost of Yerby Catalano.

11

Hannah wasn't easily frightened—not by the dead, anyway.

But waking up to find Yerby staring down at her had been a bit much. Still, she was proud of herself, because she hadn't screamed.

Seeing Dallas Samson burst into her room in pajama bottoms, a gun held at the ready, was even more disconcerting.

And yet, once again, she managed not to scream.

Dallas lowered the gun. He obviously saw Yerby, and she certainly saw him, because to Hannah's surprise she almost hurled herself into his arms as if she were still alive. Caught by surprise, he instinctively tried to catch her and pat her back comfortingly, and instead he ended up ineffectually patting his own chest.

Yerby collected herself and stepped back. Ghostly tears appeared on her face. "I don't understand. Why me? I didn't see anything. I don't know anything. I barely even saw the man who killed me. And I'm so angry and—and lost!"

Before she could go on, Melody and Hagen drifted into Hannah's room, followed by Kelsey and Logan, who were also armed.

"Yerby," Hannah said, "this is Agent Logan Raintree and his fiancée, my cousin Kelsey."

"Agents, nice to meet you—I guess," Yerby said uncertainly.

"Yerby, do you know anything at all that might help us?" Dallas asked her.

"All I know is that it was a man, and he was big and well muscled. He was wearing a full wet suit, so I don't even know the color of his hair or how old he was. He was white, if that helps. At the time I thought he was from one of the other dive boats—there were at least three more in the area—and that he was an odd man out, too."

"What about his eyes?" Hannah asked. "Do you remember his eyes?"

Yerby was thoughtful for a minute. "Blue, I think. We were underwater, so he had goggles on, but . . . yes. His eyes were blue."

"That helps," Hannah said. "Really."

"Task force meeting in the morning," Dallas said. "We'll find out if the police learned anything at all from questioning the other divers in the area and potential witnesses on the docks."

As he spoke, Yerby began to fade. "I need . . ." she began, her voice a whisper.

"Yerby, it's all right," Melody said kindly. "You'll get stronger with time."

Too late. Yerby was gone.

For a moment, they were all silent.

Then Hagen spoke. "She needs to say goodbye,"

he said. "She wants one of you to let Mark Riordan know she loved him. She wants him to be at peace."

"You can still hear her?" Logan asked.

Hagen shook his head sadly. "No. The strength to materialize—even to others of her kind—takes time to develop. I know what she wants to say because I've been there," he added softly.

"All right," Logan said. "Everyone . . . we need to get some sleep."

Kelsey gave Hannah a quick hug and left. Logan followed her. Melody and Hagen floated out.

Only Dallas was left.

"You're all right, then?" he asked.

She smiled and said, "I have three FBI agents in my house. Of course I'm all right."

"Okay."

He still stood there. She felt as if the air between them had a pulse whispering through it. She wondered if she was dreaming the way he was looking at her.

"Really all right?" he asked.

That time she shook her head. "No, not really. I . . . um, I . . ."

"Yes?"

Impulsively she said, "Don't go."

She couldn't believe she had actually spoken the words that had been pounding in her brain.

But she had been with him for most of the day,

listening to his voice, watching him move. . . .

Instinct. Chemistry. That was all it was. And yet she had just asked him to stay.

He could turn her down; he could walk away. He might not be attracted to her at all.

He stood very still for a long moment, then opened his mouth as if there were things he needed to say.

But he didn't say any of them. He simply closed the door, then locked it.

"So . . ." he managed. "Are you just looking for conversation? Human contact?"

"Contact, yes," she whispered, and offered him a small smile. "Conversation . . . well, some people talk and some don't, right?"

He smiled, too.

Hannah had barely made it to her feet by the time he reached her. She instantly liked the feel of his hands in her hair as he cradled her head. She felt a burst of warmth and life and fire when his mouth came down on hers, a liquid heat that seemed to be amplified by the strange circumstances.

Her lips parted beneath his. She was aware of everything about him in that moment: his height, the lean musculature of his physique, and most of all, the fact that everything about him was vital and vibrant and *male.* She'd almost forgotten what it was like to want someone so badly. She didn't want to question the fervor with which she wanted him. Was he simply there, eliciting desire as naturally as he breathed, an answer to the natural needs she hadn't even acknowledged lately? Or did she—God forbid—care about him?

She refused to think about that as she felt the pressure of his lips and the force of his body, and the very air around her seemed to churn with sexuality. They fell back on the bed, and longing erupted into urgency.

He caressed her cheeks as his kiss deepened, his tongue delved. The pressure of his body against hers was excruciatingly sweet. As his hands moved over her, she returned the strokes, fingers dancing over his shoulders, along his back, down his spine. She began to move against him as if they were one organism, undulating together.

He wore nothing but the cotton pajama pants, and it was easy for her to shove them away. Her nightshirt disappeared over her head. The slim lace thong panties she wore became part of their sex play as his fingers moved over the waist-band while his kiss moved down the length of her body until it met the skimpy fabric.

And then she hesitated, sanity returning.

"What is it?" he asked.

What had she been thinking?

The answer was that she hadn't been thinking. She'd been wanting.

"I don't usually do this. I mean, frankly . . . I've

never done this. I'm not . . . oh, this is so awkward. I'm not prepared."

He stroked her face. "I can be," he told her. He kissed her lips very gently. "If it's what you want."

"I . . . yes, please," she whispered.

She felt ridiculously bereft when he was gone, but he was back in seconds.

"I'm glad that you've, uh, done this more often than I have," she admitted, blushing.

He smiled. "Not often. But probably once or twice more than never," he said. He touched her face again, then drew her into his arms and pulled her closer to him.

And awkward was over.

He was the ultimate lover, knowing exactly how and where to tease. She longed to return his every touch, to taste and feel and breathe him. And there was something about the night that made each slight brush of fingers, lips or tongues more sensual and provocative than anything she had ever known. Yet it couldn't go on, and in moments he had thrust into her, leaving her wanting nothing more than every stroke that filled her and brought the night to life and seemed to clear the world of everything except for the man himself. Their loving was wet, hot and intimate, and yet as clean as a sea breeze sweeping away everything except the sweet pleasure of the moment. She climaxed with a spasm of mind-shattering force, feeling as if the world itself held still.

He eased himself to her side, still holding her. For a long while he was silent. She certainly had no words. And then he spoke.

"Why couldn't we have met at some local hangout over a few beers?" he asked.

Somehow his words were just right. They made her smile. "Rather than meeting over the dead," she murmured.

"I should go," he said, after another long silence.

"Why?"

"You want me to stay?"

"I don't see why you should leave."

He rose above her for a moment, watching her. A rueful smile curved his lips. "I do want to stay close. It's important when you're protecting someone, you know."

"Close works for me," she assured him.

He pulled her tight against him. Sex had been . . . magnificent. Better than anything she remembered. Having him stay there with her . . .

She didn't think she was a coward. She'd run a business alone for years, and she lived with resident ghosts. But she had to admit to herself that this situation terrified her.

Anyone, at any time, might try to kill her.

But with him beside her . . .

"I'm glad you're here," she admitted.

"You're glad I'm here as a shield—or just glad I'm here?"

"Both," she admitted.

She was amazed at how quickly she fell asleep.

And she was equally amazed, later on, at how quickly just turning against him aroused them both.

The second time was even better. More time to play, to re-explore territory they already knew. They reveled in the subtle touch of fingertips whispering down skin. Deeper, longer, more intimate kisses. And sex so amazing it was as if it had never existed before.

And no question, this time, as to whether he should leave . . .

She was deeply asleep when she sensed a presence. Looking up, she blinked against the early morning light and saw Melody peeking through the door. Literally. She could only see part of Melody; the rest of her astral form remained outside in the hall.

"Hannah," the ghost said.

Hannah instantly felt Dallas stir at her side. "Melody," she groaned. "Please, unless we can save a life this very instant . . ."

"I am so sorry. I did not know he was here, but they are downstairs."

"Who's downstairs?"

"Jose Rodriguez and Yerby Catalano."

"We'll be down in five," Dallas said. Heedless

of the ghost, he was already swinging his legs out of bed.

"My, my," Melody murmured.

Hannah had never imagined that a ghost could blush, but Melody did, then disappeared completely.

It was actually a wonder that there was room for the living, the parlor was so crowded with the dead. Dallas realized he should have been pleased and grateful the ghosts were there to help. Sometimes, of course, the dead actually rested in peace and never appeared. But too often they were shy, bitter, resentful—or totally lost and unable to communicate with the living other than by creating a whisper of cold air.

But, in this case, Melody and Hagen had apparently decided it was their role to help the newcomers learn to negotiate their new world. When Dallas and Hannah got downstairs they found the veteran ghosts encouraging the newcomers not to tax their strength, explaining that appearing at will took time and patience, and that speaking would tire them even more quickly.

Logan and Kelsey joined the impromptu meeting a minute later. Hagen had taken up his customary place by the mantel, Melody hovered beside the sofa and the sofa itself was occupied by Jose and Yerby. Logan, coming up behind

Dallas and aware that something was up but not sure what, raised his brows.

"New kind of task force," Dallas told him. He glanced at his watch. It was early—about 7:30 a.m. They had plenty of time to reach the police station by 9:00 a.m., the start time Liam had texted to him.

Logan nodded. "Then I guess, we'll start here."

Jose began. "I've told my story a few times, but to recap what's important, I don't know if the guys I was with the night I was killed knew what was happening and were setting me up, or if they were taken by surprise and ran like rats to make sure it wouldn't be them. I've been searching the city since then, hitting every bar and hangout I can find—even went to a few up on Stock Island—but I can't find any of them.

"As we all know—" he paused, looking at Dallas "—the real problem is finding the Wolf himself. He keeps his gang together with fear. Toe the line or you're next. Most members only know one or two others, because you have to be invited to join. And the Wolf seems to have eyes everywhere.

"And here's another problem. When he *is* caught, the only charge we'll get him on is conspiracy, and that's not easy to prove. His hands are clean. His soldiers out in the world perform all the grisly deeds on his orders. When they fail him . . . they have no idea that the friendly drunk or hot babe beside them at the bar has been assigned to take them out." He looked over at Hannah. "I'm so sorry I came here that night. If I had known what it would lead to . . ."

"So you think your killer stumbled upon you here?" Dallas asked him.

"Maybe it was planned. I don't know," Jose said. "Old Town isn't that big. Maybe he knew the route my 'friends' would take."

"So, tell us more about your friends," Hannah said. "My friend Katie saw you all at her family's bar, and she thinks one of them may have taken my ghost tour last night. She led it in my place, and she thought he looked familiar."

Jose grimaced. "Knife, Hammer, Pistol and Blade."

"Those are their names?" Logan asked.

"No one uses their real name," Jose said. "I was Pulpit. Here's another thing. The Wolf's reach stretches pretty far. Up to Miami–Dade and Broward counties, and west toward Naples and Fort Myers—then down into the Caribbean and South America. People come and go. It's almost impossible to get a real handle on someone. I was getting close, but then I gave myself away, somehow. I suspect he has people watching his people—while other people are watching them."

"What about your sister?" Hannah asked him.

Jose frowned. "Alicia," he murmured softly. He lifted his hands. "I don't know how they found her. I don't know if I'd been made before I ever came down here." He hesitated, obviously in pain. "She might have fallen in with them. If she fell in with them . . . then she might have given me up. She's a good person, but she's an addict, and addicts will do anything to get another fix. The Wolf must have known the FBI was trying to infiltrate his gang. Alicia might have innocently mentioned me—and from then on, we would both have been targeted. Anyway, she just disappeared. You can contact Miami Officer Pete Marin about her. It's still open as a missing persons case, and he's the lead detective."

Hannah cleared her throat. "Jose . . . you don't *feel* Alicia, do you? I mean, if she had been killed, you might know it. You have . . . abilities in death."

Dallas looked at Hannah. He loved the empathy in her. She honestly felt for others—maybe that was why lost souls sought her out.

Jose looked back at her. "No. I don't feel her." He looked relieved.

"And I died because . . . ?" Yerby asked.

"We think you were a warning," Dallas told her.

"A warning?" she asked.

"In case someone in your group knew something and might have talked," Dallas said.

"Oh, please! A young couple escaping their kids for a few days? A wimp like Shelly—or even Stuart? And trust me, Mark doesn't know any more than I do, and I miss him so much." She broke off with a sob.

Jose embraced her with a ghostly arm. "We're all mortal," he reminded her. "Some of us just find that out . . . early."

"Everyone dies," Melody assured her.

"I guess I just wanted to live, first," Yerby said.

Dallas cleared his throat. "All right, Yerby. We know you were killed by a big man, white, with blue eyes. We'll find out if the police came up with any leads when we head into the task force meeting later this morning. Katie will work with an artist to give us a new sketch of the man she believes was in the bar and then changed his appearance to take the ghost tour." He turned to look at Hannah. "Cancel any reservations you have for the upcoming week. Have your service do it. They can offer your guests a big discount on a later visit."

Hannah didn't argue. But then she asked, "What about the ghost tours?"

Dallas hesitated, looking over at Logan. "The ghost tours could continue," he said.

"They could?" Hannah asked.

Kelsey spoke up. "Hannah, we could close down the Siren and you could move to another state, but the Wolf would still be out there."

"In other words, our best chance of finding the man behind this is to allow the killer to come close," Logan said.

"Can't get much closer than yesterday," Hannah murmured.

"It's your call, Hannah," Dallas said.

"Why not?" she said. "Everyone loves a good ghost tour—even hit men. Now if you'll excuse me, I'll go start the coffee. And make breakfast. If there's one thing we're good at here, it's breakfast."

When she left the room, Yerby let out what sounded like a sigh. "I know you need to arrest the Wolf, but please . . . find out who did this to me, too."

"We will," Dallas said.

"Thank you," she murmured, her voice fading along with her ghostly presence.

"She's just not that strong," Jose said. "She didn't deserve this." He stood. "I'm going to go haunt the town again. It's all I can do now, but who knows? Maybe I'll find something. I'll leave you to all things physical. Dallas, my notes are in my desk at the local office. There may be something there I'm not remembering."

"Thanks," Dallas told him.

No sooner had Jose vanished than Hannah was back in the doorway between the kitchen and the parlor. "Breakfast's ready," she announced.

"Thank heaven for coffee," Logan said, heading for the kitchen.

They all followed, and for a few moments they were all silent as they filled their plates. Soon everyone had coffee and something to eat. Hannah hadn't had time to cook, but she'd set out Danish and bagels, along with cereal and fruit. She'd even come up with an assortment of power bars.

Logan filled a bowl with cereal but remained standing to eat. Kelsey sat down to nibble at a bagel. Dallas grabbed something that promised to be full of protein, fiber and Vitamin C.

Hannah herself didn't eat. She sat, cradling her cup in her hands. Melody and Hagen hovered behind her. Petrie walked over to her, and she picked him up and held him close.

"We'll get going as soon as everyone is ready," Dallas said.

"We?" Hannah asked him.

"We can't leave you here alone," he said.

To his surprise, she smiled at him. "You won't be leaving me alone. Kelsey will stay."

Dallas was startled and stared at Kelsey, who met his gaze somewhat defensively. Something in his gut seemed to tighten. He wanted to protest. He wasn't a chauvinist in any way, but he just couldn't forget what had happened to Adrian.

"I'll keep the doors locked, and we'll give Liam a call and have a patrol officer park out front," Kelsey said.

"But that means you won't be in on the meeting," he said.

She smiled. "You and Logan will be there."

Hannah stood. "You said we have to be—to be obvious."

Yes, but not when I'm not here! he thought.

He didn't say it, though. He knew he had to believe in his fellow agent's ability to do the job.

He realized something more than speaking with the dead had been going on that morning; Kelsey and Hannah hadn't talked about their plan to stay, yet they had both known it. Maybe he should have, too.

He nodded curtly. "Kelsey—"

"You're on speed dial, Dallas. And you're lead. I'll ring you before Logan if there's the slightest reason. And remember, this is Key West. You won't be far, just over on North Roosevelt."

He turned to Hannah. "Just one thing, then. Don't let anyone in while I'm gone. Got that?" She nodded, and he said to Logan, "I'm ready, then—as soon as that patrol car sets up out front."

Watch the house. Well, that was easy enough for him to do.

Machete watched.

And as he watched, he kept praying that his phone wouldn't ring.

The two men left the house, which meant the two women were alone inside. But, of course, one was armed.

The Wolf had been making mistakes recently. Until recently he'd been in control, never setting

232

a foot wrong. But every order he'd given lately had only made things worse. Machete could have handled it all so much better. He wouldn't have made a commotion everywhere. He would have taken care of the undercover agent in a very different way.

Instead, the Wolf had caused a mess.

He was losing control.

Machete took out his phone, which seemed to burn in his hands. He knew he should call the Wolf. He should tell him that the women were alone.

Machete had been contemplating his situation for a while now. He'd forced himself to admit he was obsessed with Hannah O'Brien. He warned himself that, if it came to his life versus hers, he didn't want to die.

But he was worried. He didn't want to end up like the man who had died on the bridge last night. It used to be that people only died if they were disloyal or if they failed.

Now . . .

Now they were all disposable. Send them out, let them die. None of it touched the Wolf.

The Wolf was out of control.

But . . .

His phone continued to burn in his hands. Call the Wolf?

Or just keep watching—and wait for the Wolf to call him?

• • •

There were at least forty officers gathered in the conference room at the station. Dallas spoke first, telling everyone how long the FBI had been tracking the Wolf and Los Lobos and how hard it had been to even know when a case involved them.

Katie had come in early with Liam and her husband to work with a police artist and they'd created a new image of the man she was nearly certain she had seen at the bar on the night of Jose's death and again on the ghost tour last night. Copies of the image were passed around, along with the FBI file on the case.

When Dallas had finished presenting all the information he had, Liam stood to give his report on what the police had discovered in the wake of Yerby's death. Every person on every dive boat that had been out at the time had been questioned. None of them had seen anything. The dive captains and the fishing charter captains had all been questioned, as well, but none of them had seen anything unusual, such as an unfamiliar craft or a dive boat anchored without a flag. Liam looked over at Dallas when he finished. "In short, everyone out there was accounted for, and none of them are our killer or killers."

Dallas thanked him and turned to the assembled officers again. "Someone may still know something they don't realize they know. Use the fact that we're a small community. Use all your relationships. Engage with both tourists and locals whenever you can. Remember, most members of Los Lobos are isolated. They communicate with the Wolf by cell phone, using a number that changes constantly, but if we can get just one person's phone, we'll be a few steps closer."

One of the officers cleared his throat, "Dave Levin, police diver," he said. "I have a boat at the wharf—I'm berthed next to the boat our victim went out on. I also interviewed the married couple Yerby was partnered with, since she was alone on the dive. They swear she was with them when they went by the *Jefferson*, then, when they turned around, she was gone."

"And they didn't go back for her?"

"They didn't realize she was missing 'til they were back on the boat. They're pretty devastated. I told them that they'd be questioned again and they're more than willing to help."

Dallas thanked him.

A beat cop explained that, as yet, the knife Jose Rodriguez had wielded against his attacker hadn't been found, but they were still searching the area, going through trash and brush and everything else.

Another officer stood next to tell them he'd investigated Robert Brown, the man who'd been shot down on the bridge. Amazingly, that had turned out to be his real name. He had a record for petty theft; he'd served time but been out for over ten years. He worked occasionally on construction. His apartment, however, was on Fort Lauderdale Beach—about a hundred and fifty miles north of the scene of the accident—and cost several thousand a month. He'd been living far beyond his apparent means but wasn't carrying any debt. Not married, no children, and—according to his neighbors—he kept to himself.

No phone had been found on him.

"He was probably ordered to ditch it right before the accident," Liam noted. "And that's one of the most important things. If you apprehend anyone suspected of being a member of Los Lobos, do anything you can to get hold of his phone."

"We're sure they're buying prepaid burner phones," Dallas said. "But our tech experts can learn a lot from them anyway, so let's get what we can."

As soon as he finished, Logan motioned to him from the rear of the room. Dallas thanked the attendees and walked over to join him.

"Something?" he asked.

"They've got him, the guy who was at the bar and on the tour. He's in an interrogation room now—spouting his civil rights and demanding a lawyer," Logan said. "Go see what you can get him to spill. We may not have much time if we can't find cause to hold him."

Hannah was glad she had chosen to stay at the house with Kelsey and that Dallas hadn't fought her decision.

She needed time to do what needed to be done business-wise, and maybe, if there was time, just try to calm down, chill out. She was determined not to analyze everything she had done or what she was feeling, not to mention what she thought she should or shouldn't be feeling. And she definitely didn't want to try to analyze what *he* was feeling. Besides, she was afraid she might not even have a future, so the analysis of anything was moot. Better just to keep moving.

She called her service and found out that tonight's tour was full. In fact, they'd been turning down reservations for hours. It was always popular, but her tour was the hottest thing in town these days.

She didn't go outside, and she and Kelsey were keeping the house locked, so they would hear anyone trying to enter.

"I like your guy," she told Kelsey after her cousin had done one of what she called her walk-arounds, moving through the house, checking on the patrol officer on the street and peeking out back.

"My guy? You mean Logan?" Kelsey asked, and smiled.

"You work so well together. Are you really going to get married?"

"Really."

"You don't wear a ring."

"I do." She produced her engagement ring, which she wore on a chain around her neck. It was a beautiful stone, but a sapphire, not a diamond. Hannah noted that there was a second ring on the chain.

"My favorite," Kelsey said, indicating the stone.

"Bucking tradition."

"Actually, I *am* pretty traditional. I believe in marriage."

"And you went off and got married without telling anyone—if I'm reading this right," Hannah said.

"We still plan on doing something special with our friends—soon. We haven't announced that we're married. I think our close friends have figured it out, though."

"Will the FBI let you continue working together once they know you're married?"

Kelsey smiled and nodded. "We're all hand-picked. There are dangers, yes, and we have to follow a lot of extra procedures. But because we're a special unit, we're not subject to all the same rules as everyone else. Unlike the standard field office, we're not limited to a particular territory. Since we're an offshoot of the behavioral analysis unit, we're on call, ready to go wherever we're needed. And while we're not officially 'the unit that talks to ghosts,' it's common knowledge that we handle 'special cases.' Our director knows that people like us aren't the norm, so he doesn't mess with what works. Logan and I work well together."

"But . . . ?"

"But what?"

"Do you ever feel a conflict? Like . . . it must rip you to pieces when you're both in dangerous situations," Hannah told her.

Kelsey was thoughtful for a minute. "A little. But no job comes with a guarantee. You can play it safe and never take chances, and then a car jumps a curb and crashes through a storefront, and it kills you and half a dozen others. You can die a thousand natural deaths—hurricane, earthquake, tornado, blizzard—"

"Falling piece of the space shuttle, asteroid collision?" Hannah said.

"Anything can happen," Kelsey said softly. "We had an agent survive cancer, and she was hit by a bus the week after she finished chemo. There are no guarantees. I want to make a difference and so does Logan, so . . .

"Everyone in the Krewes winds up being very close. We're different from other people, but we share that difference with each other. It's like the kinship between robotics geeks or animal trainers or . . . jugglers or specialists in any field. You speak the same language. So we tend to get emotionally involved with each other. For us, it works."

Hannah was listening to Kelsey so intently that when she heard a knock at the front door, she nearly jumped out of her chair.

At the same time, Kelsey's phone rang.

Kelsey held up a hand, warning Hannah to wait, as she answered the phone. Then she said, "That was the cop out front. He says there's a woman at the door—an attractive blonde."

"Oh, hell. It's Valeriya Dimitri," Hannah said. "I should have called her."

"And Valeriya is . . . ?" Kelsey asked.

"My housekeeper. She usually comes mornings, and we clean up the place together. I'd like to talk to her. I haven't spoken with her since right after I found . . . Jose."

Kelsey nodded. But she didn't leave her gun on the table. Instead, she slid it into the back of her jeans and let her light cotton jacket hide it.

They walked to the door together.

Valeriya looked delicate, but she could whip through a room like no one else and change beds in the blink of an eye. Once a month, Hannah had a local cleaning crew come through to give the house a thorough going-over, but on a daily basis she and Valeriya easily handled it together.

"Hannah!" Valeriya said, her eyes wide. "I

hadn't heard from you since—well, you know. I was starting to worry."

"Come in, Valeriya," Hannah said. "This is my cousin, Kelsey O'Brien. She used to live here in Key West."

"Pleased to meet you," Kelsey said.

"There's a policeman out front," Valeriya said. "Are you okay?"

"I'm fine, trust me," Hannah assured her. But *was* she?

"This is very scary," Valeriya said. "I came to America to be safe."

Hannah glanced at Kelsey. Safety was in short supply at this house right now.

"Valeriya, with everything that's going on, you don't need to come to work today. I don't even have any guests other than my cousin and her fiancée. I thought she was bringing people with her, but it turns out it's just the two of them."

"I heard you're secret agents," Valeriya said breathlessly to Kelsey.

Word was out, Hannah thought. Key West was nothing but a small town when you got right down to it.

Valeriya turned to Hannah. "Hannah, please. I have to work. I can't afford my rent if I don't work."

Hannah looked at Kelsey.

"Okay, Hannah. We've only been using three of the bedrooms, so—"

Valeriya smiled. "I will get to work right now." Still beaming, she left them and went upstairs.

"I can't let her starve," Hannah said when she caught Kelsey's dubious glance.

"No, but her behavior is pretty strange. I know you, though—you'd pay her whether or not she worked the hours."

"Yes, I would."

"So why is she staying and working?"

"Maybe she's scared," Hannah suggested. "She saw the body in the alley. And if she can't make a living and has to leave the island, I'll be in trouble when this is over and I start taking guests again," Hannah said. *If this is ever over,* she added silently.

And Valeriya's behavior *was* strange. Very strange. She had a child. Her mother lived with her and was her childcare provider. Why was she here when she could be with them?

Whatever Valeriya's reason, Hannah decided, if working was that important to the woman, she could work.

"I guess you're right," Kelsey said.

"Besides, I'm afraid, too."

"Of?"

"What if someone decides Valeriya knows something, or that I told her something?"

"First, people know she works for you, so she's in danger already. Second, we won't let her go home until Logan and Dallas get back, and then one of us will see that she gets there safely," Kelsey said.

"Yes, but she needs to go shopping and things—she has to keep living. I should have called her. I should have told her to stay away," Hannah said.

The words had barely left her mouth when they heard a long sharp scream from upstairs.

Followed by a massive thump.

12

The young man sitting sullenly in front of Dallas had neatly clipped brown hair and hazel eyes. He was tanned and fit, like someone who spent his days playing in the sun. Or working in it.

But he didn't have the hands or fingers of a working man. His palms were baby soft, and his fingertips were callus free. He had the look of many South Floridians; Dallas was pretty sure one of his parents had some kind of mixed Northern European background, while the other had hailed from Cuba or one of the other islands, or Central or South America.

His first words to Dallas were, "You have no right to keep me here."

"No? Actually, I can hold you for twenty-four hours without charging you. I understand you demanded an attorney, then decided you didn't want one after all," Dallas said.

Liam laid a file down in front of Dallas, then stepped to the back of the room and leaned against the wall, just watching. The plan was for him to stay there, silent, unless Dallas asked him something.

Logan was watching from the other side of the one-way mirror.

Dallas opened the file. "Martin Garcia. Born Miami Beach, Florida, 1991. Hmm. I'm looking at a couple of drug busts here." He looked up at the young man. "Why do I get the feeling you're lucky you were brought in for possessing the stuff rather than selling it?"

Martin Garcia smiled at him. "You can think anything you want."

"What I want is for you to tell me about the murder of a man the other night—a man you were with until he was attacked."

Garcia tried to keep up his cool, belligerent manner. He was leaned back in the chair, legs sprawled forward. Dallas ignored that and watched his eyes. As soon as the kid lowered his lids and looked to the side, Dallas knew they had him.

"Don't know what you're talking about," Garcia said.

Dallas leaned closer to him, shrugging. "I think you do. And, at this point, you should talk—and you should stay here just as long as we let you. Because I'm pretty sure the Wolf kills those he suspects of disloyalty—which would certainly include giving the police any information on him. And if you leave here, I'm going to hold a press conference and announce that we're close to finding the Wolf because of information we've received from an informant."

The blood drained from Garcia's face, and he turned a sickly shade of taupe.

"I didn't kill anybody," he said quickly. He tried to regain his composure. "And I don't know what you're talking about. Los Lobos. Yeah, I've heard of them—everybody has. So what?"

"Tell us about the Wolf," Dallas said.

"I don't know anything about any wolf!" Garcia protested.

"Well, then," Dallas said, sitting back and turning around to look at Liam. "We might as well just release him. He doesn't know anything about the Wolf. He won't wind up like Jose Rodriguez or Yerby Catalano or, more importantly, the man who died on the bridge last night. Admittedly, the Wolf didn't kill him. The poor bastard committed suicide by cop. He'd rather have us shoot him than face what he knew was coming from his boss."

"Sure. We'll let him go right now," Liam said. "Littering—what were my guys thinking, picking him up on a charge like that?"

Everything about Martin Garcia changed then. He shook his head. "Don't. You can't. I'd tell you what you want to know, but I don't have anything to tell you. Really."

"See?" Liam said. "He can't help us—really. We should just let him go. I mean, I'd offer him protection, a bunch of cops to stand around keeping an eye on him all day, but we don't have that kind of manpower. He got himself into whatever, he can get himself out."

"No!" Garcia was on his feet. "You don't understand. I don't know who the Wolf is. I got mixed up in the whole thing because of my cousin Billie."

"Billie," Dallas said. "Sit down." He indicated the chair again. "So, tell us about Billie. Would he be Knife, Hammer, Pistol or Blade? Which one are you, by the way?"

Garcia's eyes widened. "I don't know what—"

"Get him out of here!" Dallas said with disgust.

"No, no! Billie is Blade. I'm—I'm Knife."

"Knife," Dallas said. "You like knives, Garcia? Slicing people up?"

"I never killed anyone, I swear!" Garcia protested. "I just needed a name—you know, one that would make me sound tough and cool. None of us are supposed to know each other's real names—or even know each other at all, most of the time. If a job calls for more than one person, we meet at a predetermined location and use the names we've chosen."

"But you and your cousin *did* know each other. There were four of you the other night—getting to know the new guy. Jose Rodriguez. At least one of you knew him by name, because someone in the group recruited him."

Garcia nodded. "Yeah, my cousin. Billie. Blade. He recruited him."

"Great. Tell us about your cousin Blade."

"Blade didn't kill him, either."

"But you all knew he was going to be killed," Dallas said.

"No."

Dallas started to turn away in disgust.

"No, no! I swear we didn't!" Garcia cried, his voice high-pitched and tense. Sweat suddenly appeared on his face.

He was telling the truth.

"That's just it, don't you see? You have to protect me." Garcia hadn't wanted to talk, but he suddenly couldn't stop, the words pouring from him. "I never saw the guy before that night. Billie—Blade—met him in some bar. He was talking about his sucky life—how he was ready to do more so he could get more. Blade talked to the Wolf, and the Wolf said to bring him in. Blade brought the new guy—Pulpit—when we got together the other night. Wolf's orders. We were going to get our assignment when the Wolf called Blade.

"So we're in the bar and Blade gets the call. He just tells us to leave the bar and walk down Duval toward Mallory Square. Then the phone rings again, and the Wolf tells us where to turn off. We're just walking. Just walking, I swear it! Then suddenly there's this noise behind us and I . . . I turn around and there's blood and your guy is trying to fight off some guy and Blade says 'Run!' So we ran—the rest of us, we ran like hell. I have no idea who actually killed the guy. I'm telling you the truth. Finally Blade says we gotta split up. Then he tells me that I gotta look different, so I cut my hair and all. I bought preppy clothes . . . I did what I was told."

Dallas stared at him. "And you never killed anyone?"

"No."

"What happened to the girl who went diving?" he asked quietly. "Yerby Catalano."

Garcia shook his head. "I swear I don't know. I overheard one of the guys saying that call went to Machete."

"Who's Machete?"

"I swear to God, I don't know."

Liam came forward, pulled a pad from the folder on the desk and pushed it toward Garcia, along with a pen he took from his pocket. "We need names—real names if you have them, aliases if you don't."

"I'll be a dead man if I do that."

"You're a dead man if you don't. Your only hope is helping us. Then, if your info pans out, we'll bring in the U.S. Marshals and see about getting you a new identity. But first we need everything you can give us. And you'd better not lie or witness protection goes out the window," Liam warned.

Garcia winced, looking down at the paper. "My cousin . . . he's my blood," he said.

"It's your blood or your life," Dallas told him.

He leaned forward. "If we send you out there now, you're dead. I want your cousin's full name. I want to know where to find him. I also want to know about every theft you've been involved with, and I want to know everything—*everything*—you can possibly tell us about Los Lobos and the people in it. And it's in your best interest to do so, because until we get the Wolf, no matter how we try to protect you, no matter what we do, you'll be looking over your shoulder the rest of your life."

Garcia was visibly deflated. His whole face was damp with sweat. He nodded.

"There's one more thing I need to know—and I need to know it now," Dallas said.

Garcia looked at him. His eyes were wide, terrified. He nodded.

"What were you doing on that ghost tour?" Dallas asked.

Garcia froze. Then he winced as if he were in pain.

"What?" Dallas demanded.

"The house," Garcia said at last. "I was supposed to get a good look at the house."

"And what else?"

"I . . . I was supposed to get the woman alone. Wolf knew that Hannah O'Brien wasn't going to be leading the tour. That it would be another woman. Katie O'Hara. I was supposed to . . . to get her alone when the tour was over, before she headed back to the house."

"Why?"

He winced again. "I—I wasn't ordered to kill her, if that's what you're thinking. I was supposed to get to know her. Talk to her about the Siren of the Sea like I was studying local history and needed to know for a paper I was writing."

"Why?"

"So she would invite me back to see more of the place. The Wolf didn't know she'd have a cop *and* her husband with her."

"So you gave up the plan. But what *was* the plan?"

"I was supposed to get her talking. Then I was supposed to see that the doors were left unlocked."

"That's it? That was all you had to do? You weren't supposed to kill anyone?"

"No. No killing," Garcia said.

Maybe not, Dallas thought, but the kid was lying. There was something else.

Dallas forced Garcia to meet his eyes. "There's something else going on. What aren't you telling me?"

Garcia let out a breath. "Drug her coffee," he said.

"What?" Dallas said, surprised by the answer.

"Get into the kitchen and drug her coffee. But I never got the chance." Garcia stopped talking and inclined his head toward Liam. "The cop was there."

"Detective Beckett was there, you mean."

"Detective Beckett. And the other guy—lethal looking guy. He was a Beckett, too. David Beckett. The cop's brother. So when I found out she'd be surrounded all night, I shelved the plan. The Wolf isn't stupid." Garcia paused again and sighed. "He doesn't mind sending out an army to get killed. But he always has the endgame in mind, so if things don't line up, he gets it. When he called me to check in and I explained the situation, he said just to be friendly and curious and stay at the Hard Rock when the tour was over, then leave after I had my free drink."

Dallas stood and looked down at Garcia. "This better be the truth—the absolute truth," he said. "We're going to find the others and pick them up. We'll hold them, and then, most probably, they'll be charged with conspiracy to commit murder. I'm a federal agent, not a district attorney, but if you testify, I'm sure the DA will agree to relocate you."

Garcia nodded, then looked down at the pad and pen lying in front of him.

When Dallas and Liam headed for the door, Garcia laid his head down on his arms. He was shaking, Dallas saw. Despite his dangerous alias, "Knife" wasn't cut out for a life of crime, and he was afraid. Terrified. He'd been an easy mark. He almost felt sorry for the kid.

But, Dallas knew, the Wolf wouldn't feel any

such thing. Because he didn't care who he lost—who he sacrificed.

And damn it, they still weren't close to the answers they needed.

"Think we'll get anything?" Liam asked as he and Dallas met up with Logan in the hall.

"I think he was telling the truth. The Wolf is smart about only sending those out to kill who can kill," Dallas said. "Garcia, a killer? No way. The Wolf goes for the cold-blooded kind. Like the guy who came after us on the bridge. He was ready to kill or be killed. The odd thing is, I don't think the Wolf cared whether we were killed on that bridge or not."

"No?" Dallas asked.

"What he wants is to get inside the house. He knew the accident might not go his way, but he figured even if we weren't killed or in the hospital, we'd be so wiped out by getting hit, then all the follow-up with the cops, that once we got back we'd be out like lights. Maybe even on painkillers to help us sleep. Meanwhile, he would have come in through the door Garcia left open and hidden somewhere, so once we were asleep he could look around for the treasure to his heart's content."

"And then most likely kill us all," Logan finished.

"Maybe," Dallas said. "Or maybe he just wanted to get into the house and our fates didn't matter one way or the other. The Wolf steals art and artifacts. The only time someone dies is when they cross him or he wants to send a warning, or they're in his way or have something he wants. The people on the salvage boat disappeared. But Jose was only killed because he had infiltrated the gang, and maybe because the Wolf thought Jose was close to discovering something about the *Wind and the Sea*."

"Here's what I don't get," Logan said. "Why does he think the treasure's at Hannah's place? It was never there, right?"

"There are no records to show that it was ever stored at the house," Dallas agreed.

"Records can be missing or misleading," Liam said.

"We have to find it," Dallas said.

"Yes," Logan said. "And the Wolf."

"But," Logan said, "if we can find the treasure—or even make Los Lobos think we have—we just may be able to trap the Wolf."

Valeriya was in Captain Chandler's room, the room where Dallas was staying.

She was on the floor, looking disoriented. Kelsey rushed in ahead of Hannah, gun at the ready, prepared for anything. Valeriya saw the gun and let out another high-pitched scream.

"Valeriya!" Hannah cried, hurrying forward to help the girl, who was trying to get up. "What happened?"

Valeriya pointed at the bed. "I—I pulled the sheet, but it caught under the mattress and I slammed against the wall and fell down."

"Did you hit your head? Are you hurt?" Hannah asked her.

Kelsey slid her weapon back into the waistband of her trousers, snug against the small of her back, and joined Hannah to help Valeriya to her feet.

"I'm okay," Valeriya said. "I'm sorry I screamed like a baby."

"You sure did," Hannah agreed, laughing. "But that's okay."

"Let's get you downstairs, so you can have something to drink and sit a minute—make sure you're all right," Kelsey said.

"Thank you, but I'm okay."

"You may need to go to the hospital, just to make sure you don't have a concussion," Kelsey said.

"No, no, I'm okay, just . . . raffled," Valeriya said.

"Rattled," Hannah explained to Kelsey.

Kelsey smiled. "*Raffled* is good, too."

Hannah smiled, then was distracted when she realized Valeriya had slammed against the wall harder than she'd thought. False brick—really just a plaster overlay—had been applied across a section of the wall at one point, and now bits of it were chipping off.

"Kelsey, I'm going to finish making up the room. Can you help Valeriya?"

"Sure."

"No, no, I will finish cleaning," Valeriya insisted.

"No, you will sit down and make sure you're okay," Hannah told her, then walked to the hall closet to get the broom.

Back in the bedroom, Hannah struggled to move the heavy captain's bed away from the wall so she could sweep up all the plaster that had fallen. When she was done, she paused for a moment, then pushed the bed back.

The walls had been painted over the years, but she had no idea when the false brick had been added. The style had been popular during the late 1700s through the mid-1800s, so presumably it had been there awhile.

She would have to get Bentley in to repair it, she thought. He was used to working with plaster and knew the old wooden houses in the Keys like few other men. This would be a tricky job. There was actually a notch out of the wall, almost as if the false brick had been hollow.

She started to turn away but then turned back. Something wasn't right; she had just caught it in her peripheral vision.

She was trying to move the bed away from the wall again when Kelsey came back.

"You okay up here?" Kelsey asked. "What in the hell are you doing?"

"I'm fine. Moving the bed to get to the wall. There's something . . . odd. It looks like a false brick was pushed in when Valeriya collided with the wall."

"Easily fixed and easily hidden until it's fixed," Kelsey said. "Just move the bed a little to the side."

"Yeah, but . . ."

She started pulling on the bed again, and Kelsey helped her until she could reach the broken spot in the wall. Immediately she knew what had captured her attention. Something inside the wall had caught the sunlight and given off the tiniest gleam.

She poked at the plaster, and more of it chipped away.

And then she knew what she had seen. Something metal had been hidden in the false brick and revealed when Valeriya had slammed against the wall.

"What is it?" Kelsey asked.

"I don't know . . . almost got it," Hannah said. She poked around in the little hole with her finger until she touched the metal. The rest of the "brick" fell apart as she dug it out and dusted the plaster from it.

She looked up at her cousin. "It's a key."

"A key," Kelsey said. She shrugged. "Well, we've found things—including bodies—in walls before. In the past, I guess this was something like a safe-deposit box, except more permanent."

"And at least it's not a body," Hannah said.

"Yes, that's always a good thing," Kelsey assured her wryly, then mused, "but a key. A key to what?"

Hannah held the key flat on the palm of her hand. It was long and straight, with some kind of metal insignia on the top and a simple protrusion on the bottom with which to open . . . whatever it opened.

"It's old, that's for sure," Kelsey said.

Hannah looked at her and smiled, and she couldn't help responding as she sometimes had when they were younger. "Duh!"

Kelsey laughed and started to speak, but then they heard movement on the stairway and spun to face the door.

Kelsey started to reach for her gun—ever ready, Hannah thought—but it was only Valeriya.

"Is everything all right?" she asked anxiously. "Did I break something?"

"No, Valeriya, everything is fine," Hannah said, quickly slipping the key into her pocket. "How are you feeling? Did you have some tea?"

"I'm fine. I just feel so stupid for making such a fuss. And look what I did to your wall!"

"It's no big deal," Hannah assured her. "Bentley can fix it. Come on. Let's all go back downstairs."

"Let's finish in here first," Kelsey suggested.

"I will help," Valeriya said, moving to collect the clean sheets from their place on a chair.

"No!" Hannah and Kelsey said in unison.

"You can supervise," Hannah told her.

She and Kelsey had both worked for their uncle when they'd been kids. In a matter of minutes they had the bed made up with clean sheets and everything back to rights—except for the hole in the plaster. Hannah vowed to herself to come up later, when Valeriya wasn't there to feel guilty, and move the bed to hide it.

"Is someone staying in here?" Valeriya asked.

"An FBI agent," Hannah said. "He's investigating the murder in the alley the other night."

"My partner and I are staying here, too—down at the end of the hall," Kelsey told her.

"I'm glad, Hannah. This way you are not alone," Valeriya said.

"No, I'm not alone," Hannah said. "Let's go back down now."

"There are more rooms to clean," Valeriya said.

"Not today, Valeriya. Please don't worry. I'll keep paying your salary until I need you to come back to work."

"I can't take your charity," Valeriya protested.

"It's not charity. I'm being selfish. I want you around when I need you, okay?"

Valeriya looked at her searchingly, then nodded at last. "Okay. Then I'll go home now and let you and your cousin catch up."

"No!" Kelsey and Hannah spoke at the same time again, then looked at one another and smiled.

"The men will be back soon, and someone will see you home," Kelsey said.

"Why?" Valeriya asked, suddenly nervous. "What's wrong?"

"I'm just nervous," Hannah said. "I know it's silly, but after that man was killed so close to the house, I worry, that's all."

"Oh, no, that's silly. It's broad daylight, and I live a few blocks away."

"Do it as a favor for me," Hannah told her. "Let's go downstairs again. You can teach us Russian."

As they left the room, Hannah was acutely aware of the key in her pocket.

When the three men left the station, Logan headed up to Miami to find out what he could about Alicia Rodriguez, while Liam went to talk to his team about finding Blade, Hammer, and Pistol, aka William "Billie" Garcia, Reggie Arnold and Carter Addison, names Martin Garcia admitted he'd known despite the Wolf's prohibition.

Dallas headed to the other side of the island to interview the married couple who had been partnered with Yerby during her fatal dive.

He reached their hotel and paused to looked across the road to the beach and the water. He thought about growing up here and how much he still loved to feel the sea breeze, about the way the world changed in summer, cooling down just a little bit when the sun had set and the breeze came in off the water.

Key West could be a crazy place—it was a destination for bachelor parties from around the world, for one thing—and you could hear a dozen different languages being spoken every time you walked down the street. Cubans had plied these waters and landed on the island long before any real settlement had been founded, and much of the island's history had to do with the cigar makers who had made it their home. Music was everywhere and usually good, because there was so much competition and the less talented were squeezed out. Jimmy Buffet had left his mark, for sure, but you could hear anything as you passed the bars and clubs of an evening.

The Conch Train was in constant motion, touring visitors around the city and giving them a crash course in island history. Writers and readers came to pay homage to the master at the beautiful home that was once owned by Ernest Hemingway and was still filled with six-toed cats. Gorgeous Victorian homes dotted the island, and there was no end to the businesses offering diving, snorkeling, fishing and partying out on the water. The Conch Republic was like a mini United Nations, he thought, and he loved it.

And he hated the fact that the Wolf was killing on *his* home turf.

Most of all, he hated the fact that the bastard

had homed in on the Siren of the Sea—and Hannah O'Brien.

He was a few minutes early, so he decided to take a moment to call Hannah. He made his way to the hotel pool, where he was meeting the couple, chose a seat and pulled out his phone.

"Everything okay there?" he asked her the minute she answered.

"Absolutely," she assured him. "I'm having tea with Valeriya and Kelsey."

"Valeriya?" he said sharply.

"She came to clean today. She needs the work."

"Be that as it may, Hannah, you shouldn't let anyone in when you're alone."

"I'm not alone. I'm with Kelsey." Her voice dropped to a whisper. "But we're not letting Valeriya leave until one of you comes back. She's connected to the Siren, so we don't think she should be out alone."

That, he thought, was a wise decision. But he still didn't like it that the other woman was there.

Anyone—anyone—including a longtime employee, could be working for the Wolf.

"Hang on," Hannah said. "I'm heading into another room."

He waited.

A moment later Hannah started speaking excitedly. "Dallas, it's great that she came. She was making the bed in your room and fell into—"

"Wait. You let her in *my* room?"

Hannah was silent for a minute, then said, "This is a bed-and-breakfast. She didn't go in with a search warrant. She just went in to make the bed and bring fresh towels. That's what we do here."

He took a deep breath. "All right. So what happened after she fell?"

"She was pulling on the sheets, and she lost her balance and slammed against the wall where the plaster looks like bricks. You'll never guess what I found!"

"No, I'll never guess, since it's pretty impossible for a treasure chest to fit in a space that's a few inches deep, at best."

"No, not a treasure chest—but I may have found the key to one. I found a key in there, Dallas. A very old key. And I don't know why it never occurred to me 'til you just said it, but it could be the key to a treasure chest."

Dallas heard footsteps and looked up. A young brunette was coming toward him, hand in hand with a man wearing khakis and a short-sleeved shirt decorated with multicolored parrots.

They had to be the Brennans. He rose to greet them.

"Hannah," he asked quickly, "you didn't show Valeriya the key, did you?"

"No, of course not."

"And the officer is still parked in front of the house, right?"

"Yes, he's there. We're fine, Dallas. Kelsey knows what she's doing."

"I know that," he said quickly. "But I'll be there soon, anyway, as soon as I finish with this interview."

"Wait! What's happening with you?" Hannah asked.

"I'll tell you as soon as I see you, but we're finally moving in the right direction," he assured her.

The couple was almost on him. He ended the call and offered his hand. "Dallas Samson, FBI," he said. "I really appreciate your willingness to help. Sit, please." He'd found a spot near the pool that was shaded and had lawn chairs in a group.

"I really hope we *can* help," the woman said. "I'm Lottie, by the way. Lottie Brennan," she told him quickly. "We didn't know the poor girl before that morning, but she was so sweet and filled with life. She was mad at her boyfriend for not coming, but she said she wasn't missing out because of him. Another couple was supposed to have come with them, as well, but they copped out on her, too. She came anyway, because she really loved diving."

Lottie's husband, who introduced himself as Don, nodded vigorously. "She was a nice kid—a really nice kid. This is so horrible. I feel responsible."

"Me, too, even though I know we're really not,"

Lottie said. She looked at Dallas. "We were all swimming together. She was right with us. Then, suddenly, she wasn't. There were a lot of divers out—and you know how people kind of look alike in dive gear? Well, there were at least twenty people on our boat, and I don't even know how many more from the other boats anchored pretty much where we were. I thought she was still with us, because there were several pretty girls with dark hair nearby. We'd checked in with each other every few minutes all along the way, but then, when it was time to go up, she just wasn't there! We told the divemaster and the captain immediately. They called the police and the Coast Guard, then went down to look for her right away."

"Do you remember anyone on your boat who was close to my size? And blue-eyed?"

They looked at each other thoughtfully and shook their heads.

"She didn't just drown?" Don asked.

"We're investigating," Dallas said.

"Do you dive?" Lottie asked him.

He nodded.

"Then you know what it's like. You see a ray and you're fascinated, so you start following it. Then a shark swims by, and even though you know not to panic, you move away, anyway. Then you see the wreck itself and you can't stop staring at it. I have to admit, I wasn't watching the other divers. It was just too beautiful down there." She paused and ducked her head. "Not so beautiful for Yerby, though," she said. "But I can tell you this—no one anywhere near your height was on *our* boat."

"Can you think of anything that might help? Anyone you might have seen who *was* my size? Anything that struck you as out of place or different?"

"Um, yeah. One thing," Don said thoughtfully.

"What's that?" Dallas asked.

"I did notice a really big guy diving near us when we first went in. He was wearing a wet suit—not just a heavy skin, a full wet suit. It covered him head to toe. He didn't come from our boat, because he was already in the water when our group went in, but I remember seeing him kind of blend in with us. To tell you the truth, I really only noticed him because I was wishing I was in that kind of shape."

"He was well muscled?" Dallas asked.

"Oh, yeah," Don said admiringly.

"Anything else you remember about him?" Dallas asked.

Don just shook his head. "He knew what he was doing down there, but other than that . . . no, nothing. Sorry."

"I wish we could help you somehow," Lottie said. She looked at her husband miserably. "We felt guilty enough when we thought she drowned accidentally. But now that you're saying she was killed . . ."

"We don't know anything for sure. We're just investigating right now," Dallas reminded them. It was a lie, of course. But the authorities weren't giving out any information at the moment. "No matter what happened, if she was determined to go off on her own, there wasn't anything you could do."

"We keep telling ourselves that," Don said. "But she's still dead, and we were the ones supposed to be keeping an eye on her."

"Why were you asking about that man?" Lottie asked.

"Someone else mentioned him, and I haven't found him yet. That's all," Dallas said.

"Is there anything else?" Don asked. "Because I think I need a drink. I've been having a lot of them since this happened."

Dallas produced one of his cards. "No. Thank you for your time. But if you think of anything— anything at all—call me, please."

"Of course," Lottie assured him.

He nodded and headed to the parking lot.

He hadn't gone more than a dozen steps before Lottie came rushing after him. "Agent Samson!"

He stopped, waiting for her. She rushed up to him a little breathlessly. "I *did* think of something."

"What is it?"

"That man—the one my husband described?"

"Yes?"

"I remember seeing him, too. We'd been in the water about ten minutes. We were all pretty much in a group, following the divemaster, you know?"

Dallas nodded.

"When I turned back to look at a school of barracuda, I saw him. He was close to us—really close."

"Anything else?"

"Yes. He was close enough that I could see his eyes. And I remember now—they were blue. Really blue! He has to be the man you just described."

"Thank you. But you don't know where he came from? What boat?"

"No. I assume from one of the other dive boats."

"Of course."

"If I see him again—you know, if I run into him on the island—I'll tell him you're looking for him."

"No! No, please. If you see him, keep your distance. Call me or call 911 right away. But whatever you do, don't even let him know you've noticed him."

"Oh! Are you saying he—that he might . . . ?"

"I'm not saying anything. It's just better if I talk to him fresh, without him thinking about why and maybe embellishing his story because he thinks that's what I want."

"Oh. Then no, of course not. But I will call you. Immediately. I promise."

"Thank you," he told her. "What I would like to have you do is work with a police artist to do a sketch of him. Would you mind doing that for me?"

"Not at all."

"I'll set it up," Dallas promised.

She nodded. "This is so awful. But if someone did kill Yerby . . . well, then it won't be my fault anymore. Maybe I'll be able to live with myself." She looked back to where her husband was waiting for her and turned back to Dallas bleakly. "And maybe Don will stop drinking so much," she said. "He can't help it, you know. It's terrible to think you caused someone's death."

"You didn't, I promise you," he said.

"Logically? I know that. But emotionally . . ."

She gave him a smile with no humor in it and promised to work with the police artist as soon as he set it up.

They were watching an old horror movie in the back room. Hannah's phone rang just as a Godzilla-like creature stomped on a used car lot.

She jumped up and checked the caller ID; it was Dallas again. He told her he was coming up the front walk and asked her to come let him in.

"Got to go open the door for Dallas," she said.

"Want me to pause the movie?" Kelsey asked.

"No, that's all right," Hannah assured her. She hurried to the front and took the time to peer out through the glass before opening the door. She looked at Dallas anxiously. He offered her a smile but seemed preoccupied.

How quickly they forget, she mocked herself.

But that was on the far side of absurd. They were trying to solve a series of murders. Whether they did or didn't sleep with each other was not the most important thing at the moment.

"Valeriya still here?" he asked.

"Someone is here? I can go home?" Valeriya asked, hurrying through the house to reach them.

"Don't you want to see the end of the movie?" Hannah asked her politely.

"No, that's okay. I know the story. The monster will die in the end. But thank you. Thank you for keeping me here and worrying about me," Valeriya said, then looked at Dallas. "I've seen you," she said softly. "I saw you in the alley when—when the dead man was there."

He nodded. "Yes, I saw you there. I'm Agent Dallas Samson," he told her.

She offered him her small hand. "Valeriya Dimitri."

Dallas glanced at Hannah. "Shall I see Valeriya home now?"

"Yes, thank you."

He nodded. "Well then, Valeriya, whenever you're ready."

"I'm ready now," she said.

As she stepped out the front door, he turned to Hannah and said, "Lock it after us. And don't let anyone in. *Anyone.*"

"Of course."

Kelsey came up behind her as she locked the door. "I don't think he's happy you let her in."

"Worse," Hannah said. "I let her clean his room."

Kelsey shrugged. "Don't let the attitude get to you. He lost a team member not too long ago. I'm sure that had to leave a mark."

"Oh? How do you know that?"

"Logan knows about him. He's been on Adam Harrison's radar."

"And that means . . . ?"

"Adam Harrison, our director, is always on the lookout for the right people to join the unit. Sometimes he pulls people from other law enforcement agencies, and sometimes he comes across people who aren't part of any agency but they just have the right . . . talent. Dallas Samson has kept his abilities quiet. You know how that goes. Let people know, and they think you're not sane and certainly shouldn't be in law enforcement. But Adam just has an instinct."

"Do you know what happened? With his partner, I mean," Hannah asked her cousin.

"No, I don't know the details. Sorry. I just know that he must be hurting from it. We've come close a few times, and I don't know how I'd deal with it if we actually lost someone."

Hannah nodded. "But . . . that's part of the job, isn't it? You know going in that you're going to face dangerous situations."

"Of course. And we go through training to minimize the risk. The toughest part is realizing that no matter how great a shot you are, no matter how strong you are, you're still vulnerable. That's the human condition. Dallas knows that, too, but when you lose someone close to you, it just takes time."

"So there is no safe place, really, not for anyone," Hannah said.

"No. We just walk into more dangerous situations that offer more opportunities for bad things to happen."

"I guess life itself is a crapshoot," Hannah said.

"More or less. Except, in this crapshoot, we're lucky. We know there's more than meets the eye."

"Enough depressing talk. I'll start some lunch," Hannah said.

"And I'll help you."

They had barely begun when Hannah's phone rang. Dallas was back at the front door. She hurried to let him in. He still had a distant look about him. She realized she'd only known him a few days; she didn't really have any idea what made him tick. Being intimate with him hadn't opened him up as if he were a book.

"We're making lunch," she said.

"Food. Good. The couple who were with Yerby when she was killed are working with a police artist. I'll be taking the sketch to the docks. Logan is up in Miami, and Liam and his men are rounding up Blade, Hammer and Pistol."

"You know who they are?" Hannah demanded. Something inside her gave a little leap.

Maybe there was hope!

"Yeah. Where's Kelsey?"

"Kitchen."

"We'll join her, then I won't have to repeat myself."

Food and iced tea were on the table—cold cuts, cheeses, lettuce, tomatoes and condiments—and Dallas spoke as he put a sandwich together.

"The sketch Katie helped with led to the man who'd been in the bar and then on the ghost tour. He swears he didn't do any of the killing and that they had no idea Jose was going to be murdered, and we believe him. He gave us the names of the other men in the group. Also, we have his phone. The tech people will trace the call history, but the Wolf changes phones constantly and has a new number each time. After all that, I went to see the couple who were diving with Yerby when she died. They remember seeing a diver who matched the description Yerby gave, so they're working with an artist on a sketch."

"It was a good morning, then," Kelsey said.

"Except," Dallas said disapprovingly, staring straight at Hannah, "you let someone in after I told you not to."

"It was Valeriya. Seriously, Dallas, you've seen her. She's just trying to stay in the United States and find the American Dream, and if she doesn't work, that can't happen."

"Do you know how many people have seen the American Dream as a chance to get rich through illegal means?" he asked.

"I'm more afraid *for* Valeriya than I am *of* her," Hannah told him.

He shook his head. "Still," he said quietly, "no one else comes in here until we solve this."

Hannah opened her mouth to argue and then didn't. He made her crazy, coming on like a general and then softening to make his commands sound like requests.

"If you're going to blame Hannah, you have to blame me, too. I figured that, on top of everything else, there was no reason to send the woman to the poorhouse," Kelsey said.

"And don't forget, it's because of Valeriya, I found the key—for whatever it may be worth," Hannah said.

"The key . . . yes, let's see it," Dallas said.

Hannah drew the key from her pocket. "It looks really old," she said as she handed it over.

Dallas took it from her and lifted it up to the

light. Hannah studied it from that new angle and drew a sharp breath.

"What?" Dallas asked.

"The insignia on the end—I know what it is," she said excitedly.

"What?"

"It's the coat of arms of Duke Ricardo Montoya de la Geraldo."

"Who?" Kelsey asked.

"Kelsey, come on! You know the legend. Geraldo, as he was called, was the Spanish nobleman who sailed the *Santa Elinora*. The ship whose treasure started this whole mess," Hannah said.

Dallas studied her. "So," he said softly, "that could mean the treasure really *is* here."

Hannah shook her head. "No, the treasure is not in the house. I mean, feel free to look, but workmen have been in here too many times to count over the years. There is no basement, just a foundation that reaches down into the coral. You can't dig a basement here, because it gets watery as soon as you go down too far, trust me. And we used to play in the attic, so I know there are no secret walls or anything. The missing chest is not in this house."

"But this might well be the key to it," Dallas said.

"It could be the key, but would anyone—especially a man like the Wolf—risk so much and

276

kill two people just to find a key when all he'd have to do is break open an old chest to get to the treasure?"

"We're back to perception," Dallas said. "The chest may not be here, though I'm not a hundred percent certain of that. But maybe some clue to finding the chest *is* here, along with the key."

"I'm telling you, this place has been lived in continuously since it was built. It's been repaired, painted, explored, you name it."

"What was in the chest?" Dallas asked.

"As far as I know, no one's really sure. They say gold from South America, and jewels," Hannah said. "If there was ever a full inventory, I don't know about it. And I live with ghosts who were around before the treasure was lost, and even they don't know more than that."

"There's got to be someone who knows something," Dallas said.

"Archives. We could dig around in the city archives, but I think Hannah's right. If anyone knew, there would be stories about it," Kelsey said.

Dallas fingered the key. "Still, keep thinking. The Wolf has to know—or think he knows— something. Something that makes him certain the treasure is hidden here, in this house." He hesitated. "I'll keep the key with me—if I may."

Hannah lifted her hands in surrender. "Sure. Why?"

He laughed. "Because no one will expect me to

have anything on me. I'm an outsider here, even though I'm from here. Go figure. I need to head down to the station and then the wharf, but I'll be back in plenty of time for the ghost tour. Logan will be back by eight, and Liam and a few plainclothes officers will join us, as well. I'm afraid you'll have to forget that sixteen-person limit for tonight."

"Are you *hoping* something happens?" Hannah asked.

She met his eyes and realized she shouldn't have been surprised by the flash of heat that filled her. She almost blushed. He was all business right now, and all she could think about was last night.

"So we just stay here until the ghost tour?" she asked.

"Yes, but I'll be back long before that. See if you can think of anything—anything at all—that might connect the key to something in this house, some kind of clue. It could be something hidden in plain sight. Maybe Melody or Hagen could help," Dallas said. "The Wolf may be afraid of the curse, but I'm assuming you're not."

"You heard Hagen. He was the one who cursed the treasure, and he says the idea of a curse is bunk to begin with," Hannah said

"A curse *is* bunk—unless, once again, you're talking perception rather than reality. The Wolf wants the treasure, but he *does* believe in the curse, so he doesn't want to risk finding the treasure himself. If we could find it for him, well . . . we might be able to trap him," Dallas said. "Meanwhile, I'm going to show that sketch around and see what I find out, so yes, you two need to stay here."

"We can prowl around in the attic," Kelsey offered.

"We can prowl, but . . ." Hannah said.

"You never thought you'd find a key, did you?" Dallas asked.

Hannah shrugged. "No."

"Just remember, no one else in the house," Dallas said.

"Right," Kelsey said.

"All right," Hannah agreed after a moment, realizing that they were waiting for her to agree.

Then Dallas left, reminding her again to lock the door after him.

Machete watched the house, grateful for something, anything, to keep him from thinking about the trouble with his mind, something he hadn't expected.

Because he could still see her.

Yerby Catalano. He could see the trust in her eyes as he lured her away to kill her.

It was strange. He had shot a crooked cop out of Mexico and he hadn't blinked. He'd stabbed an art dealer in Florida City without a pang—but, then, he'd seen the bastard trying to seduce the thirteen-year-old daughter of a client just moments before. The man had been a pedophile. Not that he thought it was his role in life to judge.

He'd been told to kill, so he had.

But the woman . . . the first—and, God willing, the last—woman he'd ever killed . . .

Yerby Catalano. Her name, like the look she had given him, seemed tattooed on the walls of his brain.

So now he just kept watching the house.

He'd been watching it all day. He'd watched the patrol car come, and he'd watched the FBI agents leave. He'd watched the officer sitting in his car. The man had been vigilant at first. Then he'd started playing with his cell phone, and then he'd put on his sunglasses and leaned back.

Probably dozed off for a bit.

He'd seen the pretty Russian woman—Valeriya Dimitri—come, and he'd been somewhat surprised when they'd let her in. He thought about lying and not saying she'd been there, should the Wolf ask. And of course the Wolf would ask. But would he know it was a lie? How many people could he have watching?

Did he have someone else watching him watch the house?

Machete was watching when Valeriya left with the FBI agent. They weren't taking any chances, it seemed.

But, like the Wolf, just how many people could they watch around the clock?

His phone began to ring. He looked at it with dread.

Dear God, don't tell me to kill her, don't tell me to kill her, please. . . .

He realized he was praying.

He hadn't even known he remembered how.

13

Dallas had high hopes for the sketch Lottie and the police artist were working on.

He was sadly disappointed when he finally saw it.

He knew that she had tried, and he was grateful to her. But when he saw the sketch he knew it would do him no more good than a verbal description. Of course, he couldn't blame her or the artist. All she had to go on was a man in a wet suit and goggles. The entire lower half of his face had been covered by his regulator. He supposed he should be grateful she'd seen enough to know the man's eyes were blue.

He tried not to show her his disappointment when he thanked her.

And he tried not to be upset that, despite Martin Garcia's having given them the real names of the other three men who'd been with him the night Jose was killed, the cops had yet to find any of them. None of them had been at home or in any of the most likely bars and clubs. None of them had wives or roommates who could give them any leads to the whereabouts of the men. The police were still looking, but so far they had nothing.

But at least, thanks to the DMV, they had pictures of who they were looking for. When he left the police station he had images on his phone of all three.

He thought of the cases he had worked that had taken weeks—even months—to solve. That was often how it went. Following every possible lead and finding that, still, all you did was watch and wait.

The problem was, he just didn't feel that they had weeks, much less months, to solve this case.

Part of him wished that he, rather than Logan, had been the one to go to Miami to check into Jose's sister, but the truth was that he didn't want to be away from the Siren of the Sea any longer than he had to be.

Who was he kidding? He didn't want to be away from the property's owner. Hannah O'Brien.

What the hell were you thinking? he demanded of himself.

She'd wanted him to stay. They'd both felt the attraction. On some level he'd been feeling it from the first time he'd seen her. That was life. Sometimes you were just attracted to someone, right or wrong.

But now he cared about her. Too much. It was a mistake to care that way. It was a mistake to get too close. A massive mistake in the middle of a case that she was inextricably a part of.

Heading to the wharf to speak with the local

dive captains, he muttered aloud to himself in disgust, "And it's a mistake you're going to make again, given half a chance, right?"

Yes. The answer was yes.

He could argue all he wanted that she was actually safer if he was right next to her.

It was still wrong.

Or was it wrong only because he felt as if he'd caused the death of his best-friend-with-benefits?

He hadn't caused it. He knew he hadn't.

And he also knew there was no way in hell he could let himself cause Hannah's death.

There was no way in hell he would let her die. Period.

The problem was, being emotional could cause a man to make real mistakes—serious mistakes. Life-or-death mistakes.

He pushed his thoughts to the back of his mind as he reached the wharf. He parked illegally—it was hell finding parking anywhere on the island—but he had official decals on his car, so he wasn't going to come back and find a ticket on his windshield.

Walking out along the wharf, he found the *Sea Serpent*, the dive boat Yerby had gone out on—unknowingly heading to her death.

He knew he stood out among everyone else on the wharf in his tailored shirt and a casual beige jacket. At least he wasn't in a typical G-man black suit. Still, among the swim trunks and

T-shirts and colorful Hawaiian shirts, he might as well have worn a sign that identified him as agent of the law.

The captain of the *Sea Serpent*—George Howard, according to his notes—was setting up his tanks for the afternoon dive when he looked up and saw Dallas. There was something so depressed in his expression, Dallas felt sorry for the man.

"Hey," he said drearily. "You're looking for me, I guess. I'm Captain Howard. George. I gave a statement several times. The cops investigated me, my crew, the equipment, the boat—if it can be investigated, it was. We did everything by the book. They said I was cleared, but . . .

"My divemaster's been at this almost twenty years. I can't believe she disappeared on us—or that we couldn't find her in time. We do counts every five to ten minutes to make sure all our divers are with us. I tell people all the time not to go into that wreck. We can make people get certified to dive, but there's no paperwork that prevents them from being stupid."

"That's true. And Miss Catalano's spirit of adventure took her where she shouldn't have gone," Dallas said, and introduced himself. "I'm just trying to make sure I have all my information straight, and I also want to ask you about a man you might have seen."

Howard, a man of about fifty with salt-and-pepper hair beneath his captain's hat, frowned at that. "The story . . . cut-and-dried. We had an odd number of divers. The Brennan couple were real nice. They'd been chatty with Miss Catalano while we headed out. I don't let anyone go down without being partnered up in one way or another, just like I don't let anyone down if they don't have their certification on them. Anyway, as soon as the Brennans came up, they raised the alarm. I didn't even have to do a count. First thing we did was search around the ship. When we found out she was in there . . . God, we were just sick."

"It wouldn't have changed anything if you'd found her."

Howard looked more closely at Dallas. "Hell, you're the guy who found her."

Dallas nodded. "I'm trying to find out about a man, someone Lottie and Don Brennan saw. Lottie remembered him making a point of joining the group when he wasn't actually part of it."

"Lots of dive boats out there at that time. It was a—"

"Beautiful day, yeah, I know," Dallas said. "But I need to know if you recognize this guy."

He produced the drawing the police artist had made based on Lottie's description.

Howard looked at him disbelievingly. He didn't say it aloud, but clearly the man was thinking, *Huh? From that?*

"I didn't see him. But let me ask Clancy, my

divemaster." He turned around and shouted, "Hey! Clancy!"

Clancy was about forty, fit and bronzed to the color of coffee from years in the sun. He recognized Dallas, too. "Hey. You're the Fed who found Miss Catalano. Man, I'd give my eyeteeth to go back—hell, I'd give my life to go back. I've never lost a diver before. Ever."

"Agent Samson wants to know if you saw this man," Captain Howard told him, handing over the sketch.

Clancy stared at it and then at Dallas. "Yeah. Yeah, I *think* I saw him down there. I figured he was off one of the other boats. Some of the divemasters give instructions and hang out but don't really lead the dive. The divers can go where they want on the reef. We're a really tight operation, especially compared to some of those guys. But, yeah, I'm pretty sure I saw him hanging around our group. Right near the ship."

"Thanks," Dallas told the two men. "Do you remember which other dive boats were out at the same time you were?"

Clancy pointed down the docks. "All five. Captains, divemasters, crew—we're all pretty friendly around here. We have to be. If one of us ends up overbooked, the others pick up whatever we can't handle. *Sunset Dream*, *Magic*, *Aqua*, *Matty May* and *Twilight*—all of them were anchored near us."

"Any other boats—boats you didn't know?" Dallas asked them.

Both men looked thoughtful, but it was Captain Howard who answered. "Actually, yes, but not that close to us. Two private boats. I don't know if the cops spoke to their captains or whoever else was aboard. One was just a fishing boat, but the other was a really nice vessel. It was a Sea-Doo, I think. Maybe a Donzi. I don't remember, really. Not a dive boat either, really, more a pleasure craft. But, where to find them or who owns them, I don't know. Oh! I think the fishing boat's name ended in 'sun.'"

Dallas nodded. He knew how hard they were trying to help. Unfortunately, the word *sun* was in the name of lots of boats down in the Keys.

He thanked them both. For the next hour, he went along the docks, speaking with captains, crews and divemasters. Everyone was devastated by what had happened and wanted to help, but no one actually knew anything.

At the end of the last dock he hit a crusty divemaster named Jimmy Jones who told him, "Man, am I sorry for those people. We lost a man once. I was working out of Key Largo then. We were at the Spiegel Grove dive site and some old fellow who shouldn't have been diving—had a pacemaker he didn't tell us anything about—wound up panicking and coming up with the bends. By the time we got him in and to a hyperbaric chamber, well, it was too late. I know what Cap Howard and Clancy are going through. You can do all the right things, but if someone goes off where they shouldn't be . . .."

"I'm not here to blame Captain Howard or Clancy," Dallas assured him. He produced the sketch and asked, "Did you see this guy out there yesterday?"

"Yeah, I remember that guy. He was down there. I just saw him kind of peripherally, you know?" Jones said. "I remember wondering why he was all covered up like that. In the heat we've been having? Crazy. But I had twenty divers down with me. I didn't have time to waste thinking about him."

"What about other boats in the area?" Dallas asked.

"Yeah, there were a few. But, you know, there are always a lot of boats out. Especially on a beautiful day."

Dallas sighed. If there was anything he knew really well by now, it was that Yerby Catalano had died on a beautiful day. "Right. But do you remember anything about any of them?"

Jones was thoughtful. "There were other dive boats, of course. And a few other boats that came and went. A couple of fishing boats. A speedboat. Now that I think about it, that was kind of odd. Speedboats don't usually just sit out there."

"What kind of a speedboat?" Dallas asked.

"Donzi, I think."

"What about the fishing boats? Did you notice a name? Did you see a boat with the word *sun* in the name?"

"Yeah, come to think of it. Something like . . . no, wait. It wasn't *sun.* It was *sin.* Something *sin.* Like *Evening Sin* or something like that."

"You're sure? *Sin, not sun?*"

"I'm absolutely sure."

Dallas thanked him and called Liam, giving him all the information he had so far. They needed everyone out there—cops and Coast Guard—looking for those boats.

Dallas started walking back along the docks, studying every boat as he went. Every captain and crew member on the dive boats now knew who he was, of course.

He'd nearly reached his starting point when he saw a man walking down the dock toward him carrying a toolkit. At first, he barely noticed him; he had been looking for a big, strong guy with blue eyes.

But then he remembered the pictures he had in his phone, pictures of Blade, Hammer and Pistol.

Men who couldn't be found at home or prowling the city's hot spots—or even the down-and-out establishments that tourists seldom saw.

The man looked up just as Dallas neared him.

It was Blade, Billie Garcia, Martin Garcia's

cousin, the man who had enlisted Jose in Los Lobos.

Billie looked up just as Dallas recognized him. He took one look at Dallas and knew.

He was a thin, wiry man of about twenty-eight. He produced a knife seemingly from nowhere, and with it grasped tightly in his hand he lunged for Dallas, who moved in the nick of time. Garcia plunged past him and into the water.

Dallas didn't hesitate. He dived in after the man, blinking to clear his eyes against the water.

Garcia was right in front of him, still wielding the knife. Dallas surged back, crashing into one of the pilings supporting the dock, and slipped to the side.

Garcia drove his knife into the piling. As he tried to wrench it free, Dallas clutched him around the throat.

The knife came free.

Garcia knew he was caught, but he still had the knife.

He raised it again, and Dallas realized Garcia wasn't trying to kill *him* anymore, he was trying to kill himself.

Hannah headed up to the captain's room again. She tried not to notice that Dallas Samson had somehow already made it his own. There was a light scent of some woodsy cologne in the air, something she'd missed when she'd been rescuing Valeriya, shoving the bed around and finding the key.

The scent naturally made her think of him. She hadn't realized it until that moment, but she was even familiar with his scent.

And she liked it.

Worse . . . she was drawn by it.

The man was an enigma to her, she had to admit.

Yeah, an enigma she wanted to sleep with again.

She gave herself a mental shake and walked to the side of the room where a number of old books were carefully kept in glass-fronted bookshelves. Dark wood, of course, in keeping with the room's resemblance to a captain's cabin.

She looked through the titles and found the two books she wanted. One was titled *Spanish Treasure Ships* and the other was *Key West: Dirty Days of the Territory.*

Taking them both, she curled up on the bed. Petrie jumped up beside her, and she smoothed his beautiful fur.

She thought she knew almost every legend about Key West and treasure that it was possible to know, but maybe some of her facts were rusty.

She started with treasure ships. A fleet of twelve ships had left Havana, Cuba, in 1715, bound for Spain. A devastating storm had cropped up, and all twelve ships had gone down on July 31, 1715, off the east coast of Florida. Most of their silver and gold coins and other treasures had been discovered. But the *Santa Elinora* had headed out of port late, accompanied by one gunboat. They'd been behind the fleet by a day or two, so they'd been caught by the storm not long after leaving port. The *Santa Elinora* had gone down in the Florida Straits, not ten miles from Key West.

She'd been discovered, as well, though not until almost a hundred years later, by one of Commodore David Porter's ships.

Porter had never been popular in Key West, despite the fact that he'd been the one to rid the island of pirates. Residents despised the man for his rigid rule; he was against alcohol and fun in general. Before his arrival, Key West had been claimed by individuals rather than nations, although at various times those individuals had been Spanish, British and American. Since it was only a small island, people mainly used it for fishing and birding, or as a stopover on a longer trip. Finally John Simonton had purchased the island from Juan Pablo Salas, who had owned it through a Spanish land grant. But everyone had lived reasonably happily together—until Porter clamped down.

He was an interesting man, strong and determined, and intent on providing what profit he could to the United States government—at least at first. Later he would be court-martialed for demanding Puerto Rico return one of his men, who'd been sent there to retrieve a treasure he believed belonged to the U.S.

Rumor was he also knew something about salvage, and what he didn't know, his men did. One way or another, he managed to bring up most of the treasure of the *Santa Elinora*.

But there was a rumor, which arrived in Key West via Cuban fishermen, that the *Santa Elinora* had also carried a sea chest filled with gold and the jewels belonging to the mistress of a high ranking official in Cuba. The poor woman, after being discovered by the official's wife, had faced a trumped-up charge of treason and been hanged.

The jewels the official had showered her with when he'd first been smitten were set to become gifts of atonement to the man's wife. Among those jewels was a medallion known as the Zafiro de Seguridad, a huge sapphire set in gold and surrounded by a ring of diamonds and supposedly blessed by a priest to bring safety from all evil to those who wore it.

The book contained a drawing of the piece, which was beautiful and looked as if it would have fit right in with Britain's crown jewels in their tower.

But though there were rumors about the chest, it hadn't been on any official logs.

The rumor sprang up among the navy men assigned to Commodore Porter that he had found it and was keeping it at Fort Zachary Taylor.

Then, years later, rumors rose up again and claimed that it had been on the *Wind and the Sea* when it went down.

That was the age of salvage, and the locals had done their job well before the ship finally sank beneath the waves. So questions remained. Had the treasure been aboard the vessel when she'd gone down? Had it been salvaged and secretly stowed somewhere in Key West once again? Or had there ever even been such a treasure to begin with?

Hannah set that book down and picked up the other. Commodore Porter had reigned over Key West with a heavy hand. She'd known that. He'd basically hated the place, so there had been no love lost on either side.

There was nothing about the treasure, though.

Hannah closed that book, as well, and then remembered that Jose had told her about an article about the *Discovery*, the ship that had gone out in search of the remnants of the *Santa Elinora* and then gone down in a storm itself.

"Hey, you okay up there?" Kelsey called to her from downstairs.

"Yep, fine—just reading."

"Okay."

"I'm coming down, though. I want to get on the computer."

Hannah stood and put the books back. The sun was streaming heavily into the room. In the interest of preserving the air-conditioning, she walked over to the window to close the drapes. As she did so, the cat made a mewling sound.

"What's up, Petrie?" she asked.

He was staring at the windows as if he were looking out. As if he had seen something there.

Hannah paused. She really hated it when he stared at things. He frequently saw the ghosts before she did. And sometimes he just stared when she didn't see anything at all.

Animal instinct.

"Okay, Petrie. I'm looking."

At first, she didn't see him. If it hadn't been for the cat, she wouldn't have kept looking.

But she continued to search until, finally, she was certain she saw a man.

He must have moved slightly, or else the breeze shifted the branches of the big old banyan tree beyond the sidewalk, and that had drawn her attention. She still couldn't see him clearly, though.

But *he* was there. Looking up, just watching.

"Kelsey!" she called.

She heard her cousin coming up the stairs. But by the time Kelsey reached her, a horde of bachelorette partiers—the bride was wearing a headband with a veil—was walking by, giggling.

Hannah blinked.

And the man was gone.

Liam had done his work well, getting his officers to cover the docks and, Dallas was certain, the whole of the island.

Five minutes after he'd dragged Billie Garcia out of the water and wrested the knife from him, there were officers on-site, ready to take him in.

Dallas said he'd be along as quickly as he could get changed. He also asked one of the officers to call Liam and tell him to put Garcia alone in an interrogation room after getting him dry clothing. He was to be watched but left to sweat for a while, wondering what was going to happen to him.

Once Billie was safely in a patrol car and being driven away, Dallas reached for his cell phone to make a call and then realized that it was as drenched as he was and didn't work. He cursed the ruined phone as he drove quickly back to the Siren of the Sea.

Since he couldn't call to say he was there, he stopped at the patrol car. The officer had just come on duty and quickly dialed for him, too well trained to ask about Dallas's condition. The front door opened as he approached the house, his feet sloshing in his shoes.

Hannah stood there watching him approach, Kelsey right behind her.

"You decided to go for a swim?" Hannah asked casually, but he saw the concern in her eyes and heard a deeper question in her tone.

"Hey, it's a beautiful day, right?" he asked drily. As he stepped inside, though, he set his hands on her shoulders. "We're getting closer. I found Blade."

"Oh?"

"I'm going to clean up and get down to the station. I have him on hold until I get there," he said.

"So you caught him in the water," Kelsey said.

"Uh-huh."

"Hand me your phone," Hannah said. "I'll put it in a bowl of rice right away to dry it out. Believe it or not, it usually works."

He produced his phone—and then his wallet and keys. She smiled as she took them.

"Thanks," he told her briefly.

"Anything else we can do?" Kelsey asked him.

"Have you heard from Logan?" Dallas asked.

Kelsey nodded. "He's fine. He's on his way back. He says you should go up there with him tomorrow." Kelsey inhaled deeply, then let her breath out in a sigh. "Also, I got a call from Mark Riordan, Yerby's boyfriend. He wants to know when he can have her body."

Dallas paused, frowning. He'd been so intent on the hunt that he'd forgotten about Yerby's boyfriend, along with Judy and Pete Atkinson. As far as he knew, Shelly Nicholson and Stuart Bell were back in Miami, and none too anxious to return to Key West anytime soon.

"Mark Riordan called you here?"

"He tried the police station, and all they told him was that she was still at the M.E.'s office up in Marathon, and they would provide more information in a timely manner. Then they referred him to me and gave him my cell number. He sounded pretty broken up. Yerby's parents died when she was a baby, and she bounced around from foster home to foster home. He's all she had."

"I'll talk to him. Not a bad thing to talk to him anyway," Dallas said. "He and the Atkinsons are still down here, I take it?"

Kelsey nodded.

"Would you mind giving him a call and telling him I'll see him in the morning? Right now I've got to get back to the station," Dallas said.

He looked at Hannah again. She seemed grave and quiet. He wanted to hold her and tell her that everything was going to be all right.

He didn't touch her.

And to be honest, he didn't know if things really would be all right. The Wolf had been operating Los Lobos for quite a while, and they hadn't so much as laid a hand on him.

But they were getting closer.

Maybe the Wolf was finally losing control and they would get the break they needed.

"Are you all right?" he asked Hannah.

"Yes, of course," she said, and offered him a

smile. "Go get changed, and I'll go take care of your phone."

She turned away, and he hurried up the stairs to shower and find clean, dry clothing. As he got dressed, he noticed the books on his bed. Someone had been doing research.

He couldn't stay; he needed to get to the station before Billie Garcia bashed his head into a wall or injured himself in some way so he wouldn't be able to talk.

Hurrying back downstairs, he found Hannah and Kelsey in the kitchen. "Was that you doing research earlier?" he asked Hannah.

"I'm looking for any clue I can find, but so far I haven't found anything that gets us any closer to solving Jose's death. There may or may not have been a treasure. It may or may not have been found by Commodore David Porter. It may or may not have been kept at Fort Zachary Taylor. It may or may not have been on the *Wind and the Sea* when she went down. Oh, I did find out that part of the treasure is supposed to be a medallion called the Zafiro de Seguridad. A massive sapphire set in gold and surrounded by diamonds. Priceless, I imagine."

"That means something like *sapphire of safety*, doesn't it?" Dallas asked.

Hannah nodded. "Didn't do much for Hagen Dundee, assuming they were both aboard the *Wind and the Sea*," she said drily. "But I suppose if it was going to protect you, you probably needed to be wearing it."

"A priceless gem of protection that did nothing against a curse," Dallas said.

"No object can guarantee your safety," Hannah said. "Not even a gun."

"Or a knife. And speaking of knives . . ." Dallas glanced at his watch, glad it was a diver's watch and his recent dousing had done it no harm. "I've got to get going and talk to our buddy Blade. I'll be back as soon as I can, and I'm sure Logan will be, too, but even with both of you here, no one for the ghost tour comes in until we're here, okay?"

"You got it," Kelsey agreed.

"Come with me and—"

"Lock the door," Hannah said. "I know."

He smiled at her, but she didn't notice. He knew something was disturbing her, and he didn't think it was him. Unfortunately, he had no idea what it was. No matter, it had to wait. First things first.

He drove back over to the station.

Liam was watching Billie Garcia through the one-way glass.

"Has he said or done anything?" Dallas asked.

"He tried to take the table apart. Maybe he thought he could skewer himself with a leg, I don't know. He gave the guards hell when they got him into dry clothes. He doesn't have a belt or shoelaces or anything, so we're pretty sure he can't hurt himself. For the past fifteen minutes he's just been sitting there as if he's catatonic. But there's nothing wrong with him."

Dallas nodded. "Thanks."

He walked into the room and sat down across from Billie, who looked back at him warily. Dallas smiled. Then he leaned forward. "Want to talk?"

"I have absolutely nothing to say to you," Billie said.

Dallas shrugged. "You might as well talk to me. Your cousin has already fingered you for enough crimes that we can put you away for years."

Dallas knew instantly that word of Martin being picked up by the cops hadn't reached Billie yet. He paled to the color of ash.

"Martin is a sniveling liar," he said.

Dallas shrugged. "Maybe, but Martin will probably live."

"Martin is already a walking dead man," Billie told him.

"We can protect you."

"No one can protect anyone from the Wolf. He has eyes everywhere."

"The Wolf is a man—just a man. And he only has power because he keeps secrets and convinces other people to keep them, too. People start telling those secrets and he won't have any more power. We'll pick you off, you know, one by one. And we'll get to the heart of Los Lobos. We'll get to the Wolf."

"Fuck you! I'm not saying nothing."

"That's a double negative, but whatever." Dallas smiled again and said icily, "You are responsible for the death of my friend Jose, *Blade*. You led him straight into an ambush. Now, you can help me, or I'll do one of two things. I'll let you out on the street and make sure the newspapers print something about you being a snitch—"

"I'm not a snitch!"

"Ah, but will the Wolf believe that?" Dallas mused. "Or I'll see to it that you spend years and years—the rest of your life—in prison for conspiracy to commit murder, at the very least. What I won't do is let you die easily. You'll help me now, and if you don't, you'll spend every minute wondering how and when the Wolf will get to you. I know the way he works, and it won't be pretty, I can promise you that much."

14

"You're going to learn how to fire a gun," Kelsey told Hannah.

"I don't own a gun," Hannah said.

"And I'm not giving you one—not right now, anyway. But you need to learn how to use one in case there's ever a need."

Once, Hannah thought, she would have argued. She'd never been fond of guns—not even spear guns. She dived for pleasure, to see fish, not shoot them. Not that she didn't like to eat them, too; she just wanted them on her plate, a nice filet, or maybe some sushi.

"All right," she agreed.

"This is my service weapon," Kelsey told her, placing her gun on the table. "It's a Glock 19. It uses a magazine. Right now it's loaded, but I'm going to unload it. To do that, you push the little button right here, on the side, by the handle." She demonstrated. The magazine fell into her hand. "Okay, you can't be certain at this stage that there isn't a round still in it—that it's really unloaded—so you bring the slide back. With the magazine out, you should be able to look in the hole and see clear through the gun—unless there's a round in it. If there *is* a round, once you hit the slide, it will empty. It's crucial that you always make sure." Kelsey demonstrated, and the bullet emerged. "Okay, my mags have fifteen rounds. That's a new one, and I want you to put it back in the gun. That notch goes forward. The number on the back goes to the rear. Now you take it."

"Wait. Where's the safety on this thing? Shouldn't I check that first?" Hannah asked, tucking her hands behind her back to avoid taking the weapon.

"It doesn't have a safety."

"What?"

"Not all guns have a safety, per se. But this one does have a safe trigger. You could throw this gun across the room and it wouldn't go off. It can only fire when the trigger is fully depressed—that's the 'safety' on this model." Kelsey pointed. "There's the trigger, now see that little piece in the middle? The gun can't fire if you aren't squeezing the trigger firmly. If it's nudged on top, no. If it falls, no."

She held out the Glock again, and this time Hannah took it.

It felt funny to handle the gun. It wasn't that she hadn't touched firearms before. It was just that they were usually harmless flintlock reproductions that were used for Key West's famous Pirate Days.

She loaded the gun just as Kelsey had instructed her. She wasn't sure whether she was glad it was so easy—or disturbed.

"That's it—you're ready to shoot," Kelsey told her. "In fact, we should go to a range soon so you can learn."

"We should?" Hannah said. "Already?"

Kelsey said, "Okay, let's have you do the whole thing first. Take the clip out, check that the barrel is empty and there isn't a round remaining. There won't be, of course, because you saw me take it out, but you need to learn to check it. Then slide the magazine back in again."

Hannah did as she was told.

Kelsey nodded approvingly. "Good. I bet you won't have any trouble learning to aim, either. When we were kids, you were great at those carnival shooting games."

"Hey, don't forget. I'm good at darts."

"Always an important talent," Kelsey said. She picked up her gun and slid it back into her waistband. "I usually have this on me. Logan carries a Glock plus a little Smith & Wesson, and I think Dallas carries the same model Glock I do. Not that it matters. They all load the same. The number of rounds in the mag is always on the back end and the notch always goes forward. Got that?"

"Got it," Hannah promised.

Kelsey seemed tense, she thought. She realized that her cousin had seemed jittery ever since she'd run upstairs in answer to Hannah's call, only to find that the watcher—if indeed there had been a watcher—was gone. "Are you okay?" Hannah asked.

Kelsey nodded. "Of course I'm okay. I wish I could have seen what you saw, that's all. I'm not surprised. I figured someone was watching the house round the clock, and I don't mean the officer out front. You didn't catch any details at all?"

"Not of his face," Hannah said.

"But it *was* a him?"

"Or a big her."

"What about Melody and Hagen? Where are they? And Jose and Yerby?" Kelsey shook her head. "We're in a very lucky position to have them, but it would be nice if they showed up more often."

"They're probably watching the grounds," Hannah said, and smiled. "But I know they're somewhere nearby. We can ask if they saw anyone next time they materialize."

Kelsey nodded. She walked to the front door and looked out. Then she moved through the house to look out back to the pool and patio. "It's so beautiful back there," she said.

"Want to go sit outside for a while?" Hannah asked.

Kelsey lifted a brow at her.

"Oh, yeah. I'm supposed to stay in the house," Hannah said. "Out there we'd be sitting ducks for a sharpshooter or a bush vaulter or whatever."

"Cabin fever already?" Kelsey asked her. "You'll get out tonight for your ghost tour."

"Please, Key West History and Legends Tour," Hannah corrected with a smile. "In deference to Melody and Hagen. They don't like being called ghosts."

Kelsey smiled. "I didn't mean to be rude."

"Seriously, sometimes we're all so politically correct we don't know what we're talking about. But in my experience, most ghosts prefer the term *spirit*."

Almost as if the word had summoned them, Hagen and Melody materialized, entering hand in hand from the backyard.

"Did you find out anything?" Hannah asked them.

"No, but Hagen and I have been walking the trail from where Jose entered your yard, met Shelly and Stuart, and then staggered out to the alley to die," Melody said.

"And?" Hannah asked.

"The killer must have followed him," Hagen said.

"We'd figured as much," Kelsey said. "But where is Jose's knife?"

Hannah shook her head. "The crime scene techs searched everywhere. They even went through bins of garbage. The killer must have taken it with him."

"All right, that makes sense. But what about the blood? The only reason for the killer to take the knife is if he was cut, and that means his blood has to be somewhere," Kelsey said.

"But unless the lab found his blood, we can't even test the DNA," Hannah said.

"The knife was dripping blood—that's what Shelly Nicholson said, right?" Kelsey asked.

"Right, but she was pretty freaked out, I don't know whether it was really dripping. There might just have been blood on the blade," Hannah admitted.

"And there's another problem with DNA evidence," Kelsey said. "Even if we find the killer's blood, we need something to compare it to. If he's not in the system, we're screwed."

"On another topic, have you two seen anyone watching the house?" Hannah asked.

Melody looked questioningly at Hagen. "I haven't seen anyone," she said. "And at night Hagen takes the front and I take the back. It's odd, though."

"What?" Hannah asked her.

"I *feel* something. I *feel* that we're being watched, that someone is always out there all the time. And I don't know why I can't *see* him."

Billie Garcia wasn't as easy to break as his cousin.

But, in the end, he broke all the same.

It happened when Dallas threw up his hands and told Liam that he was through and the cops could take Billie. As soon as Liam thanked him and said that Billie would fit right in with the general population at the correctional center on Stock Island, Billie suddenly decided he liked the concept of living after all.

Unfortunately, he wasn't even as helpful as his cousin had been. He swore he hadn't killed anyone. He knew that he might have been asked to. He listed the relatively few robberies he'd taken part in, and explained that he'd mainly been responsible for transporting stolen goods.

From where to where?

He'd been told where a van would be and then told where to drive it.

Not much help, Dallas was forced to admit. The Wolf was meticulous, using several people on a haul, none of them knowing who had left the truck for them or who would be picking it up after they left it in turn.

"The four of us that night . . . we're all from here, so we go way back," Billie explained. "Martin picks up work as a dishwasher at different restaurants. Reggie plays a mean guitar. He hangs at Mallory Square a lot. Carter does odd jobs, pretty much whatever he can find. We mostly work gang jobs on our own, like everybody else, but when the Wolf needs a group effort, he comes to us."

"How do you get paid?" Dallas had asked him.

"Cash, of course. We get a call about where we can pick up the green."

"What about Jose Rodriguez?"

Billie grew visibly uncomfortable. He let out a sigh. "I met the guy at a bar on Duval. He'd been scrounging money from tourists over on Duval near Front Street. As soon as he got enough, he came in and asked for a drink. He told me he'd been let off from some kind of a computer job, and the more we talked, the more he seemed like a guy we could use. I told the Wolf about him, and he told me to feel him out. I did. The night he met with the four of us, I was supposed to give him a phone. I guess the Wolf had done some research on him in the meantime and didn't like what he found out. And . . . well, you know what happened next."

"Give it to me from your point of view. The five of you were seen walking along Eaton Street from Duval. You were ahead of the witnesses. Then you turned and went back the way you'd come," Dallas told him.

"Yeah. When we were walking down Eaton, I got a call to circle around. When we got close to Duval the next time—" Billie broke off. There was a fine sheen of sweat on his forehead. "I didn't know. I swear I didn't know. I was scared to death when the guy came up behind us. All I remember after that was someone shouting *run,* so I ran. I ran like a jackrabbit." He was trembling as he spoke.

"You heard from the Wolf after that?"

"Yeah," Billie said dully. "Yeah. I got a call. It said I had done a good job, and that I'd get a bonus." He let out a mirthless laugh. "Blood money, I guess."

Liam had handed Dallas a file, and now he opened it slowly, taking out an eight-by-ten picture of a beautiful young Latino woman. He put it down in front of Billie.

Unless the guy was really good, the picture meant nothing to him.

"Is she dead, too?"

"We don't know. Do you know her?"

Garcia looked up at him. "I've never seen her. Who is she?"

Dallas shrugged. "If you haven't seen her, it doesn't matter."

Billie looked up at him. "I really hope she's not dead," he said.

Dallas believed him. He didn't think Billie was the diver who had killed Yerby. He wished he were, that he had gotten somewhere on this damn case. "What about your boat?"

"What about it?" Billie asked. He looked genuinely confused.

"Did you have it out recently?"

Billie shook his head. "No—oh, man, you think I killed that woman, the diver. That wasn't me. I swear it. I haven't even been at the dock in over a week."

"Who knows you have a boat?" Dallas asked him.

Billie shook his head, looking cornered and beaten. "Everyone. Everyone knows I have a boat." Now he looked genuinely frightened.

Dallas noticed and almost felt sorry for the guy. "They'll keep you in a safe house tonight," he said. "And while you're there, try to think of anything—anything at all—that might help us. Your life depends on it."

Billie nodded and dropped his gaze. After a long moment he looked back up at Dallas. "I knew that people died. But only people who deserved it. People who didn't listen to the Wolf. People who were thieves, too—and worse. People like me. I figured this guy, Jose, was just another no-gooder who wanted more than what he was going to get. But then . . ."

"Then?"

"That girl who died on the dive . . . she didn't just drown. There's a guy—Machete, they call him—he's the enforcer down here. I'm pretty sure if you can figure out who Machete is, you'll have your killer. *Her* killer, anyway."

"Why did the Wolf want her dead?"

"To make an example of her. To keep anyone else from talking. She was with that group staying at the Siren of the Seas. Kill her, and if one of the others thought of something, well, they'd think twice about calling the authorities. Murders cover up murders."

"Did Machete kill Jose?"

"I think so," Billie said. "But I don't know."

"What did you really see that night, Billie?" Dallas asked.

"A guy—a big guy."

"Did you see his face?"

"He was wearing a hoodie. I couldn't see a thing under that."

Back to basics, Dallas thought wearily. He knew more than Billie, in fact, since he knew the guy he was looking for probably had blue eyes.

He glanced at his watch and was shocked when he saw the time. Time to go.

As he rose, Billie gripped his arm. "You won't—you won't let them put me in gen pop, right?"

Dallas shook his head ruefully. The Wolf didn't pick the bravest or the best, he thought.

But then, the Wolf didn't care. His people were expendable.

"For tonight, no one will know where you are. You'll be protected. And I don't care how many people the Wolf has, the man doesn't command an army. You'll be safe. There will be two officers with you at all times."

"That's just it," Billie said, looking up at him. "Cops don't get paid that much. How do you know one of the cops isn't in on this?"

Valeriya Dimitri tied the plastic handles of the garbage bag and headed for the kitchen door.

She'd barely stepped outside when she felt rough hands on her shoulders, pulling her back into the shadows of the carport. The hand over her mouth was massive; she couldn't breathe, much less scream.

A voice, a harsh whisper—sandpaper scratching the air—spoke to her.

"What did you find?"

She was so terrified she could barely stand, but she needn't have worried. The man was strong. She wasn't standing on her own at all. He was holding her up.

He shook her until she thought her neck would break.

"What did you find?" he repeated.

What did she find? What was he talking about?

Oh, Lord, she should have known!

She'd been left money at the house—"tips" that were far larger than anyone left a maid. Money—and cryptic little notes.

Actually, they'd been scary notes.

She should have known better than to accept the money. She should have known there would be a price to pay. Even in the United States, nothing was free or easy. And she should have been smart enough to know that. Maybe she had been. Maybe she'd forced herself to be blind because she wanted things to be good—even when she'd known something wasn't right.

There was no way she could answer him. He

seemed to realize that, but before he eased his hold on her mouth he told her, "I can snap your neck in an instant and be gone before your body hits the ground."

His hand eased far enough away for her to draw a deep breath, then try to stutter out an answer.

"F-find? I don't know what—"

"You went in to clean today. You were there a long time. An FBI agent walked you home. There's only one reason for that. You know something. So I repeat—*what did you find?*"

She tried to shake her head in denial.

He repeated the question yet again, shaking her harder.

"I didn't find anything. I got hurt making the bed. She made me sit. Hannah made me sit. And then they made me wait."

"You're a liar," he said, and she felt his grip tighten.

"I'm not a liar."

"Your mother and your baby are just inside," he reminded her. "You don't want anything to happen to them, do you?"

Valeriya thought first about her baby. Kirin. He was just a year old, stumbling around and staring at everything with his big eyes and happy smile. She would gladly die for her child. This man knew it. And her mother! When Valeriya's husband had died of a sudden heart attack before they'd left for America, it was her mother who had held her up.

"I would tell you if I knew. I would tell you anything!" she sobbed.

"You get back in there. You get back into the Siren of the Sea, and you look until you find it. Somebody found something in there, and now you're going to find it for me."

"They won't let me back in! They told me to stay home until—"

"Get in. Get in again, and I don't care how. Even if it kills you. You get in—even if you die in the process—and your baby will live. You will get back into the house. You will find it. Or when I come back next time I will not leave you standing, and I will not stay outside your house— and I *know* you know what I mean. And one more thing. I'll be watching you, so don't think you can lie to me. I'll see everything you're doing, and if you don't do what I told you to . . ."

His hands moved around her neck and squeezed tight, then tighter. She couldn't breathe. Darkness punctuated by bursts of stars started to descend around her. Then she felt herself being shoved forward, and she slammed against the side of the house.

She was scared, hurting. But she was alive.

She turned quickly, but she was too late.

He was gone.

Just as if he'd never been there at all.

She closed her eyes and prayed her thanks to God.

She was alive!

She was filled with dread, but she was still alive—for now.

From never really liking guns, Hannah had become determined to master one.

She practiced with Kelsey's Glock in the kitchen, loading it, unloading it, taking lessons on aiming from Kelsey.

Melody and Hagen were out, patrolling the grounds. Melody, in particular, was determined that she was going to find whoever was watching them.

Kelsey's phone rang. Logan had returned.

Hannah accompanied Kelsey to the door. Looking out, she saw that Logan had stopped to speak with the officer out front. The minute he came up the walk, Hannah asked anxiously, "What happened? Did you find out anything?"

Logan stepped in and closed the door behind him, locking it, while Kelsey waited patiently for him to speak. "Dallas here yet?" he asked.

"He's back at the police station."

Logan nodded. "I know. I just thought he might be back by now."

As Logan spoke, Hannah saw Dallas's car coming down the street.

"He's here," she said, surprised at just how much pleasure his return gave her, and equally surprised by the thundering of her heart. It was so loud she found herself hoping no one else heard it.

"Good, we're all here," Logan said.

Dallas saluted the officer in the patrol car, and a minute later they were all in the kitchen, since the day was hot and everyone was ready for something cold to drink.

"Please, tell us what's going on," Hannah pleaded.

"You start," Dallas told Logan.

"All right," Logan said, pulling out a chair at the table.

The others joined him.

"I don't think Jose's sister is involved with Los Lobos, other than that she might have met someone who's a part of it," Logan said. "She's been missing several months now. The police had her things moved into storage, and her apartment's been rented, so there wasn't anything for me to find there."

"Why do you think she's not involved? Where do you think she is?" Hannah asked. She didn't like the way Logan's expression clouded over as she asked, "You think she's dead, don't you?"

"I don't know what to think. She didn't take her car or any of her belongings. Her keys were there, her makeup. Even her contact lenses. I talked to her neighbors. They've been worried about her. She'd told them about her past and that she'd gotten clean, but they thought she was on something the last time they saw her. So what I think is that Jose was right. Someone in Los Lobos got to her and found out she had a brother in the FBI."

"So they took her to get information on Jose?" Kelsey asked, but her tone said she already knew the answer.

"That's what I think, yes," Logan said. "I think initially the Wolf was hoping to use her as leverage to get Jose to be his inside man at the Bureau. But from talking to her, he realized no one was ever going to be able to turn him. Then, when Blade brought Jose into the fold, the Wolf figured out that he was the brother she was talking about, and realized he knew too much and had to die."

"Where do you think she is?" Hannah asked.

Logan let out a breath. "The Wolf doesn't leave things where they can be found. Keeping a hostage would be dangerous. I believe he had her killed once he got what he needed from her."

"But her body has never been found," Hannah said.

There was silence at the table for a minute.

"Hannah, it would be great if she were alive, if we could find her," Dallas said. "But you've got the Gulf of Mexico, the Florida Straits—hell, the whole Atlantic Ocean. He could have disposed of her at sea and no one will ever find her."

"But you're not just going to give up on her, are you?" Hannah asked.

"Of course not," Dallas said.

"Why don't you come back up to Miami with me tomorrow?" Logan suggested to him.

"I have a better idea. Let's go through all the right channels and get a search warrant for the apartment. Even with new people in there, the crime scene techs can pull up the carpet, go over everything with luminol. Who knows? We might get blood. That would help us know what happened, whether she was grabbed there or not, and whether she was . . . hurt."

"Good idea. We'll call tomorrow and get it done," Logan agreed.

"What about the guy you were questioning earlier?" Hannah asked Dallas. "Did you find anything out from him?"

"A few things," he said. He looked over at Kelsey. "I hope your buddies over at the U.S. Marshals' office have plenty of money for witness protection," he said.

"I'm willing to bet that they'll have money to stop the Wolf," she said.

"Basically, what I've gotten out of everything today is that our guy is big and strong and has blue eyes. He also knows how to dive. He has a private boat or access to one, because he wasn't out with any of the dive captains I spoke with. They gave me some leads on other boats that were in the area that day, and the Coast Guard is looking for them now," Dallas said. "That's going to be tough, though. The boat could be unregistered, or he could just paint out the name and call her something different. And there are miles of coast and open water to cover. The killer could have headed into the Florida Straits or into the Gulf to make for port on the west coast of the state, up the panhandle to another state entirely . . . even to Mexico. Hell, he could have headed up the entire east coast to New England."

"Or he could be down on the docks past Front Street," Hannah said. "This guy is obviously one of the Wolf's key men here. He's the one who does the dirty work."

"He goes by Machete," Dallas said.

"Whatever his name is," Hannah said, "I'm willing to bet he's in so deep, he's still around."

"That's a good theory," Dallas told her. "And I hope you're right—that he's here in the area somewhere and we can find him—but it's still just a theory."

"He's not leaving. The Wolf wants something, and that something is here. That means Machete will be here, too, until he's caught, killed or finds it," Hannah said determinedly.

"One problem," Kelsey said.

"What's that?" Logan asked her.

"If we find Machete and he's as much in the dark as the others, we still won't have the Wolf," she said.

"Yes, but the Wolf's local army is disintegrating,"

Dallas said. "He lost one man at the scene of the accident, we've taken two more off the streets here and I believe—now that we have names—we'll pick up the other two tomorrow or the next day. That means he's down five men."

"He'll just recruit five more," Kelsey said.

"It's not that easy to find the right people," Dallas reminded her. He looked at Hannah. "We're going to get him. So who should I dial for some dinner? Your people will start arriving for the tour soon."

She quickly rose, feeling like an awful hostess. She'd forgotten that they would need dinner.

"I'm sure I can throw something together," she said.

"Hannah, we'll call for delivery," Kelsey said. "It's already six-thirty."

She nodded. "Yeah, sure. We can call Joe's. Pizza, subs or pasta. They're not gourmet, but they're good, and most of all, they're fast."

They called Joe's. It was strange. As they were ordering, Hannah felt almost as if they were a couple, although she realized one night of sleeping with him did not mean they were in a relationship. And she doubted Kelsey or Logan had any idea of what was going on between the two of them.

In some ways, last night seemed as if it had happened long ago. Maybe she'd dreamed it.

When the food came, she set it up in the back

room where they could look out over the pool and patio. It was beautiful out there, lush with croton bushes, palms and more. She had a sea grape tree and a banyan, an avocado and two banana trees, all of them making the pool area almost irresistibly inviting.

"It's strange," she commented, twirling a forkful of linguini. "I can go days without hopping in the pool, but now that I shouldn't be out on the patio, all I want to do is swim."

"Of course," Dallas said. "Forbidden fruit always looks the most luscious." He smiled at her.

Was that all it was? Were they forbidden fruit? she wondered. Thrown together in the midst of a tension-filled life-or-death situation?

Or had she really fallen for him?

"Well, when this is over, I'm diving straight in," Kelsey said. "I love the ocean, but when you're hot and sticky, there's nothing like a freshwater pool. And this yard is amazing."

"Did you put the pool in, Hannah?" Dallas asked.

She shook her head. "Our uncle put it in about a decade ago. Kelsey and I were in our teens, and he was already running it as a bed-and-breakfast. We'd come and tell ghost stories to the guests, along with cleaning for him, and he'd let us have the run of the place."

"Ronin O'Brien, his name was," Kelsey said.

"Our parents were great, but Ronin was *cool*. Being here was fun."

"I apologize if this is a rude question," Dallas said. "But, Kelsey, did you mind that Hannah got the house? I guess he didn't have children of his own?"

Hannah said, "No. He was married when he was young. His wife died of cancer when she was in her thirties. He never fell in love again."

"He dated, and Hannah and I would judge the women for him. Oh, and no, I didn't mind. Hannah was always the historian, and I wanted to be a U.S. Marshal from the time I was a kid. He left me some bonds. But the bottom line is that we both loved him and we knew he loved us. He didn't need to leave either of us anything."

Petrie suddenly jumped up on Hannah's lap, and she let out a little gasp of surprise. She was amazed at the way the other three jumped into motion, rising, drawing their weapons.

"Sorry! Sorry! It's just Petrie," she said.

"Petrie!" Kelsey said, walking over to scratch the cat on the head. "You little mongrel. You scared us all to pieces."

"I think he just wants to be fed," Hannah said. "I'll be right back."

She took the cat into the kitchen. Petrie was beautiful. As big as a Maine Coon and just as bushy, he had paws that looked gigantic because each one had six toes.

"I'm really not forgetting you, but no more just staring out of windows, okay? It freaks me out," she told him.

He rubbed against her as she prepared his food, then dug right in when she left to rejoin the others.

There was a knock at the door just as they finished eating. The first people to arrive were four middle-aged women on a reunion trip together. Three couples followed them, and then a group of six students who were down from Tallahassee.

"None of them looks dangerous," Hannah told Dallas in the kitchen as they gathered water bottles to hand around.

"No," he agreed. "But Liam and David are on the way, and they'll be coming with us. We're not taking any chances. And tonight I'm not so worried about who's *on* the tour. I'm more worried about who may be *following* it."

"So should we bait him?" Hannah asked.

"If we're going to bait him, we have to figure out the right way to do it. And it's too dangerous to do it out in the open, where we have no control of the scene. Tonight we'll just be watching, too."

She couldn't help noticing how close he was to her, how he was smiling at her. She felt as if the world should know there was something special about him, something that called to her, as if she'd longed for him forever somewhere in her soul. He was . . .

. . . leaving the kitchen without a second glance her way.

She followed him, mentally kicking herself for being an idiot. Liam and David had arrived by the time she reached the parlor, and she found herself more than usually glad to see them. She was relieved that she would be surrounded by law enforcement tonight. It would be suicidal for someone to go after her.

Then again, the Wolf's crew seemed to *be* suicidal. Maybe it was a requirement of the job.

As she always did, Hannah began with the history of her own house. One of the women was delighted to tell her that she was certain she had seen Melody Chandler up on the widow's walk the night before.

When they left the house, she walked them to Duval and told them stories about the hanging tree in Captain Tony's Saloon. The building had been erected in 1851 as an icehouse, but it had doubled as the morgue. Sixteen pirates had been hanged from the tree, as well as one woman, who had killed her own family. She was known as the Lady in Blue, some said because she had worn blue when she died, while others said it was because she had turned blue when she was hanged. She was buried beneath the pool table and was known to haunt the bathroom. The late

Captain Tony himself had been like a Hemingway character, engaged in all kinds of enterprises, as well as being the mayor of Key West. But it had been a woman, Josie Russell, who had first opened the building as a saloon. It had been called Sloppy Joe's until a rental dispute had driven the owner to move the well-known Hemingway haunt across the street. Josie packed up all her equipment and alcohol in the middle of the night and moved over to the current location of Sloppy Joe's on the corner of Duval and Green Street. Key West, however, was a haven for bars. The old Sloppy Joe's reopened as Captain Tony's.

They moved on to St. Paul's, where an old sea captain haunted the graveyard where he remained along with a number of children who'd died in the fire at the theater nearby. Most of those buried in the graveyard had been moved to the Key West Cemetery, but a few remained. The sea captain was known to have haunted a down-and-out traveler who had decided to sleep there; the children were heard to cry and sing. From the church they moved to the theater where the children had died. That was followed by the La Concha hotel, haunted by both old and new ghosts. The group was delightful, asking questions, commenting and staying close.

One of the women asked her specifically about the Artist House bed-and-breakfast and one of Key West's most famous—or infamous—residents,

Robert the Doll. Hannah led them down Eaton and stood across the street from the beautiful old Victorian house.

"Some of you may already have heard of Robert the Doll," Hannah said. She tried not to be distracted by the crowds streaming past. She told herself that she was virtually surrounded. The Beckett brothers—Liam and David—were there. Kelsey was right at her side. Logan was standing at an angle just in front of her, almost blocking her tour group. And Dallas was so close behind her that he was nearly on top of her.

"Robert is an interesting case. The natural need of a child for an imaginary friend? Or truly a cursed object? Robert Eugene Otto grew up in the gorgeous Victorian manor across the street from us, now a charming bed-and-breakfast called the Artist House, because Robert did, in fact, grow up to be an artist. Born in 1900, he was a six-year-old boy known as Gene when, in 1906, he was given the doll—which he named Robert—by a Bahamian servant. According to the story, the servant was unhappy with the family. Perhaps they had somehow slighted her. At any rate, she gave the doll to young Gene, and soon afterward his parents would hear him talking to it. The strange thing is, they swore they could hear the doll talking back to him. Sometimes at night Gene screamed. The parents would find him cowering in bed with the room in disarray. No matter what happened, he would always say that Robert the Doll did it." She smiled and paused.

"Did Gene Otto just use the doll as an excuse? Or was something strange really going on? He'd walk all over town, dressed in a sailor suit like Robert's, carrying the doll. Eventually Gene went away to school, and later he married another artist, Anne. There were a number of strange rumors after that. He built a nursery, and Anne thought they were planning for children, but the room was for Robert. There were disturbances at the house, and the police would come and find Anne looking . . . a little the worse for wear, but Gene would tell people that Robert did it. Truth? Or just a story embellished through the years? No one knows. What *is* true is that Gene died in 1974. Anne moved back north, where she was from, and she rented out the house with one stipulation. The doll was to go in the turret room, and the door was to be kept locked at all times. Anne died in 1976.

"The first family to own the house after Anne died had a little girl. In interviews as an adult, she claimed that the doll was cursed, that it spoke and did evil things. Workmen claimed that Robert moved their tools. Robert wound up at the Fort East Martello Museum, where he remains today. You can visit him there, but beware. Word is that you must ask Robert's permission to take his picture, lest your camera be cursed."

Dallas suddenly whispered in her ear, "Keep talking, keep them here," he said.

Trying to hide the tremor that ran through her at his words, she went on. "Another reason to visit the museum is to take the nighttime haunted tram."

"You're saying we should take another ghost tour, too?" one of the college boys asked her.

"Absolutely. And by day you definitely have to see the Key West Cemetery. Be sure to get your picture taken in front of the stone that reads 'I told you I was sick,'" she said. "The cemetery exists because in the mid-1800s a storm raged through Key West. Bodies and bones literally came flooding down Duval Street, washed out of the original cemetery by the storm, so it was decided then to create a cemetery on the highest point on the island. They reburied what bodies they could there, and used it for all future burials."

That left her with nothing else to say; she'd finished her story, and it was time to move on. But Dallas was gone—just gone. He had disappeared after whispering to her.

She looked for Logan, and realized he had stepped away and was on his phone.

She started ad libbing, pulling up whatever facts she could. "The body of Ian Chandler, the first owner of my home, was one of those that was found after the flood, and though his marker is gone, his remains are still there somewhere," she said, wondering when someone would grow impatient and ask her what they were seeing next.

Luckily Logan caught her eye just then. He nodded to her, and gestured. She read his mind.

Move on, but slowly.

"And now," she said, "it's time for us to head back toward Duval, where I'll leave you all at the Hard Rock. You can indulge in your complimentary drink and a meal, and perhaps see a ghost on the second floor—especially you ladies, since it's said that a man named Robert Curry haunts the ladies' room, where he hanged himself."

Where the hell had Dallas gone? she thought with an increasing sense of panic.

Something had happened. She knew it, and she had a feeling Logan knew exactly where Dallas was, and that someone *had* been watching them. She just had to finish the tour and then she could get back to the safety of the Siren.

As always, she left her group at the Key West Hard Rock Cafe. As soon as she'd said her goodbyes, she turned to Logan. "What's going on?"

"Dallas saw someone following us, so he went after him."

"And?"

"He found Hammer."

15

Logan and Kelsey accompanied Hannah back to the Siren of the Sea, but Dallas wasn't with them. He was at the police station.

At midnight, Hannah decided to give up waiting for him and go to bed, but she didn't sleep. Petrie came into her room and she invited him up on the bed, stroking him as the hour grew later and the tension inside her grew.

Then Petrie did just what she'd hoped he wouldn't.

He moved to the foot of her bed and started staring out the window.

Hannah told herself to stop worrying. She knew she was safe. Kelsey and Logan were just down the hall, and Melody and Hagen were somewhere on the property, keeping watch. A patrol car with an officer sitting in it was still parked in front of the house.

But Petrie's behavior was getting on her nerves, so she walked to the window and pulled back the drapes.

She thought she saw the shadow of a man in the yard, but as she stared into the darkness she realized it was just the way the street light fell on the banyan tree.

"Petrie, I love every cell in your furry little body, but you're out," she told him.

Just as she opened the door to put him out in the hall, she heard her cell phone ringing on her bedside table. She unceremoniously dropped the cat and hurried to answer.

It was Dallas.

"I'm just letting you know that I'm almost done," he told her. "I already spoke with Logan. We're well trained, and it's unlikely we'd shoot each other, but just in case . . ."

"Thanks for letting me know."

"I'll see you in a few minutes," he told her.

"Wait! Did you find out anything?"

"More of the same," he told her. "But . . . just hang on. I'll be there in a minute."

Seconds later she heard the front door open and rushed out to meet him. As he came up the stairs, she noticed that the door to Kelsey and Logan's room stayed firmly shut.

A moment later Dallas was striding toward her. She stepped back into her room, hoping he would take the hint and follow her.

He did.

She watched anxiously as he slid out of his jacket. She saw that there were grass stains on it, and some mud, as well.

"Talk to me," she told him. "How did you know some—"

"As we went from block to block, I saw a guy

who kept appearing. Once I knew he was following us, I went to talk to him and he took off running." He looked at his jacket ruefully. "We cut through a few yards."

"And then?"

"Then I caught him and took him to the station. And it was the same old story. Yes, he was one of the men with Jose that night. He was terrified when Jose was killed. He didn't know anything about Yerby Catalano. What we do have is another cell phone, but it's the same deal, of course. The Wolf supplies his men with phones but changes his own all the time. They receive calls from him and do what he tells them to do. I guess he's smart as far as that goes, because he knows men can break down and betray him. He's careful with who knows what, and he uses his people according to their strengths.

"This guy, Hammer, isn't capable of killing anyone. He broke down faster than anyone I've ever seen, especially after he learned that we had Blade and Knife already. I actually have a feeling that we're not going to have to look for Pistol. At this point, I believe he'll turn himself in. *If* he's still alive. And I believe the empire is vulnerable. We have three cell phones now, and though they're untraceable, the techs are triangulating the calls. They may be able to find out where a lot of them originated, and that could be where the Wolf is holed up."

"So there's hope," Hannah said.

He nodded. "You must be tired."

"Yeah, but I'm not the one who chased someone halfway across town. You must be tired, too."

"Actually, I'm a little wired."

"Want something? Hot tea? A drink?"

He shook his head, looking at her.

"Do you want to talk?" he asked her.

"About . . . last night? No, not particularly. Do you?"

"No, not unless you do."

They both hesitated awkwardly, and then Hannah didn't know if she moved forward or if he did.

It didn't matter.

No, she didn't want to talk. They were adults. They had chosen their course.

Just as they were choosing it again.

She wanted to feel him in her arms, wanted to feel his hands on her, easing her nightshirt over her head before tossing it to the floor, and then she wanted to feel his fingers teasing over her naked flesh.

She wanted the crush of his body against hers, his hot liquid kiss, his mouth pressing down on hers, the way that simple touch seemed to ignite every atom of her flesh and blood. He broke away to remove his gun, and then they were together again, struggling to rid each other of their clothing until they could come together naked, flesh against flesh, all down the lengths of their bodies.

They fell onto her bed together. There were long frenzied minutes when they struggled to touch each other as if they might never get another chance. Then the frenzy passed and he raised himself over her. She marveled at the contours of his face, lost herself in the shadows in his eyes as he studied her. Then he moved against her, his kiss finding her throat, her collarbone, her breast and midriff and beyond.

She threaded her fingers through his hair, her body alive and electric as she fought to keep silent while he did intimate things to her that drove her to the brink. He knew when to tease and when to pause, how to elicit the kind of response she'd never known herself capable of. Finally he took her lips once more as he settled against her, then slid into her at last. She couldn't get close enough to him, couldn't breathe in his scent deeply enough. . . .

They climaxed almost as one, and after the explosion of release swept through them and she settled into his embrace, she heard the settling of the house, a sound that had always soothed her. A dog barked somewhere down the street, and she felt the sweat-dampened sheet beneath them, heard the steady throb of the air-conditioner.

He held her tightly against him.

After a moment he asked, "Do you want to talk yet?"

"No," she told him.

They fell asleep together, cradled in each other's embrace.

That night she dreamed there was someone outside in the street. Someone big, with well-muscled arms, wearing a wet suit, and cloaked in darkness and shadows. He suddenly grew large beneath the streetlight and rose to the window, like a vampire floating on air. Then he was in the room and reaching out for her. His hands closed around her throat until she couldn't breathe, and he shook her, shouting, *The treasure! Where is the treasure?*

She tried to fight. She thrashed and struggled and finally woke up.

And found that Petrie was meowing and protesting as she pushed him away from her.

She was alone in the room with the cat. Dallas was gone.

Another day had begun.

Kelsey already had the coffee going by the time Dallas came down. Logan was on his computer, going through his notes on the case, trying to see if they'd missed anything. Dallas had just poured himself his second cup of coffee when Hannah made her way to the kitchen and headed straight for the coffeepot. Her giant cat followed her in, and as soon as she'd greeted them all and poured her coffee, she fed the cat. She glanced Dallas's way, gave him a weak smile and then turned away as if preoccupied.

"All right," Logan said. "We're rounding them up. We know that the Wolf has people covering Fort Lauderdale and Miami, but his reign in Key West is about to become history." He looked at Dallas. "You were right. Liam just called me. Pistol threw a beer can at a cop car so he'd be arrested and brought in. He didn't like being the last man standing, got a little worried for his health. He's in holding now, waiting for whenever you want to go in. Now our number-one target is Machete, the man the Wolf has committing his murders for him."

"Well, we have a description, verified by a number of witnesses, of a big, powerful man with blue eyes," Dallas said. "So I'm going to assume that's him."

"Big man, that's probably half the male population. Blue eyes, well . . . that could bring it down to a quarter," Kelsey said, then shrugged apologetically. "Math was never my strong suit."

Dallas smiled drily at that, watching Hannah. She looked tired, drawn. Despite that, he still thought she was stunning, somehow graceful even when she was pouring cat food. How had all that happened so quickly? He felt as if he knew her better than he'd known anyone before. Friends he'd known for years. Friends he laughed with, worked with, spent his down time with . . .

a friend with benefits he'd genuinely cared about and yet . . .

Never been in love with.

He couldn't be in love with Hannah.

Maybe not, but he could be falling in love.

He gave himself a mental shake.

"Hannah?"

She turned to look at him, a question in her eyes.

"How much do you really know about this place?"

"The Siren?" she asked, frowning. "Well, ask Kelsey. I do know there are no secret rooms or sliding panels. And no bodies in the basement, since there isn't a basement. The attic is clean as a whistle. No mysterious nooks or crannies. No skeletons anywhere, I swear."

"What about the yard?" he asked her.

"The yard? I can't imagine there's anything buried in the yard," she said. "Kelsey, remember all the workmen when they put the pool in? Half the yard was dug up."

"There *was* a lot of digging going on," Kelsey agreed.

"A lot of digging—and half the yard dug up. Still, I'd like to get a look at the plans."

"Easy enough. Everything is on file," Hannah said. "Uncle Ronin never did anything that wasn't entirely on the up and up."

Dallas looked over at Logan, who shrugged and

said, "Who knows? Maybe there *is* a treasure buried in the backyard."

"Maybe. Meanwhile, I just had an idea," Dallas said.

"We're listening," Logan said.

"Yesterday I caught up with Blade at the wharf, where he has a boat. We know that our killer went out on a private boat. I'm thinking that was Blade's boat. We need to get back to the station, Logan, and find out where that boat is."

Logan rose. "Let's get going. Kelsey?"

"Yes, we got it. Don't go out, don't let anyone in," she said.

"Anyone," Dallas repeated, looking at Hannah.

"Anyone," she said, her tone cool.

"And call," Dallas said.

"If anything happens, we will," Kelsey said.

"Hey!" Hannah said.

"Yes?" Dallas said.

"You call, too, if anything happens," she said, determined.

Dallas and Logan hadn't been gone long when the patrol officer in front of the house called to tell them that they were getting a visitor.

Hannah opened the door carefully, with Kelsey right behind her, after looking out and seeing that it was Valeriya.

"Valeriya, I told you that I'll keep paying you even though I don't need you right now."

"Please, you don't understand," Valeriya begged.

"Hannah," Kelsey warned her softly.

"I just can't," Hannah told her. "Valeriya, I can even get you a check now for the next week if you're that worried."

"No, no, it's not about the check."

"I'm sorry, but I just can't have anyone in here right now, Valeriya. Not even you."

Tears suddenly streamed down Valeriya's cheeks. "You don't understand," she said desperately. "You have to let me in. I'm begging you. If you don't let me in, he's going to kill my baby!"

Sergeant Mallory from the technical division was skinny as a reed and looked like the stereotypical nerd. He had a thatch of reddish hair, freckles and giant glasses. But the minute he opened his mouth, Dallas liked him. The kid was good.

He gave them a few technical details as he explained what he had found out from the cell phones. They were prepaid and available across the country, but he had managed to discover that they'd been bought at different times at different stores in the southeast part of the state, from Palm Beach to Miami.

But the most important discovery he had made was where the bulk of the calls had come from. Most had been made from a point just southwest of the Seven Mile Bridge, which made Dallas wonder just how much time the Wolf even spent in Key West. But it was the next thing Mallory told him that gave Dallas the chills.

Pistol had revealed another detail of the Wolf's security precautions. He didn't just replace his own phone on a regular basis, he had his men trade phones between themselves, too. Just that morning, right before Pistol had gotten himself arrested, he'd been ordered to pick up his new phone. Mallory had traced and dated and cross-referenced calls and figured out that most on that particular phone had come from Key West. He had narrowed it down to somewhere around Duval, northwest of Front Street.

Dallas had a sinking feeling that the man who'd owned that phone up until that morning was Machete, and that meant a killer had been making calls from very near Hannah's house.

When Mallory finished his report, Dallas, Liam and Logan all commended him. The man turned a bright red and told them he was glad to help, then headed back to his computers.

Dallas immediately filled the other two men in on his conclusion—and his fears.

"I'm going to call the cop on duty out front right now and tell him to be on high alert," Liam said.

When Liam left, Dallas turned to Logan. "I want to interview Billie Garcia again. I want to ask him about his boat."

"If Machete had taken his boat, don't you think Billie would have told you?"

"I think he would have if he knew," Dallas agreed. "But, what if Machete took the boat and Billie didn't know about it?"

"How would Machete even know Billie had a boat?" Logan asked.

"The Wolf would have known. He knows everything about everyone he hires. He would have sent Billie somewhere on some pretext or other, then told Machete where to get a boat."

Logan reflected on that. "Let's get him in here," he said. "With this case, anything is possible."

Hannah didn't even have to look at Kelsey to know they were in agreement. She opened the door wider and let Valeriya in.

Valeriya was still sobbing, so Hannah led her into the kitchen, sat her down at the table and quickly found a box of tissues for her.

"Tea?" Kelsey suggested.

"Sure. And the Jameson's might be good, too," Hannah said.

It took them a few minutes and a big mug of tea laced with whiskey to get Valeriya calmed down. "Thank you," she said, then winced. "Someone is watching. Someone is always watching. If they see me crying, it will be even worse."

Kelsey was seated across from Valeriya. "You

have to tell us what happened. Who's threatening you and why?"

"Last night," Valeriya said, huge tears welling in her eyes again, "I went to take the trash out. Suddenly he was there. He could have killed me then. He is a big man. Strong—powerful."

"What did he look like?" Hannah asked, then looked at Kelsey, pretty sure she already knew the answer.

"I don't know!" Valeriya wailed. "He grabbed me from behind. He—he was strangling me, but then he told me what to do and let me go. He said I had to get back here, back in the house, to find something. He thinks there's something here. Something valuable. I told him you wouldn't let me back in, but he said I had to make you. He said if I didn't get in and look for this . . . this *thing,* he'd kill my baby and my mother. He said if I try, even if I die, then at least my baby would still live."

"What is 'it'?" Kelsey asked.

Valeriya shook her head. "I don't know. And I don't think he believed me when I asked what he was talking about. I am so frightened! I don't know what to do. We don't have money. I can't just go away." She laid her head down, sobbing again.

Hannah and Kelsey exchanged a look, and then Hannah said, "There, there. We're going to make sure you're safe."

"We just need to know everything that you can tell us about this man," Kelsey said. "Have you been threatened before? Did anyone ever ask you to look for something in this house before?"

Valeriya looked up, wiping her cheeks, a frown creasing her face. "Oh, God," she whispered.

"What?" Kelsey asked.

"He knows me," Valeriya said. She turned to look at Hannah. "And he knows *you*. He knows this house."

"How do you know that?" Hannah asked. She felt rivulets of ice creep along her spine.

"Because he left me money once—here. In a room in this house."

Billie Garcia's boat was an old fishing rig refitted with a diving platform. It was a twenty-two-footer with a small tower and smaller cabin. There were slots, four on each side, to hold dive tanks.

Her name was *Original Sin.*

Logan headed off to find out if anyone had seen who had taken the boat out and brought it back in, and when.

Dallas stepped from the dock to the deck and took a look around. There were no tanks in the slots now. The boat had been hosed down. There wasn't so much as a speck of dirt on the deck.

He headed up to the helm. There was no radio, no GPS, nothing that would allow them to trace the boat's movements. He headed down into the small cabin. It held a table that converted into a bed, a small head—complete with a shower hose positioned right over the toilet—and a small galley. There were cabinets above the sink; opening them, he found some basic supplies: canned goods, mac 'n' cheese, and cereal and other nonperishables.

He didn't think the cabinets would yield anything useful, but he moved cereal boxes around anyway, looking behind everything.

He gasped when he moved the corn flakes and found the treasure he'd been seeking.

There was a knife. His heart quickened. Of course, it could be any knife.

But it wasn't. It was a bowie knife.

It had a nine-inch blade, the handle was polished wood, and it was about fifteen inches total in length. It had been washed clean.

But . . .

That didn't mean that it wouldn't yield something. If Jose had cut his attacker deeply enough, blood could be soaked into the wood or lurking in the slot where the blade was attached. It wasn't likely, but it was possible.

"You down there?"

He heard Logan shouting to him from the deck, and a moment later, Logan appeared on the steps that led down to the cabin. "Anything?" he asked.

Dallas produced the knife.

Logan whistled softly. "We need to get that to a lab quickly."

Dallas nodded. "Agreed. What about you?"

"Big guy brought the boat in yesterday. Wearing, of course—"

"A hoodie," Dallas finished for him.

"A dark hoodie. And he kept his head down. They noticed because they know the boat belongs to Billie Garcia."

"And this knife," Dallas said, "could—with any luck—be another piece of evidence tying Machete to this boat *and* Jose's murder."

Machete was still watching. And waiting.

And watching a house—even Hannah O'Brien's house—was, frankly, boring.

At least he had different hiding places from which to watch. Buildings, the alley, sometimes under trees. And he was the one person who could get away with being where he was. He was perfect. Maybe the Wolf had known that from the beginning. But in the beginning it had been fun. It had been thwarting the police and riding the waves and finding treasure, tricking people, tricking governments.

Then it had been killing. But killing those who needed to be killed. It had been exhilarating. And it had been justified.

But then the Wolf had become obsessed. And

Machete's job had turned into watching. It strained the eyes, cramped the body. . . .

Toyed with the mind.

Except for those rare times when something happened.

And now, finally, things *were* happening. This was it.

Valeriya Dimitri was in.

But even while he was pleased, he was also worried. He'd thought Valeriya was one of them, at least in a way. He'd thought that, now and then, he'd heard the voice of a woman speaking softly in the background when the Wolf spoke to him. And he'd thought that woman was Valeriya.

He'd heard her often enough, knew her voice. And she was in the house the Wolf considered the key to the treasure. It had made sense that she had a connection to the Wolf.

He'd even left her money once, because of that. He'd told the Wolf that he'd left money for the housekeeper, and the Wolf had been pleased with him.

Now he wondered.

A mistake. A major mistake. You couldn't make mistakes in the Wolf's world. Then again, the Wolf had been pleased when he left the money, so what did that mean?

There had been a time when it had been easy to slip into the house. He was a neighbor, liked and respected, and no one had been afraid. It was a bed-and-breakfast—people came and went.

He'd left her the money and the note, thinking she was part of the gang. *Thank you for all you've done for us—and all that we know you will do when we ask.*

Whether she was part of the Wolf's team or not didn't matter. Because she was doing what he'd told her to do, and that was what mattered.

She didn't know she was looking for a treasure. But she would be looking for anything valuable, and that was good enough.

Just a little more waiting. And watching.

He knew what he had to do. And the time was coming.

Soon. Very soon. In fact, he suddenly decided, he'd had enough waiting and watching. The time was now.

Machete walked across the street, waving to the cop in the patrol car. He walked over to the window and leaned against it, as if he just had a friendly question to ask.

It was so easy. . . .

Dallas couldn't help but think about what Billie Garcia had said to him: that the police themselves might be involved. The thought worried him. No one knew who the Wolf was, and no one knew who else might work for him.

He didn't want to believe the Wolf had law enforcement in his pocket, but he had to acknowledge the possibility.

While he and Logan were in the car, taking the safely bagged knife to the lab, Dallas's phone rang. It was Dirk Mendini.

"You're going to want to get up here," the M.E. told Dallas.

"What's going on?"

"I heard you were looking for a young Hispanic woman, the sister of your man Rodriguez. I have a woman here who fits the general description. She was fished out of the water off Grassy Key. No ID. She's pretty bloated. I'm thinking she's been in the water at least a week. She may have nothing to do with your case, but . . . you might want to take a look."

"Yeah. I didn't know Jose's sister, but . . . yeah, I've seen her face in the file photo. We'll be there," he told Dirk.

When he hung up, he started to recap the call, but Logan had overheard.

"She might not be Alicia," Logan said. "Odds are against it. Alicia disappeared months ago."

"I know, but hell, we're heading north anyway," Dallas said. "And," he added, "whoever she is, she was someone's daughter, lover, friend."

"You know how people tip me sometimes for cleaning the rooms?" Valeriya said to Hannah.

"You told me that the tips were mine to keep, that I didn't need to share."

"I'm not worried about people leaving you tips," Hannah told her. "I'm trying to figure out how a guest leaving you a tip meant that you were somehow being threatened."

Valeriya let out a breath and looked at them, realizing how stupid she'd been in her eagerness to accept the money.

"It was a really big tip," she said. "Two hundred dollars."

Hannah's brows shot up with her surprise. She held still a minute, willing her temper to cool before she spoke. She needed to keep Valeriya as calm as possible. She glanced at Kelsey, but her cousin was waiting for her to speak.

"Someone left a two-hundred-dollar tip and you didn't think to at least mention it to me?" Hannah asked quietly.

Valeriya lowered her head. "I needed it. And there was a note with it."

"What did the note say?" Kelsey asked.

" 'Thank you for your service, now and in the future,' " Valeriya said as if by rote.

"Do you still have the note?" Hannah asked her hopefully.

Valeriya winced and shook her head.

"Okay," Hannah said slowly. "You got a two-hundred-dollar tip but you didn't keep the note that came with it."

"I threw it away as soon as I got it. I mean, it might not mean anything, but it . . . it scared me."

"Valeriya," Kelsey said, her voice low and controlled. "When was this? It's important that you remember when it was."

Valeriya shook her head. Her fingers were clenching her teacup so hard that her knuckles were almost a solid white. "I'm not sure. Maybe a month ago? Yes, before the first. I used it to help pay for my rent." She looked at the two of them. "It's bad that I kept it, isn't it? I do get nice tips, though. Guests who only stay a night leave me twenty dollars sometimes. I thought maybe he had miscounted. Or he was really rich and the money didn't matter to him. Or . . ."

Her voice trailed away, and she let go of her cup and looked at her hands. They were just shaking.

"What is it that he wants so badly?" she asked.

"A treasure chest," Kelsey said.

"A treasure chest?" Valeriya echoed. She frowned and looked at Hannah. "But a treasure chest is big. If there was a treasure chest here, we would have seen it."

Hannah didn't intend to tell her that while they hadn't found a treasure chest—and she agreed that it would have been found if it had been in the house—they *had* found a key. "What should we do?" she asked Kelsey.

"First, we have to act as if everything is normal.

Then we need to get someone over to Valeriya's to keep an eye on her mother and her baby."

"He'll see. He sees everything!" Valeriya said.

Kelsey stood. "You're right. So, we'll make it look as if you're doing exactly what he told you to. Let's go up to my room. I actually think I've seen him standing by the banyan out front, looking up and watching the house."

The three of them went upstairs.

"I'm going to slip into the captain's room and watch from that window. I won't let myself be seen," Kelsey said.

Hannah nodded, then led the way into her room.

"You already made the bed," Valeriya said.

"Yes, but . . . pretend to straighten it or something."

"I will get the vacuum," Valeriya said.

"Valeriya, we don't really need—"

"I need to do something! I must." She hurried downstairs to get the vacuum from the downstairs utility closet.

While Valeriya was gone, Hannah realized that she needed to call Dallas. They needed to make sure that someone was watching Valeriya's house, so as soon as her mother left with the baby they could intercept her and get them somewhere safe.

She had just pulled her phone from her pocket and punched in Dallas's number when she was startled by the sound of the doorbell.

She paused, frowning. The cop in the patrol car

out front usually called to warn her before some-one came to the door.

"Wait!" she called, aborting the call and shoving her phone back into her pocket.

But it was too late.

"Hello, how are you?" she heard Valeriya say, her tone surprised but friendly.

Hannah waited. Waited for someone else to speak.

Nothing.

Holding her breath, she walked to the landing, but she couldn't see anything.

Kelsey silently joined her on the landing, frowning. She drew her Glock and motioned to Hannah to get behind her. Hannah obeyed, reaching into her pocket and feeling for the button that put the phone in silent mode. All she needed was Dallas calling her back and alerting whoever was at the door.

They went down the stairs slowly, cautiously.

"It's just me, Hannah."

She knew the voice instantly.

"It's okay," she told Kelsey, pushing past her as Kelsey slid her Glock back into her waistband.

But then they reached the foot of the stairs and saw Valeriya—saw why she hadn't answered them.

Saw the massive knife that was pressing so tightly against her throat that a thin trickle of blood was already oozing slowly down her neck.

16

"Stop!" Dallas told Logan.

"In the middle of the road?" Logan asked.

"No, but turn around," Dallas said, staring at his phone. He looked over at Logan. "Hannah called me, but the call cut out before I could answer. And now, when I try her back, I'm not getting an answer."

Logan pulled off on the side of the road. Luckily they had only gotten as far as Stock Island. It wouldn't take them more than twenty minutes—maybe less—to get back to town. He used his Bluetooth device to call Kelsey, and Dallas saw the worry on the other man's face when she didn't pick up.

"I'll call Liam," Dallas said.

In a minute, he had the detective on the phone.

"Hannah and Kelsey aren't answering their phones," he said without preamble.

"I drove by not ten minutes ago," Liam said. "Officer Bickford was sitting in his car, right where he was supposed to be. Hang on. I'll get him on his radio."

Long seconds went by. Logan was already turning the car around.

Liam came back on. "I can't rouse my officer.

I'll get a couple of patrol cars over there right away."

"No, don't," Dallas said. "If someone *is* in there, he thinks he got in clean and now he's in control. Tell your men to park around the corner and approach the house on foot, but tell them to make sure they're not seen and not to go in. See if you can find a way to reach the patrol car without being noticed, though frankly, I'm afraid you're going to find your officer dead or dying. Get help for him quickly, but do it without being noticed."

"I'll get it done carefully," Liam promised. "Unless someone's watching from a distance, I'll get my man without being seen. But as for the house . . ."

"Liam, please, play this my way. Unless you hear screams or shots fired, don't go in. That's the best chance they have of staying alive. I'm begging you. Hannah and Kelsey have to play along, make him think they can and will help him. They have to pretend to give this guy what he wants."

"Do they even have what he wants? Did you find something?"

"No, but he doesn't know that. And—" He broke off, looking at Logan. "They're smart. They'll keep him talking. They'll play the game."

"Sweet Lord, I pray you're right," Liam said.

"Hannah tried to call me," Dallas said. "She'll

know I saw and we're on the way. Hold off, please."

"I'll call you back the second we're around the corner, getting ready to approach the house."

"If you burst in—"

"We won't. Your case, your call," Liam promised quietly.

"Thank you. I'll go in myself and—"

"How the hell are *you* going to get in?" Liam asked.

"Well, I could just use my guest key. It's a bed-and-breakfast, remember? I'm a guest," Dallas said. "But I'll play it by ear."

"I'll have my men placed discreetly as near the house as is safe. They won't go in, but they'll be ready."

Dallas thanked him and hung up.

Logan drove fast, but with a dead-steady hand. "I'm going to park one street over. We'll go through the alley."

Dallas nodded. They were back on Roosevelt already. Logan had a true talent for dodging through traffic.

"You're taking the back door?" Logan asked.

Dallas shook his head. "There's a big avocado tree in the back. I'm going to climb it to the widow's walk and go in through the attic, then play it by ear from there."

Logan didn't argue with him, and Dallas felt a solid sense of gratitude. Logan Raintree was a hell of a guy and the kind of leader a man could respect. He meant what he said when he handed over the reins, and he didn't micromanage.

Dallas smiled grimly. They were going to pull this off. "I don't think he wants to kill anyone, at least not until he has what he's looking for—though why he thinks we have it, I don't know. I need you to distract him while I come. He's got some kind of a hostage thing going on. I'm sure of it."

"So am I," Logan said. He looked over at Dallas quickly. "If not, Kelsey would have shot him by now."

Logan parked a street away, as planned. They made their way to the alley, then split up.

Logan headed to the rear door, moving silently through the foliage.

Dallas slipped around to the avocado tree and hoped the tree would hold him and get him where he needed to go.

"Bentley Holloway, what the hell are you doing?" Hannah asked.

It was so damned obvious, but at the same time it was ridiculously impossible to believe that the next-door neighbor she'd known since she was a kid was a killer.

A big guy with blue eyes. Hell. They'd never even suspected. . . .

He ignored Hannah and looked at Kelsey. "Put

your weapon on the ground. Now. Slowly, calmly and easily. I'm pretty much past caring whether I live or die, but this woman is a mother. She wants to live. Don't you, Valeriya?"

Valeriya didn't make a sound. She seemed barely able to breathe. Her terror was almost palpable.

Kelsey turned, then carefully lifted the Glock from her waistband for him to see.

"Down. Right there . . . yes."

Kelsey set the weapon on the floor.

Hannah prayed that her cousin had something else in her arsenal.

"Step back," Bentley said.

Kelsey obeyed.

"You always were a smart girl, Kelsey. I remember you both as kids. Hannah, you were like a light in the darkness. Even then, you knew every story about Key West. You knew all about the soldiers, the pirates, the spongers and the salvagers. You were like a sponge yourself, soaking up every piece of information that came your way."

"I think he likes you best," Kelsey said drily.

"Shut up, Kelsey. Try anything and sweet Valeriya dies," Bentley said. "And you know I'll do it. I've killed before. I won't blink at doing it again."

Hannah noticed that Hagen and Melody had materialized by the kitchen door. Hagen looked furious, as if he would have ripped the man in two if he could. He strode angrily toward Bentley—then walked through him.

Bentley, however, felt something. His grip on Valeriya tightened, and Hannah flinched as she saw the necklace of red at Valeriya's throat darken.

Bentley's eyes narrowed. "What the hell is going on in here?" he demanded.

"The ghosts," Hannah said.

"What?"

"Melody and Hagen. They really do haunt the house."

Bentley smiled and shook his head. "Amusing, Hannah. As always, I do like you best," he told her.

Kelsey shrugged. "It's okay with me. But you should let Valeriya go. She's useless. And if you have to worry about anybody, it's me, so you should have that knife at my throat."

"Hannah, check your cousin's pocket. I'm betting you'll find some of those plastic zip-tie cuffs. Am I right, Kelsey?" When she nodded, he smiled.

"Bentley, you weren't listening," Kelsey said calmly.

"I heard you. But you're going to try to save the day. So you need to be cuffed. Much easier for me than trying to hold on to you," Bentley said.

"You want something from me, Bentley,"

Hannah said thoughtfully. "And I don't believe you want to kill us. So why don't you tell me what you want and I'll help you if I can."

"Aren't you nice, Hannah. Yeah, right. In real life, what do you see? The big sweaty construction guy next door. Well, Hannah, you know what? You're right. I don't want to kill you. I've made mistakes because of you. And it will hurt me—it will *haunt me*—if I have to kill any of you. But I will if I have to. Kelsey, make things easy. Give her the cuffs."

"So it will be easier for you to shove me to my knees and shoot me in the back of the head?" Kelsey asked.

"I told you, I don't want to kill you. I just want the treasure. I know you know what's going on. The Wolf wants the treasure, too, but he wants *me* to find it because it's cursed. But I don't believe in curses. I have a way out. I just need one particular piece. And I really want to leave you alive. So come on, help me out here."

Kelsey produced the cuffs from her pocket.

"Put them on her," Bentley said to Hannah. "And be sure they're tight enough. You don't have to hurt her, but make sure she can't slip out of them."

"How on earth do you think this is going to work out?" Hannah asked. "I don't have the treasure chest. You've worked in this house long enough to know that. And Dallas and Logan will be back soon, not to mention there's a policeman out in front. He'll be in here—"

"No," Bentley said quietly, "he won't."

Hannah felt a horrible chill.

Hagen said, "The bastard killed him. Why didn't we know it was him? He was right next door!"

"I didn't know, either," Hannah said.

"Who are you talking to?" Bentley demanded. "Your 'ghosts'?" He laughed. "Handcuffs. Now. And cell phones, while you're at it."

Kelsey nodded and told Hannah, "Pull them on. It's easy. They're like garbage bag ties."

Hannah looked at her worriedly but did as she was told.

"Cell phone this pocket," Kelsey said.

Hannah got out Kelsey's phone and then her own. She saw that she had missed five calls from Dallas.

He would come save her, she thought.

"Bentley, you need to get out now. Dallas and Logan—"

"Can't possibly get back here in time to do you a damn bit of good," he said smoothly.

"You can't know that! They're close," Hannah said.

"I'm afraid not. The medical examiner has found another body," Bentley told her. "The Wolf," he added quietly, "makes sure of all things."

"What can we do?" Melody asked. She was

trying to shove Bentley, but needless to say, he wasn't moving.

He felt something, though, Hannah thought. He just didn't know what it was.

"Nothing," Hannah said.

"Don't do that—just don't, Hannah," Bentley said. "I'm not one of your ghost-tour guests."

"It's a history and legends tour," she corrected. "And the spirits are real, Bentley. Not to mention there are more of them. Melody and Hagen are here now, but Jose Rodriguez is around somewhere. So is Yerby Catalano. They're both pretty bitter. Let Valeriya go. Make me your hostage. I'm the one you think has what you want."

"I don't believe in ghosts any more than I believe in curses. Get that straight. And, by the way, you definitely have what I want."

"How can you say that?" Hannah demanded. "You've been in this house more than almost anyone."

"As a matter of fact, I actually know the house better than you do," he told her, suddenly thrusting Valeriya away from him. Sobbing, she fell to the floor in front of Hannah, who instinctively reached down to help her.

When she looked up again, Bentley had slid the knife back into a sheath at his calf and was holding a gun. She didn't know what it was, but it certainly looked lethal enough.

"Now, Hannah, where is it?"

"If I had it, I'd give it to you!" she shouted.

He stepped toward her, so she backed away, holding Valeriya, who was trembling and trying but failing not to make any noise as she sobbed.

Then she realized he wasn't coming toward *her,* he was heading for Kelsey.

Kelsey saw him and lunged, kicking out viciously. He grunted in obvious pain when she connected, but he didn't stop.

He used the gun to crack Kelsey hard on the side of the head. Hannah heard the impact of the gun against her cousin's skull.

Melody rushed over and tried to catch Kelsey as she fell, and Hannah thought maybe she did soften the impact slightly, but Kelsey still went down in a heap.

Hannah let out a cry of protest.

"Shut up! I didn't shoot her, did I? Do you want me to?" Bentley demanded.

"You're going to kill us, anyway. You'll have to."

"I plan to be long gone before you can sic your cop buddies on me. Now for this one."

He reached for Valeriya, who promptly fell to the floor in a dead faint.

"Now, where is it?" he asked Hannah. He held the gun on her, the muzzle never wavering, as he bent down by Valeriya, pulled his own set of plastic cuffs and bound her wrists.

"Human life means more to me than any object,

Bentley. Don't you think I'd give you what you want if I had it?"

"Then you'd better think quickly and figure out where it is," Bentley said. "Because in a minute I'm going to start motivating you. I'll start by slicing your cousin's fingers off."

"Do you see a treasure chest anywhere?" Hannah demanded desperately. She realized that she was shaking. There was no way out of this. She should have thrown herself at him the second he released Valeriya. She would have died, but maybe Kelsey and Valeriya would have made it. Kelsey had been trained in combat skills and could have taken advantage of the distraction. She had no idea how to fight.

All she had was the instinct to survive.

"Hey," Hagen said suddenly. "Someone's coming." He raced toward the back of the house.

Hope revived her spirit as if she had grown wings. Suddenly Hagen returned and rushed upstairs.

"Hang on!" he shouted over his shoulder.

"Tell me why you think I know where it is and maybe I can help you," Hannah said desperately to Bentley.

"There was a letter. Your uncle left a letter," he told her.

"To me?" she asked, stunned.

"I'm surprised you never found it, but I did, and

I read it. He said he'd figured out that the treasure was here and where it was hidden. He wouldn't write it down. He planned to tell you."

"He never said a word. I know it's not in the house. And I don't see how it can be in the yard—everything was all dug up for the pool and the patio."

Bentley looked stunned. "He really didn't tell you?"

The timing couldn't have been more perfect.

She heard a noise from the rear of the house. Bentley heard it, too. He grabbed her and spun her against his body as he trained his gun on her skull.

"Come in, Fed. Come on in!" he called.

"I'm not armed!" Logan said as he walked into the room. He saw Kelsey on the floor and, ignoring Bentley, hunkered down next to her. "She's breathing," he said quietly, staring at Bentley. "You're lucky."

"Oh, really? Or you'd kill me?" Bentley demanded.

"In a heartbeat," Logan assured him evenly.

Bentley eased the gun away from Hannah's head and leveled it at Logan.

"I don't need you. I already have plenty of leverage to keep Hannah doing whatever I ask," Bentley said softly.

Oh, God, Hannah thought. He was going to do it. He was really going to shoot Logan.

But just as that thought came to her, she heard thunder on the stairs. Bentley tried to swing the gun around. Too late.

Dallas was there.

He fired, and the bullet winged Bentley's arm, sending him spinning. The gun flew from his hand. Hannah screamed and tried to wrench free, but he went down, dragging her with him.

And there was Kelsey's gun, just inches from Bentley's outstretched arm.

He reached for it, but Hannah scrambled desperately, got free and grabbed it herself. She was just a foot from him.

Dallas was racing down the stairs, and Logan was on his feet, but then Bentley pulled his knife again, ready to stab Valeriya.

Was it too late to save her?

There was something cold in Bentley's icy-blue eyes. Something that meant he intended to go down fighting. He was big and powerful, and she gasped as he raised the knife over Valeriya.

"Drop it!" she commanded him.

He didn't.

She squeezed the trigger firmly, just as Kelsey had taught her. The gun recoiled in her hand. She felt the force almost bending her wrist back.

And she saw the red stain appear on Bentley's shirt.

She saw his eyes as he died. They weren't so

cold or so icy now. They held a look that she could have sworn was relief. . . .

And then there was nothing in them. Nothing at all.

"Go figure," Kelsey said. She was lying in a hospital bed, wearing a stupid hospital gown with little blackbirds all over a field of blue, but with the way her red hair framed her face she seemed especially beautiful to Hannah.

The confusion that had reigned after she'd shot Bentley was at last over. It had seemed like forever, yet it had happened so fast. Armed men had burst in through both doors and down the stairs. Dallas had taken the gun from her, turned her face to his and asked, "You all right?"

She had nodded and murmured, "Not a scratch."

He'd had to leave her then to reconnoiter with Liam and his men, and then the paramedics had arrived. Soon the parlor was being cordoned off and Liam had taken over her phone. She tried to get to her feet and found she couldn't stand, but then Dallas appeared from somewhere and helped her up. She was happy to see that Kelsey was already groaning and protesting the need for an ambulance.

Dirk Mendini arrived. "Hell, I'm trying to get you up to my office to see if you can identify one corpse and instead you offer me another," he told Dallas, who wasn't amused.

"Nobody else?" Dallas asked worriedly.

Liam was the one to answer. "Not so far," he said. "Officer Hannigan—he was on duty in the patrol car when Bentley made his move—is hanging in. He may not make it through the night. He's a tough old bird, though, and Bentley missed the artery."

"Thank God," Hannah whispered.

By then the paramedics were ready to take Kelsey and Logan away. Hannah insisted on going with them, but she was torn, worried about Valeriya.

Valeriya was going to be okay, though she was still terrified. She'd overheard some of the cops talking and kept saying that the Wolf was out there and coming to get her. Liam was working on calming her down, promising that two of his best officers would take her and her family to a safe house, then stand guard through the night.

Just as she was getting ready to go with Kelsey, Liam walked over to Hannah and stopped her with a hand on her shoulder. "Sorry," he said, "but you can't go yet. You have to give a statement."

She looked at Dallas, a little dazed, then followed Liam to a relatively quiet spot and started answering his questions. The whole time she was aware of Dallas standing nearby and watching her with a concerned expression.

As soon as she'd finished and signed, he strode

to her side and took her to the hospital to visit Kelsey.

She understood why he was so worried.

She had killed a man. A man she had known most her life. She knew that even policemen had to get psych clearance after killing someone, and she would probably need help, too.

But all she felt right then was numb.

And grateful that everyone who mattered to her was still alive.

The hospital wanted to keep Kelsey overnight to watch for aftereffects of the concussion she'd sustained, so she was all set up in a private room by the time Hannah and Dallas arrived.

"Here I am, a Federal agent, and there's my cousin the innkeeper bringing down a hired killer before he could claim another victim. You okay, cuz?" Kelsey asked with a stern look.

Hannah nodded, aware that Dallas and Logan were watching her as intently as Kelsey was. "He was going to kill Valeriya," she said. "I didn't have a choice."

"You didn't," Logan said. "But killing a man, even when it's a righteous shoot . . . it's never easy."

"You all need to stop looking at me like that," Hannah said. "I'm okay. I'm fine. Really."

"He was our friend, but you and he were especially close, with him working for you and all," Kelsey said.

Dallas slipped his arm around her shoulders where she sat at the bottom of Kelsey's bed and pulled her against his side. "You handled yourself remarkably well," he told her.

They stayed a little while longer, and Hannah told them what Bentley had said about the letter. "He couldn't believe Ronin never told me."

"Are you certain he didn't say anything? Anything at all?" Logan asked.

"I'm pretty sure I'd remember if he'd told me the location of a priceless treasure," Hannah said, too drained to bother hiding her sarcasm.

"He died unexpectedly," Kelsey said. "He dropped dead of a heart attack."

"So maybe he meant to tell you," Dallas said to Hannah.

She nodded. "Maybe. But at least now we know he was sure the treasure is on the property somewhere. And I swear it's nowhere in the house."

"Then we start digging tomorrow," Kelsey said.

Hannah laughed. "If we start digging up the whole yard, I'll need a treasure to put it all back when we're finished."

"Whatever it takes, it needs to be done," Dallas told her.

She met his gaze, and she knew then what he was thinking.

They had survived Machete.

But the Wolf was still out there, and he had to

be thinking of revenge. One way or another, they'd cost him six of his men, four in custody and two dead, not to mention he still didn't have the treasure.

"We'll dig up the yard," she said. "And worry about fixing it afterward."

They stayed at the hospital well into the night.

Katie led the ghost tour again—with Liam and David watching over her.

Dallas and Hannah kept tabs on Kelsey while Logan went to eat something, and then they grabbed a meal there themselves. To Hannah's surprise, the food tasted delicious.

Because I'm alive to eat it, she thought.

They didn't return to her house that night. The hospital was in Marathon, and they just didn't feel like making the long drive back.

They took a little room at a mom-and-pop motel just a few blocks away on the beach. Their room opened out to the sand. Hannah asked Dallas if they could just walk out and sit by the ocean. She lay back and felt the dampness of the sand against her, relaxed at the sound of the water washing onto the shore. The sky above her was beautiful, a perfect Keys night sky, shrouding the world in black velvet and shining stars.

"It's hard to believe Jose and Yerby didn't show up for any of this," she murmured.

"I doubt we'll see them tonight," he told her. "They don't know where we are."

She smiled. "That's a little sad, isn't it? They're ghosts, but they don't get to be omniscient."

"No," he agreed. "If so, Hagen and Melody would have known that Bentley was out there watching."

"Just bad timing, I guess," she said.

"They were there when we needed them today," he said. "Logan and I had our entrances planned, but thanks to Hagen I knew what was happening when I made it from the widow's walk into the attic."

"They *are* wonderful, aren't they? They don't have the ability to fight physically, but they make their presence known."

It was beautiful by the water, but with his arm around her, she found herself wanting more.

"Let's go in," she said.

She hit the shower first; she couldn't wait to wash away the feel of the day.

He joined her. She felt the thrill of his body, hot, steaming and naked against her own.

She turned into his arms and kissed him. They left the shower, damp, glowing, and then they made love, touching, kissing, as if they were enjoying a feast of passion.

Afterward they lay in bed, listening to the sound of the surf.

She turned to him then and asked, "Do you want to talk?"

"What do you want to know?"

"About your friend, your coworker. The one who was killed."

She could just see his face in the moonlight streaming in. There was pain in his expression, but acceptance, too.

"We really were friends, best friends. And her death came close to wrecking me."

"I'm so sorry."

"I am, too. One day we wouldn't have had the benefits anymore. She would have found the right guy for her. She would have been a great mother. She deserved that." After a long silence, he spoke again. "What about your past?" He touched her hair.

"Nothing dramatic," she told him. "Just . . . not the right guy. I don't know what else to say."

"What you've said is enough," he said.

She kissed him, and they made love again.

It was good.

In the morning, they collected Kelsey and Logan from the hospital. But they didn't head right home.

They went to the morgue. There was a body they needed to see.

Hannah couldn't help but pray that they hadn't found Jose's sister.

17

Dallas stood looking down at the body in the morgue.

Every member of law enforcement the world over, he was certain, hated a floater.

Water creatures nibbled on the flesh. Most of the time the body had been intentionally sunk, and it was the gases forming in the body during putrefaction that caused it to rise. Decay never had a pleasant smell, and the human body was no different than any other, but the stink of a floater was something much worse.

He had a mask over his nose and mouth, and spoke through it when he looked over at Dirk and asked, "You really think we might be able to recognize her?"

"I'm hoping. My cabinets are filling up, guys," Dirk said. "I'll release Yerby Catalano soon, and I'd be happy to release Jose Rodriguez, too, except his only next of kin is his sister, and . . ."

"And this may be her," Logan muttered.

Despite the grayish hue of the corpse's bloated flesh, Logan had laid a hand on her, and Dallas intended to do the same. Every once in a rare while, it was possible to make contact with the deceased that way.

Dirk had finished the autopsy, so she wasn't as grossly swollen as when she'd been found. Even so, she looked like some kind of monstrous hybrid. There was nothing left of her nose or lips. Dallas wasn't sure that her own mother would have recognized her.

With gloved hands, he inspected her neck. The bruising around the throat was like a black collar. He looked at Dirk. "Strangulation?"

Mendini nodded. "Yes."

Dallas surreptitiously removed a glove and laid his palm on the body, but he didn't feel anything at all. He prayed the poor woman's soul had moved on.

"We can try dental records," Mendini said.

Kelsey stepped into the room. She had on a mask and gloves. Before Dallas had a chance to ask her where Hannah was, Logan's shocked expression posed the question.

"Don't look at me like that. Hannah is fine. She's in Dirk's office with the door locked," she said.

"You think you might recognize her?" Mendini asked.

"I'm just interested in a challenging autopsy," she replied.

But Dallas knew the truth. She, too, had come to touch the body. But he could tell from her expression that she didn't get anything from the corpse, either.

• • •

Hannah looked around Dirk Mendini's office. Nice. He had a gold coin from the *Atocha* displayed in a glass case on his desk. His many framed certifications hung on the walls, along with seascapes and old photos. She was sitting in a chair in front of his big pine desk, but there was also a comfortable sofa against the wall. She wondered if he sometimes slept in his office.

There was a book on the lower Keys on his desk; she thumbed idly through it as she waited. She got so caught up in it that she was startled to hear a knock at the door.

"Hannah, it's me. Logan."

She rose and opened the door.

"You up to seeing a corpse?" he asked.

"Do you think I might recognize . . . her?" she asked.

He shook his head. "I don't think anyone would recognize her. I thought you might—well, your ability to communicate with the dead is better than any of ours. Stronger. Kelsey's told me about how when you were kids she 'met' people through you. I know you're a civilian and this is a lot to ask, but . . ."

"You want me to touch the corpse, don't you?"

He nodded.

Reluctantly, but knowing she had no choice but to do the right thing, she accompanied him down the hall and through a door marked Autopsy: Staff Only.

Kelsey was asking Mendini something technical that Hannah was perfectly happy not to understand.

Dallas was standing by the corpse, waiting, watching her. He looked regretful. She had a feeling he wasn't happy about the decision to ask for her help, even if he'd agreed with it because it was the right one.

She walked up to the corpse, telling herself not to look closely.

"Do you know her?" Dirk asked.

She shook her head as she touched the woman's flesh where he couldn't see. It just felt cold.

She looked at Dallas and shook her head again.

Turning, she noticed another body.

Bentley Holloway.

She felt nothing when she looked at him and wondered if that meant something was wrong with her. She was sorry, of course; she hated the idea that she had killed anyone. But the idea was intellectual, not anything that came from her heart.

Overall, she still felt numb. She'd simply done what she had to do.

She turned away from the body and said, "I'll be back in the office."

"I'll walk you out," Kelsey said.

Hannah didn't know how much longer the others were going to be, so once she locked the door behind Kelsey, she chose a seat on the sofa and picked up the book on the lower Keys again, turning to the section on Key West. She was just thinking how much she loved her home when she heard sobbing.

She looked up. The ghost of a young woman was sitting in Dr. Mendini's chair, at least as much as a ghost could sit anywhere.

The ghost was naked, and she hadn't fully materialized, which somehow made her both more beautiful and more pathetic.

"Hello?" Hannah said softly, rising.

The sobbing stopped, and the ghost looked at her in shock.

"Hello. Please don't be afraid," Hannah said. *How funny,* she thought. *I'm the living person, and I'm telling a ghost not to be afraid.*

But the ghost *was* afraid. She disappeared completely for a minute, then began to slowly reappear.

Hannah stood and walked toward her. "It's all right. I'd like to help you if I can."

"No one can help me. I saw . . . myself," the young woman said.

In life, she had been beautiful. Long, curling dark hair tumbled down her neck and over her shoulders. Her eyes were large and dark and stunning. And given that she was naked, there was no way not to notice that her body was absolutely perfect.

"I'm Hannah." She prayed she wasn't going to get the reply she was expecting when she asked, "Are you . . . Alicia?"

To her relief, the young woman shook her head. "Alicia is so kind. She tried to keep us believing that help will come. Then, a few days ago, we heard that her brother was dead. She always believed he was coming for us, that he would save us."

"Who are you?" she asked.

"Maria Lopez. Alicia and I . . . we were best friends. We grew up together in Miami. When we were older, we worked in one of the clubs together and . . ." Her voice trailed away.

"And?" Hannah encouraged.

"There's money at the clubs. All the beautiful people. And . . . and cocaine. A lot of it. And before you know it . . ."

"I understand," Hannah said.

"So then, you do things. You sleep with repulsive men and you don't even care. And you . . . move things for people."

"Move things?"

Maria nodded. "A diamond one time, artwork another. Hidden in shoe boxes in the back of your car or inside a suitcase. You go down the street and get into a van and move it where you're told. And then one day . . . one day I got a call about another van. I got there early and saw two men in it, and I heard them talking. What they were saying scared me, so I went to leave, but one of them saw me. He said something that scared me even more, so I hit him and tried to run. But he was faster than me, and stronger. I ended up in the back of the van, and the next thing I knew, I was in a cabin by the water. I think it was on an island."

"Tell me about the cabin," Hannah demanded. "Do you know where it was?"

Maria began to weep. "I don't know. But Alicia was there, and one other girl. Alma. And one old man who watches over us. They kept us in a room together. Alicia said her brother would come, but I couldn't stand it. I got out and tried to swim away. I saw a man in a boat, and I thought he would save me, but he dragged me out of the water and . . . here I am."

"Was he a big man, with blue eyes?"

Maria nodded.

"He's dead now, too," Hannah said.

"Good!" Then Maria lowered her head and wept. "Why am I still here?" she whispered.

Hannah didn't have the answer to that. "Do you think you could come with me?" she asked. "I have friends like you at my home in Key West. Do you think you could follow me?"

"I . . . can try."

As she spoke, the key turned in the door. Dirk and the others were back.

"I'm a busy man, you know, Dallas," Dirk was

saying. "Keep the body count down, will you?"

"It's not like we go looking for them," Dallas said. "Hannah, you ready?"

She looked from him to Kelsey and Logan. She could tell that none of them saw anything unusual. Then again, neither did she at that moment.

"Yes, ready, let's go," she said.

"I wonder if we'll make it back without incident today," Logan said, looking at Dallas in the rear-view mirror. "To tell you the truth, I'm kind of hoping for something," he admitted.

"Actually, we do have something. Some*one,*" Hannah said.

Maria Lopez was sitting uncomfortably at her side. Naked.

"What?" Logan said.

"She's very shy and uncomfortable right now," Hannah said, smiling at the young woman who, so far, only she could see. "But she's coming with us. Melody may be able to help her."

"Is it—is it Alicia?" Dallas asked.

"No," Hannah said. "But she can help us find out where Alicia is."

Nothing happened on the way back to Hannah's house. The Siren of the Sea had never looked more beautiful, she thought, as she stood on the street and looked up toward the widow's walk. Of course, when they went in, there was still blood on her parlor floor.

"What should I do?" she asked Dallas.

"There are special companies that specialize in cleaning up crime scenes. I'll call one for you," he told her.

So for now, she decided, they were simply going to avoid the parlor.

She headed to the kitchen, calling for Melody and Hagen, who appeared immediately. Dallas was right behind her, and Kelsey and Logan went up to their room.

For a brief moment Maria Lopez fully materialized. Then she saw Dallas and disappeared, but from his gasp, Hannah knew he'd caught a glimpse of her.

But Melody and Hagen had turned to the spot where Maria had been. From the look in Hagen's eyes, they apparently still saw her.

Melody slammed him with an ectoplasm elbow.

"Sorry," he murmured, and then he said kindly, "I'm truly sorry, Miss. Do not be embarrassed. I will leave now, but please, trust Melody. I know she will help you."

"Why don't you all come with me?" Hagen said to the others, and they followed him to the back room.

"Who is she?" Hagen asked, and Hannah explained.

"I still haven't seen her," Kelsey said as she and

Logan walked into the room in time to hear Hannah's explanation.

"Me neither," Logan said.

"Just as well," Dallas murmured. He looked at Hannah and smiled. She smiled back, and then both their smiles faded. Maria had fallen easily into a trap tailor-made for a woman who had grown up poor but beautiful—and innocent.

"The thing is," Hannah said, "I think she might be able to help us figure out where Alicia was—and hopefully still is. She said the two of them and another woman named Alma were kept in a cabin by the water with one old man to take care of them."

Jose Rodriguez suddenly materialized in front of them. Yerby appeared a second later, clinging to him.

"My sister?" he asked. "You know something about Alicia?" he asked.

Hannah explained again. By the time she finished, Melody had joined them. A moment later Maria Lopez appeared behind her, now clad in a casual white dress and sandals.

"It's all up to the power of the mind," Melody explained briefly.

Dallas and Logan rose politely, and introductions were made all around.

Maria joined Jose and Yerby on the sofa, and the others took the various chairs. The sun was streaming in, the water in the pool glistened, and

Hannah finally dared to relax, feeling oddly . . . *good.*

She had killed a man. A man she had known for years. And yet she hadn't known him at all.

"The man who killed me—the dead man," Maria said, "he was the one they called Machete, yes?"

"Yes," Logan said.

"There were others like him," Maria said. "That's what the men in the van were talking about. There was one called the Bomb in Miami. He died in one of his own explosions."

Hannah caught Dallas and Logan looking at each other and read the message they were sharing.

It was going to take a long time to end the reign of Los Lobos.

"You knew my sister?" Jose asked.

Maria smiled. "She is so good. I should have listened to her. I never even said goodbye."

She began to sob softly. Yerby laid an arm around her shoulders. "We never know when it's the last time," she said softly. "But you'll see her again one day."

Maria smiled and nodded. Along with the dress, she was now wearing a little gold cross. She fingered it with a ghostly movement.

"We have to find that cabin," Dallas said. "And it won't be easy. There are about seventeen hundred islands in the Keys. It could be on any of them."

"But we can narrow it down. Maria was found in Marathon," Logan said. "Gulf side."

"I think we need to press Pause on looking for the Wolf," Dallas said. "If he's killed first, I'm betting the other two women will be killed, a clean-up operation."

"No!" Jose said. "You can't let that happen."

"We won't," Dallas said. "I promise."

They retrieved their agency laptops, settled around the kitchen table and got to work, looking at maps, tide charts, weather reports from the past ten days . . . anything that could help them figure out where Maria's body had been thrown in the water before it washed up in Marathon.

At one point Dallas put his computer down and stretched. "We need to know who owns the private islands out that way."

"I'll call HQ and get a few interns busy searching the records," Logan said.

Hannah, who'd kept herself busy making coffee and lunch, decided it was time to check on the ghosts, who'd remained in the back room. Melody and Hagen were playing host, she saw. Yerby was still clinging to Jose, and Maria was just sitting quietly, as if drinking it all in.

Hannah decided to let them be and headed back to the kitchen.

"There's something you can help us with," Dallas told her as she walked back into the room, rising and slipping his arms around her. "Along with everything else, we need word to get out that you're looking for the treasure of the *Santa Elinora* here on the property. You need to start digging right away, because even if it does turn out to be in the house—" he held up a hand to silence her when she started to protest "—digging will be obvious to anyone walking by, so the news will spread quickly."

"How do I do that?" she asked.

"I'll get ahold of Liam," he said. "He'll pull strings and get the permits expedited. We'll have a backhoe out here by tomorrow."

She nodded.

"Logan and I will rent a boat in the morning and head out with the information we have so far and start searching for that cabin," he told her.

She nodded again.

"But this evening . . ." he began.

"Yes?"

"Well, I'd officially like to invite you to dinner. You're free to say no, but just so there's no misunderstanding, I'm asking you out. On a date." He lowered his voice and said in a conspiratorial whisper, "Well, okay, a double date with Kelsey and Logan. But it would be my pleasure to take you out to a restaurant tonight. Anyplace you choose. If, of course, you'd like to go. I'll tell you my sign and everything."

Hannah laughed. "I would be delighted to go on a date with you, Agent Samson. Even a double date."

After all, the house would be well watched, given that there were currently five ghosts in residence, though with all the agents away and the Wolf down so many men here in Key West, it was likely to be a quiet night.

That night they headed first to the western waterfront, where one of Hannah's friends was performing, for a round of predinner drinks. After that, they dined at Turtle Crawls. It was an amazing evening. Hannah realized that she'd forgotten how to have fun, and suddenly it felt so good simply to be alive and out on the town.

Better yet, to be out on the town with Dallas. She couldn't help smiling every time she looked at him. He was . . .

Thoughtful, intense—sometimes too much so—more than a little bit autocratic, capable of apology, always ready to explain and, she thought, perfect. For her.

He caught her looking at him at one point and tilted his head at an angle, slowly arching a brow.

"Spinach in my teeth?" he asked her.

"We didn't have spinach," she told him.

"Ketchup on my chin?"

She smiled and shook her head. "I just . . . I was

just thinking that it was nice to talk about movies. And music. And that . . ."

"I could sound normal?" he asked her.

She flushed. "And even nice."

"Hey!" he protested, and then grinned. "And may I return the compliment?"

"I haven't been normal?" she asked him.

"No—I mean that you can be nice, too. You know—friendly, without attitude."

"Hey, I wasn't the one who came in like a thunderstorm."

"No, but . . ." He slipped an arm around her shoulder and pulled her close. "Let's face it, we didn't meet under normal circumstances. And yet I wouldn't trade having met you for anything," he finished softly.

She smiled and touched his cheek, and she wasn't even worried that she was certain he had to have seen the wonder in her eyes.

Back at the house, they retired early, made love—and talked. He liked black coffee, rare steaks and really hated wearing a tie. They were both into history.

"Will you stay down here?" she asked him.

"I don't know, but . . . I've spoken with Logan. Apparently I've been on his boss's radar for a while. I suspect I'm going to be asked to join the unit."

"And that means . . . D.C.?" she asked.

"Just outside. In Virginia," he told her.

Hannah kept silent. She didn't want to think about him leaving.

It would be the right thing for him to do.

"Have you ever thought of leaving?" he asked her.

"I could never sell this house."

"But other people could run it."

That was as far as they got. He'd been running his fingers lightly down her back. Now, eager to avoid a difficult topic, she slid closer to him and moved provocatively. That stirred something in him.

In seconds they were making love again and for a little while the real world fell away.

The backhoe and a small crew of workers arrived by the time Hannah had the coffee brewed in the morning. Kelsey was in the kitchen with her, and they went together to look out back, where Logan was standing with the foreman and a copy of the original plans for the pool.

There was also a reporter in the yard. Hannah had seen her before, the morning she'd found Jose Rodriguez's body.

Today Dallas was talking to her.

He really did want everyone to know about the dig.

"Do you think this will ever really be over?" Hannah asked.

Kelsey slipped an arm around her shoulders.

"Do you know why the Krewes are so well respected even though they like to joke and call us the ghost-hunter division?"

"Why?"

"Because we haven't failed yet."

"That's good. So . . . I hear Dallas might join you guys."

"He and Logan work well together," Kelsey said. She smiled at Kelsey. "But then, so do he and you."

"I, uh . . . I'm sorry. I should have said something to you."

"Why?" Kelsey asked, laughing. "It was obvious from the beginning!"

"You mean you knew when we . . . ?"

"Of course. The house isn't that big," Kelsey told her.

Embarrassed, Hannah fell silent as Dallas came in.

And he was all business. "All right. Liam will be here with a few officers to keep an eye on things. Logan and I are going to take a boat out of Marathon. We'll have our phones and try to stay in touch." He smiled at her. Finally. "Can you talk to Maria and Jose? See if they'll come with us?"

She nodded. "Yes, of course. Follow me."

They were still in the back room and readily agreed to help. Yerby insisted on going, too, having developed something of an attraction to Jose.

Dallas looked at Melody and Hagen. "Okay, officially we're leaving Liam in charge, but—"

"Don't worry about a thing," Hagen said. "We'll keep an eye on everyone. We won't fail you again."

"Can Kelsey and I come, too?" Hannah asked.

Dallas smiled. "What the hell. I don't like leaving you, so yes, come on."

The water wasn't quite as blue on the Gulf side of the Keys compared to the Atlantic side. As they hugged the coast of one island after another, they saw an incredible array of bird life.

Dallas was glad that Hannah and Kelsey were there, because they remembered more than he did about the area.

They knew which ones were the private islands, who lived where, what movie star was rumored to own which massive house, and where there had been trouble with wild parties and reported drug deals.

They'd been out for hours when suddenly Maria Lopez, who had been sitting in the bow, leaped to her feet. "There! There . . . where the trees are growing in the water. I know that place. I saw it when I tried to get away. If you go that way . . ." She pointed.

Dallas was piloting the boat; Logan had told him that he was the Florida boy, so he should take the helm.

He followed Maria's instructions, and there it was.

Close to the edge of Grassy Key, it was hard to see, even from the water, and almost completely hidden by the mangroves surrounding it.

There were no boats in sight, but he couldn't see whether there was a car out back because of the trees.

"I'll bring her in as close as I can," he told Logan, "but we'll have to anchor and hop out."

They were prepared, with everyone wearing swim gear and shorts. Dallas drew the boat in as close as he dared and droped the anchor.

"You must be ready," Maria said. "Tio, the man who watches us, may be old, but he loves guns and knives. He has them everywhere."

They hopped out of the boat. Dallas was carrying his second weapon, having decided that Hannah shouldn't go in unarmed. Hell, she'd shot Bentley, so he had to trust that she wouldn't shoot any of *them*.

It was slow going, maneuvering over and between the roots. Little crabs scurried out of the way as they drew closer to the shore.

Eventually they made it through the trees. And there, ahead of them, was a roughly hewn fisherman's cabin. It stood on crude pilings and was surrounded by sea grape trees, blending in completely.

There was no indication that anyone was at home.

"Kelsey, Hannah, stay back," Dallas said, looking at Logan.

"Front or back?" Logan asked him.

"Your call," Dallas said.

And he and Logan began moving carefully toward the little cabin.

Hannah hung back with Kelsey and watched the men sneak toward the cabin. It was hot, and she was sticky with salt and sweat after struggling through the trees. Something moved a foot away, and Hannah started, but it was only a crane walking curiously past them.

Above them, a giant cormorant moved across the sky.

She jumped again when her phone vibrated in the pocket of her shorts. She glanced at the caller ID.

It was Liam.

She answered it quickly. "Hey."

Just as he started to speak, the phone went dead. "Damn it!" she muttered.

"Someone is coming," Kelsey said, instinctively stepping around her, ready to face whoever was approaching.

"Hello, there!"

The voice was male, but the speaker was still hidden in the mangroves. It was familiar, but Hannah couldn't place it, even though the man swore and went on speaking.

"This is ridiculous. Why in God's name send a man like me out here on my own? You'd think they'd have sent the damned Coast Guard with me or something."

The speaker came into view at last, and she was relieved to see it was the M.E., Dirk Mendini. His white lab coat was already dirtied and wet. He had his black bag of crime scene supplies in his hand.

Kelsey lowered her weapon and asked tensely, "They? What's going on?"

"I got a call from the cops. They told me to come out here. Gave me some GPS coordinates. Said there are bodies out here somewhere. But damn it, I can't get my cell to work. I'm trying to get back to Liam."

"Liam? He just tried to reach me," Hannah said. "He sent you out here looking for bodies?"

"I was ordered to come here," he said. "Ordered to get out here, on my own, thank you very much. They said there was some kind of shoot-out."

Kelsey turned to look back to the house. "The guys haven't come out yet, and we haven't heard any shooting." She turned to Dirk. "Who did you say called you?"

"I just told you. Detective Liam Beckett."

"I'm going in," Kelsey said.

"You're the only Fed here—you're not leaving us alone," Mendini protested.

"Follow me, then, but stay down and keep quiet," she said.

Kelsey started to move, and they followed, Dirk went first, holding tight to his black bag. Hannah crept along behind him. When they reached the raised porch on its moldy pilings, Hannah's phone started to vibrate again. She cursed, reaching for it. As she pulled it out and noticed that it was Liam calling, Mendini suddenly lifted his bag and slammed it against Kelsey's head.

She fell face-first onto the marshy ground.

For a moment Hannah was so stunned she couldn't move, then she remembered the gun. But first she had to get to Kelsey, who was lying with her face in a pool of water and possibly drowning. Fumbling for the gun tucked against the small of her back, wondering whether Liam was calling to warn her about Dirk, she rushed to her cousin and dragged her to one side, relieved to see that Kelsey was still breathing.

She straightened as she pulled the gun free, turning to face Dirk, only to see him standing firmly, steadying a gun on her.

"Give me your gun," he said in a tone that sent chills up her spine. "Never thought I'd be worrying about you shooting me, but then, you brought down Machete, didn't you? Who would have thought?"

"What are you doing?" she demanded. "After everything you've seen, why would you work for

400

the Wolf? He doesn't care anything about the people who work for him. He uses them up like tissues and throws them away to die. You'll die, too, as soon as he's got no more use for you," she told him furiously.

Mendini laughed at her. "For God's sake, how stupid can you be? Don't you get it? I *am* the Wolf."

The cabin was empty, though there were signs that people had been there recently. There were two rooms, a living room that had apparently been lit by candles and a bedroom with mattresses on the floor.

"No blood anywhere," Logan announced.

"Going to check the front," Dallas told him.

He stepped out the front door and, as soon as he saw that the area was clear, jumped down to the marshy ground from the porch. He rounded the corner of the house, using what trees he could find for cover. When he reached the back he searched the trees for the women, even though he knew he wouldn't be able to see them in the thick mangrove growth.

A flash of movement caught his eye, and he realized there was a small beach to one side of the mangroves. They'd missed it on the way in. Two women huddled together on the small patch of ground, their backs to him, and an old man was pacing in front of them—the movement that had caught his attention—and wielding a knife.

The man began to speak, and Dallas strained to hear.

"You hear? They found . . . body . . . wretched Maria. You think you . . . run like Maria?" The old man's voice grew louder, his movements more agitated. "No, no. You will stay here. You will be ready when the Wolf wants you. Maybe you'll go live in Colombia, huh? They like pretty girls there. And at least you will get to live."

Dallas shifted carefully to get a better view of the two women. Yes, one was Jose's sister, Alicia, and the other must be Alma. He wished Tio would turn his back, giving Dallas a chance to rush him and take him down without shooting him. He needed to take Tio alive, so he could find out what the old man knew about the Wolf.

"I can try to distract him."

Dallas heard the whisper at this back and turned to see Jose looking grim and determined.

The ghost strode toward the water, moving toward Tio—and then through him.

The old man swatted at his back, as if he thought there was a bug on him.

Jose began punching the man over and over, wafting through him to attack first from behind, then from the front, then from behind again.

Baffled, Tio spun around, trying to see what was happening.

Dallas took advantage of the split-second distraction and rushed forward, tackling Tio to the ground. The man was old, but he was a fighter. They struggled in the sand, and Dallas managed to break his grip on the knife. Then, when the old man looked up at him, he couldn't resist.

He slammed him with a right hook to the jaw.

Tio was out.

Dallas slipped the plastic cuffs from his pocket, rolled the man over and secured his hands.

Tio wasn't going anywhere.

The two women jumped to their feet and ran over to him, sobbing, talking at the same time, nearly knocking him over.

"I'm Agent Dallas Samson, and we're going to get you out of here. Alicia Rodriguez?" he asked.

He didn't need to. Jose was standing by her, trying to touch her, and he was sobbing, as well. His tears looked real.

The pretty brunette nodded. "And this is Alma White. Where did you come from? How? Do you know my brother, Jose? They told me he was dead, but—"

"I'm so sorry. Jose *is* dead. But he helped us find you," Dallas said. "Now—"

He broke off when he heard the sound of a shot being fired.

And then a scream.

Hannah put down the gun and was desperately trying to figure out what to do next when Dirk grabbed her hair and twisted so hard she nearly cried out in pain. He dragged her in front of him as a human shield.

"Now, I want you to talk to the boys in there, Miss O'Brien. Tell them that you're coming in. Do it and do it right, and maybe I'll let you and your cousin live. You can take Maria's place. Defy me and your cousin dies, right here and right now."

She didn't know what to do! If she didn't do as he said, he would shoot Kelsey. If she lunged at him, he would undoubtedly shoot her, but Dallas and Logan would be out in a flash and at least have a chance to kill him.

Suddenly she heard a creak and the cabin door swung open, though no one was visible. "Come in, Mendini," she heard Logan call from the cabin.

How had he known? she wondered. Had one of the ghosts seen what was going on and given him the info?

"Do you think I'm stupid? *You* come out *here*. Now," Mendini said.

"Don't be ridiculous. So long as I stay in here, I just might get the chance to kill you."

"How about I forget about you and just shoot your woman?"

"Kelsey is an officer of the law. She knows the risks that come with that life," Logan said smoothly.

"Come out. My patience isn't going to last long."

"I have a few questions first. How the hell did the Wolf get you, of all people, into his orbit?" Logan demanded.

"Lord, you people. Who do you think you're looking for? A street thug? A dumb down-and-outer? *I'm* the Wolf, you moron. Did you think some stupid punk would know what to go after? If you thought about it for a single second, you would have known the Wolf is a man of intelligence and education. One with access to police information. It was so easy to keep tabs on you. Who in the hell would suspect a respected member of the team?"

"You did have it covered," Logan said.

"I did—and I do. Now put your gun down and come out here." As if to emphasize his words, he shot toward the cabin, and a chunk of wood came flying off the doorframe.

Hannah couldn't help herself. She screamed.

To her surprise, Logan's Glock came sliding out to the little porch.

And then Logan himself walked out calmly.

"Get your friend out here," Mendini ordered.

"My friend?" Logan asked. He looked at Hannah, and something in his eyes warned her to keep quiet, because he knew what he was doing.

"Samson—Dallas Samson. Tell him to get his sorry ass out here, too."

"Oh, my friend isn't in here," Logan said. He indicated the scraggly beach in the distance. "You can tell him yourself what you want him to do with his sorry ass."

It was well played. Mendini jerked around.

And there was Dallas, his gun aimed straight at Dirk's face. He was flanked by Yerby Catalano and Jose Rodriguez.

"I think you should have paid attention to the curse, Mendini," Logan said quietly.

Dallas fired.

And Hannah screamed again as, right next to her, Dirk Mendini's head exploded into a mist of blood and brain matter.

Epilogue

Hannah was the first one downstairs on the Monday morning after the death of Dirk Mendini and the de facto dissolution of Los Lobos. She started the coffee and went outside for the newspaper. She smiled as she came back in, waited on the coffee, poured a cup and went out back to drink it while she read the paper.

She'd always enjoyed sitting by the pool while morning broke, enjoying a cup of coffee and with a real newspaper in her hand.

It was even sweeter when the headline and half the front page were dedicated to explaining the mess in her backyard: 1715 Treasure Chest Found.

It had, indeed, been there. They'd unearthed it not long after they'd started digging, about ten feet past where they'd excavated when they put in the pool.

Liam had been there to see it happen, and he'd tried to reach her to tell her the news. He'd gotten a call from Dirk just after dialing Hannah and, thinking he might have come up with valuable information, he'd cut off the call to her and taken the M.E.'s. Liam had mentioned that Dallas and the others were headed up to Marathon following a lead, at which point Dirk's entire tone changed and he'd started pumping Liam for more information. Then he made an excuse for getting off the phone without ever explaining why he had called in the first place. Liam had been called away by one of his men at that point, but he'd tried Hannah again, planning to mention Dirk's strange behavior. He'd never gotten the chance to talk to her, of course.

After that, everything was conjecture. Their best guess was that Mendini had already been on his way to the cabin, so he'd simply changed his plans and decided to kill the agents if they were already there and wait for them to show up if they weren't. As to whether he might also have killed Tio and the women to prevent them from revealing anything about him if everything fell apart, who knew?

Tio, it turned out, was Mendini's actual uncle on his mother's side. The best they'd been able to fathom about the island and the women was that Mendini kept them there because he could and he liked the rush of power that gave him, and because there were times when he could exchange a woman for a treasure he wanted from some less-than-honorable seller in the Middle East or South America.

They would never have all the answers, of course. The FBI and local law enforcement would probably be cleaning up the remnants of Los Lobos for years.

But, as Dallas put it when the shooting was over, the head was off the snake.

As for the treasure . . .

The priceless Zafiro de Seguridad had been in the chest, and it was now being cleaned and prepared for display at the Smithsonian while ownership of the treasure was settled between Spain, America—and Hannah.

Truthfully, she didn't want any of it. Too many people had died for it. And she had never been interested in *things,* anyway.

Just people.

She was startled when she heard someone calling her name from out front.

She rose and walked slowly around the house. She moved warily, still a little paranoid after all the things that had happened.

There she found a tall, very distinguished white-haired man studying the house with true appreciation for the architecture. He was dressed in a suit—a light, handsome, charcoal-gray suit, but a suit nonetheless.

FBI, she thought.

He was old for an agent. But there was a younger man at his side, pointing up to some architectural detail on the widow's walk. Hannah realized that the younger man looked a lot like the older one—and that he was dead.

"Miss O'Brien? Yes, you have the look of your cousin about you," the older man said. "Different hair color, of course, but there's a definite resemblance," he said.

"Yes, I'm Hannah O'Brien. May I help you?"

"I'm Adam Harrison," he said, stepping forward to study her further with a smile.

"Oh, Kelsey and Logan's boss."

He nodded. "Though I tend to let Logan handle the Texas Krewe without interference. I don't go into the field much anymore. Not the micro-manager type."

"Well, it's lovely to meet you. I'm the first one up today. If you'll come in, I'll get the others for you."

"Actually . . . would you mind if we walk around back?"

"If you wish."

"I'd like to speak with you."

"Oh?" she asked, surprised, and led the way.

He smiled, taking a seat on one of the lawn chairs. She joined him, noticing that the younger man was still with them and looking around the yard—the pristine pool area contrasting with the raw dirt where the treasure had been found—with interest. "Can I get you some coffee?" she asked Adam.

"In a minute." He smiled. "I've received some interesting reports regarding your abilities."

Ignoring that for the moment, she looked at him sympathetically and asked softly. "Is that your son?"

"So you do see Josh," he said.

The ghost turned to smile at her. "She's got it, Dad. She's really got it."

"I can see Josh now, though I couldn't at first. But love is strong, as I'm sure you know. I don't see others, however. But you—well, they tell me that you were able to communicate with Maria Lopez when no one else could even see her . . . And without her help . . . well, the outcome would have been quite different, I imagine."

"I don't know about that. Your agents are very good."

"Yes, they are. I also hear that you took a ten-minute course in handling a Glock and then took down a murderer with your first shot."

She reached for her coffee and shook her head. "I was just lucky," she said.

"I think it's more than that. And I'd like you to think about joining us," Adam Harrison said.

She nearly dropped her cup.

"Just think about it, no need to decide this minute. It's a difficult decision. It's a tough job, and some days it's life or death, but we have good days, really good days, especially when we take down someone like the Wolf."

She certainly understood that. It had been a really good day when they'd saved Alicia and Alma, a real emotional high seeing Jose standing by his sister, knowing he'd been instrumental in saving her life.

"Adam!"

Kelsey hurried over to Adam and hugged him as though he were her grandfather, and then she welcomed Josh, although her hug went right through him. A minute later Dallas and Logan joined them. Kelsey made the introductions.

"So, are you joining us, son?" Adam asked Dallas. "I know Logan told you I'm eager to have you."

"I don't know," Dallas said, and he looked at Hannah.

She felt poleaxed by the entire situation, torn in two as to what she wanted. But she knew what the look he had given her meant.

Yes, he wanted to go.

But he wasn't going anywhere without her.

"I've been thinking," she said. "Valeriya and her mother could manage this place. I'll never sell it, and it will always be my home. But, frankly, I'd like to get away from everything that's happened and all the crazy attention that's coming, at least for a bit."

Dallas smiled at her. Lord, but the man had a great smile.

"Let's go in and have breakfast," Hannah said. "The Siren of the Sea is a bed-and-breakfast, after all, and we're known for our breakfasts."

They all talked over breakfast, though it quickly became clear that Dallas would be accepting Adam's offer while she still wanted to think for a bit before she committed to a career change. Going with him, however, had never been in doubt. Still, there were things that had to be done first; a move would take some time.

Hannah didn't know yet whether she was right for the academy, but she did know that Dallas was right for the Krewe of Hunters and she was right for him.

Adam and Josh left around twelve.

When they had gone, all the Siren's ghosts, the old and the new, gathered with the living in the back.

There Melody announced to Hannah that she wanted to visit her father's grave. Because his stone was old and weathered and no longer legible, no one even realized that it was his, but she knew where it was.

"We'll all go with you," Dallas said.

"Jose, Yerby and Maria wish to move on," Melody said.

"What about you and Hagen?" Hannah asked. She wanted them to move on, too. She wanted them to find peace and happiness. But seeing them go would be like losing beloved relatives.

Melody smiled. "We're not quite ready. Valeriya might need us for a while. But when we're ready, I promise, wherever you may be, Hannah, we will find you and say goodbye."

They went to the cemetery. Hannah was surprised to find Alicia Rodriguez—who had decided to make the island her home—sitting on a bench there. She heard Jose gasp, and Alicia looked around, almost as if she had heard him.

She looked at Hannah. "It's almost as if my brother were here. I wish I could thank him. I know he died because he came here, and I know he came here because of me. I was always afraid he would think I betrayed him, that I joined Los Lobos, but I would never have done that. I loved my brother—he was always the one constant in my life, the one good thing I could hold on to."

"He knows you didn't betray him, Alicia," Hannah assured her.

The young woman smiled. "I'm going to have him buried here," she said. "He loved Key West."

"I think he'd like that," Hannah replied.

Jose stood next to his sister. For a minute they were silent as they looked out over the cemetery with its many above-ground vaults, its stones, its strange mausoleums, and even one grave that looked like a redbrick fire pit.

"It's almost as if I can feel him," Alicia whispered.

"You *do* feel him," Kelsey said gently.

"Love doesn't die, it lives in the heart," Hannah assured her.

Hannah felt the other ghosts behind her. She heard Melody whisper encouragingly to Yerby.

Jose stepped away from his sister at last and reached for Yerby's hand.

She took it, meeting his eyes. "I'm afraid," she said.

Jose smiled. "So am I."

She moved closer to him. Then, together, they turned around and Jose took Maria's hand, as well. The three of them turned toward the north.

Hannah could have sworn she saw a soft golden light streaking across the sky in a glimmering arc, but when she tried to look closer, the fierce Florida sun was in her eyes.

She tried to watch them move away, but one moment they were there, and then they were just . . . gone.

The sun continued to beam down.

It was just another Florida day.

That night they went to Mallory Square. They watched the balloon man and the statue lady, laughed as the cat man had his felines perform their delightful antics. They watched the sunset, and it was glorious, filling the sky with streaks of gold and red and mauve, like a preview of heaven.

As they sat there, Dallas slipped an arm around Hannah and asked her, "Can you really leave all this?"

"I'll always be a Conch," she told him. "Always. And so will you. But can I live somewhere else? Yes. I've never been a big believer in things or even in places. I'm just a believer in people."

He nodded, whispering, "Am I a person you believe in?"

"To me, you're that sunset we just saw."

"I love you," he told her.

She kissed him and whispered the words in return.

And she knew that she would follow him anywhere.

Center Point Large Print
600 Brooks Road / PO Box 1
Thorndike ME 04986-0001 USA

(207) 568-3717

US & Canada:
1 800 929-9108
www.centerpointlargeprint.com